FINDER'S FEE

Also by Alton Gansky

The Prodigy

The Madison Glenn Series

The Incumbent
Before Another Dies
Director's Cut

J. D. Stanton Mysteries

A Ship Possessed
Vanished
Out of Time

altonGANSKY
FINDER'S FEE

ZONDERVAN®

ZONDERVAN.com/
AUTHORTRACKER
follow your favorite authors

ZONDERVAN®

Finder's Fee
Copyright © 2007 by Alton L. Gansky

Requests for information should be addressed to:

Zondervan, *Grand Rapids, Michigan* 49530

Library of Congress Cataloging-in-Publication Data

Gansky, Alton.
    Finders fee / Alton Gansky.
        p. cm.
      ISBN-10: 0-310-27210-6
      ISBN-13: 978-0-310-27210-6
      1. Women executives — Fiction. 2. Kidnapping — Fiction. I. Title.
PS3557.A5195F56 2007
813'.54 — dc22

                                                    2006037576

All Scripture quotations are taken from the *New American Standard Bible.* © 1960, 1962, 1963, 1968, 1971, 1972, 1973, 1975, 1977, 1995 by The Lookman Foundation. Used by permission.

Interior design by Michelle Espinoza

Printed in the United States of America

07 08 09 10 11 12 • 22 21 20 19 18 17 16 15 14 13 12 11 10 9 8 7 6 5 4 3 2 1

To Brad and Travis, two great sons-in-law.

acknowledgments

Special thanks goes to Kenny Adams for taking my calls about determining property ownership and Lieutenant David Cavanaugh of the San Diego Police Department for insight into police work. As always, any mistakes are mine.

FINDER'S FEE

one

May 12, 9:30 a.m.

A phone rang.

Not quite a ring.

More of a chirp.

It sounded muted.

Judith Find looked at her desk phone. No lights shone on any of the lines.

It chimed again.

Snapping open her handbag, she removed a thin cell phone. The display was dark and empty.

Again she heard the tones.

"What—"

She let her ears lead her, turning her head slightly. The sound came from the top of her desk. She pushed over a neat stack of padded envelopes. She always had padded envelopes on her desk—fabric samples, videos of her television ads, samples of paints, finishes, and more. It was part of being America's interior design diva. She glanced at the labels. Two she recognized from furniture design firms she worked with. One package had been marked PRIVATE. It bore her name and company on a plain three-inch-by-four-inch adhesive label. There was no return address.

The ringing stopped.

Judith stared at the package. Why would someone put a cell phone—

The sound resumed, pushing its way through the paper and plastic that sealed it in.

"This is nuts." She lifted the package. It felt light. Without another thought, she ripped open the envelope then stopped. Her mind raced back to that guy who sent bombs to people in the mail. What was his name? Kuzy ... Kinsey ... Kaczynski. That was it. Theodore Kaczynski.

Thoughts of biological contaminates, bombs, and worse flashed on her mind. She should have been more careful. The world held a lot of nutcases who hated the successful and wealthy, some enough to wish someone like her bodily harm.

But the deed had been done. The open package rested in her hands. No dust emanated from the ragged opening, no fire started, and thankfully, no loud boom announced the loss of her limbs and life.

Again the phone sounded.

Judith peeked in the package and saw a small flip cell phone. "In for a penny, in for a pound." She extracted the noisy device.

Ring!

The small monochrome screen read, Unknown.

Ring!

She snapped the phone open and held it to her head. "Who is this?"

Silence.

The vague hum of an open line wafted from speaker to ear. "I said, who is—"

"If you hang up, then he will die."

A pause.

Judith's gut twisted and squirmed as if filled with wriggling worms.

"What? I don't—"

"This is not a gag. This is not a prank. If you hang up, he will die. If you do not do exactly as I instruct, then he will die. If you understand say, 'Yes.'"

"I demand to know who is speaking."

Pause.

She started to speak again when—

"This is not a gag. This is not a prank. If you hang up, he will die. If you do not do exactly as I instruct, then he will die. If you understand say, 'Yes.'"

Word for word, the same message. Even the inflection remained consistent. No sign of annoyance. A recording. A computer-operated recording with voice recognition like those used by the phone company and other businesses.

"This is not a gag. This is not a prank. If you hang up, he will die. If you do not do exactly as I instruct, then he will die. If you understand say, 'Yes.'"

"Yes."

"February 27. You know the date. You know what you did. If you understand say, 'Yes.'"

Judith's stomach stopped turning. It seized as did her heart and lungs.

"February 27. You know the date—"

"Yes." She snapped the word like a knife thrust.

Pause.

"At precisely 11:00 a.m. you will drive alone to Hutch's Diner. You will order a bowl of chili. A man will meet you. Wait for the envelope. If you understand say, 'Yes.'"

Judith melted into her chair, her legs no longer able to support her. "Yes."

"I know your secret. If you defy me, then the world will know. If you go to the police, then he will die. If you talk to the media, then he will die. If you talk to anyone about this matter, then he will die. If you understand then say, 'Yes.'"

She did. Questions flew through her mind. Who would die? Why her? How did the person who set up this call know her secret? Why go to such elaborate means? Asking questions was useless. She wasn't talking to a person; she was listening to a machine. Nothing of heart and blood there. The same could be said for whoever thought of this game.

A game. In the center of her mind she knew this wasn't an amusement.

"You have a gas fireplace in your office. Place the phone and envelope in the fireplace. Close the glass screen. Turn on the fireplace gas and igniter. If you don't, then he will die. If you understand—"

"Yes."

The connection dropped.

Judith rose from her chair feeling as if she had gained five hundred pounds in the last sixty seconds, retrieved the envelope, dropped the cell phone in it, and walked to the fireplace.

She felt stupid obeying an electronic voice as if the man behind it were standing in the room with her. Was she being watched? She stopped and looked around the office. Everything looked in place, but then again, if a professional industry spy had infiltrated her office and planted a camera or listening device, she wouldn't be able to tell. What did she know of such things? Still, she forced her eyes to trace every foot of the expansive room. If she was being watched, then she had better comply.

Compliance did not come easy to her. Independent most of her life, she had developed a stubborn streak, something only her late husband had been able to control.

A sense of defiance rose within her and she felt the heat of anger radiate from her face. For several long seconds she considered returning to her desk and calling the police, despite the vile warnings. But something—intuition?—warned her not to.

She finished the last few steps to the fireplace and set the package down on the marble hearth, pulled open the glass shields, and pushed back the chain-mail screen. The shaking of her hand surprised her. At the moment she felt only fury, but fear had not let go.

Lifting the envelope, Judith studied it, looking for any clues she might be destroying and found none. She set the package with its cargo of cell phone on the simulated wood logs. The logs were made of concrete but looked as real as anything found in a forest.

Judith closed the metal link screen and the glass doors and stepped to a control panel mounted on the wall to the right of the fireplace, then punched two buttons: HIGH and IGNITE. The soft hiss of natural gas reached her ears then the snap, snap, snap of the electric igniter. Two seconds later, flames erupted from the burner and lapped at the concrete logs and the envelope they supported.

Judith watched, stunned into inaction, as the fire ate at the edges of the package. The paper burned in odd colors, green and blue, then erupted with enough force to rattle the glass screen.

It had been no ordinary envelope. Within a minute's span, the envelope and cell phone were engulfed in a furious blaze that burned hotter than it should. Three minutes later all that remained were ashes.

And the day had started off so normal.

May 12, 9:10 a.m. — twenty minutes earlier

The brass-clad elevator doors parted and Judith Find poured from its compartment. Unlike the elevators others used in the Find, Inc., building, this conveyance carried only her or one of her three vice presidents. That perk came with owning the ten-story building. Ten stories might be small compared to other office structures in the megalopolis of Los Angeles thirty-five miles to the west, but here in Ontario, California, it stood proud.

"Oh, you're here," a familiar voice said.

"I'm that obvious, am I?" Judith glanced up to see Terri Penn standing just three feet away.

"You know what I mean."

Judith did. Terri stood the same five-foot-eight as she, but the similarities ended there. Where Judith moved through life with a reserved confidence, Terri buzzed from event to task to conversation to problem to whatever else might arise. At forty-eight, the personal assistant reminded Judith of a teenage girl still full of unbounded energy. Still, Judith didn't see it as a fault. Terri's administrative skills were legendary. No one could want or find someone as talented as she. Her brown hair bounced an inch-and-a-half above her rounded shoulders. As conservative in dress as in language, Terri wore a plain white blouse, black skirt, and bone pumps. The blouse hung open only one button. No one ever used the word *risqué* to describe her.

"I want to bring you up to date."

"You think I'm out of date? And I try to be so hip ... or is it cool?"

"In my book, you are forever cool."

"You're just saying that because I sign your paycheck."

"That's so very true." Terri smiled with innocence for a second then allowed the grin to erode. "Marlin called first thing this morning. He sounded irritated."

"Terri you know to never begin my day with 'Marlin called.' And he always sounds irritated. It's a gene on his Y chromosome."

The routine played the same every morning. Judith would arrive at 9:10 with a cup of vanilla latte, extra shot in one hand, and her gray leather briefcase in the other. Terri would be waiting in the lobby as if the boss couldn't find her own way without an escort. As they moved from the elevator, Judith would say, "Good morning," and then plow through Terri's office and into her own.

Today followed course.

"The ad agency sent the preliminary videos over as you asked, but they seemed very uncomfortable. They offered to come over and make a presentation."

Judith nodded. "I expected that. They're trying to win our business and want to be present when I view the mock-ups so they can try and sell me."

"They don't know you very well, do they?"

No one knows me very well. "No, they don't. There's nothing worse than sitting in some ad agency's office or having them invade our conference room only to have them show a commercial then explain what we just saw."

"I told them you were too busy for a meeting right away, but that you were eager to see their concepts. They gave in."

Judith had made certain that Terri's office stood as a showpiece. After all, decorating was what Find, Inc., was all about. Since visitors saw Terri's office first—the "portal" she called it—Judith felt it had to be spectacular. It was. More than one CEO who had come to pay a visit assumed the assistant's office with its blue suede walls, handcrafted maple furniture, frosted glass-topped desk, deep-pile cobalt rug, artwork on the walls, and a stylish, iron sculpture of a giraffe in the corner was where Judith commanded her international home decorating enterprise. They were wrong.

"They didn't have a choice." Judith opened one of the two doors to her office and plunged in, Terri one step behind.

"No, ma'am, they certainly didn't."

Terri's office had a touch of the contemporary to it. Judith's did not. The floor was a blend of hard maple slats laid in a herringbone fashion, bordered by twelve-inch wide ebony. Mahogany panels lined the walls and paintings of classic mansions hung at eye level. A large mahogany desk, wide and deep, rested eight feet from the exterior wall. A matching bureau sat next to the wall, a laptop computer rested patiently, waiting for attention. A green-veined marble lined fireplace gave the large space a homey feel. A marble topped, curved wet bar, used only at gatherings with key suppliers and CEOs of retail outlets, marked off the third corner of the room. The only two windows, both less than five feet wide but reaching from floor to ceiling, remained covered by thick drapes holding insistent daylight at bay. Judith liked to work in a dim room.

Judith approached her desk and set her briefcase on the surface. After popping the latch, she removed a leather clutch purse, a handheld computer, her favorite fountain pen—a gift from her husband—and a short stack of folders. Once empty, she moved the briefcase to the floor.

"Cue it up, Terri. Let's see what the creative minds of Bonner, Taylor, and Lennox have for us."

Terri moved to the seating area at the right of the office. Two long, leather sofas and two reading chairs populated the sitting area. A flat-screen television rested on a tall, narrow rosewood table. A sleek DVD player opened its drawer at Terri's touch.

Judith glanced over at her desk. Four "While You Were Out" slips waited her attention. Three padded envelopes rested to the right of the desk. Two had been opened, one remained sealed. The only mail Terri ever left unopened were envelopes marked private.

"Ready," Terri said.

Judith walked to the sitting area and stood just behind the glass-and-iron coffee table. She would be sitting all day, so she appreciated the opportunity to remain on her feet.

Terri punched play.

A woman dressed in an unbuttoned brown-and-white checkered shirt over a thick white T-shirt, jeans, and cloth garden gloves appeared on the screen.

"Is that supposed to be you?" Terri frowned. "It looks like she's wearing a wig."

The woman had shoulder length black hair, high cheekbones, and straight white teeth—a pretty good representation of Judith. Of course, the ad firm had hired an actress or pulled one of their employees in as a stand-in. Not unusual in a proof-of-concept video. If she gave approval, it would be Judith in front of the camera lens.

"At least they used someone younger than me. I don't think I could stand seeing someone older hocking our product."

"You're only forty-five," Terri said.

Yeah, only. "I just feel seventy."

"You work too hard."

It was true. She did work too hard.

"The garden," the actress said, "is more than flowers in our backyard—it's a place of refuge."

"Refuge?" Judith said.

The actress continued. Terri had been right. Clearly, she was wearing a wig—a cheap wig. "I love the time I spend communing with the plants that make my garden an outdoor home. That's why I'm so happy to introduce our new classic line of outdoor furniture—"

Judith stopped listening. "Turn it off."

"Don't like it?"

"Do you?" Judith asked.

Terri shook her head. "Not in the least. Exactly what is new classic furniture? Isn't that an oxymoron?"

"It's some kind of moron."

She stepped back to the desk but not before hearing, "I'm Judith Find—Find everything you need at Judith Find's."

"Send it back, Terri. It stinks. Tell them I'll call later this week. Let them stew awhile."

Terri retrieved the DVD. "Will do. Anything else?"

"Not now. I have plenty of work to do. Please shut the door on the way out." She sipped from the coffee.

"Oh." Terri pulled up short of the door. "Marlin called and would like some time this morning."

A hot coal dropped in Judith's stomach. Marlin Find was her stepson and her biggest critic. "I'll think about it."

"And if he should call again?"

"Tell him you passed on the information and that I haven't got back to you yet."

"Got it." Terri started to exit. "One last thing: could I leave a little early today? There's a baby shower at my church this evening and I said I'd swing by and help decorate if I could."

"I don't see why not." Judith knew the next comment before Terri uttered it.

"How about going with me? I'll introduce you to some of my church friends."

Judith smiled. "Thanks, Terri, but no." Her assistant had been trying to get her to attend church for the last year. She always refused. Business and faith never seemed like a good mix to Judith.

"Okay. Let me know if you change your mind. We have a woman who makes the world's best deviled eggs."

"They allow devil eggs in your church?"

Terri grinned. "Cute. I'll have to remember that."

Judith thought she heard a phone ring.

two

Hutch's Diner sat at the north end of the Ontario Mills Mall near Fourth Street. The mall complex was one of the Chamber of Commerce's talking points. One point seven million square feet under a single roof provided a home for two hundred retailers that saw over twenty million visitors each year. Judith knew the stats because one of Find, Inc.'s stores took up its share of the complex.

Major chain restaurants dotted the perimeter of the parking lot. Only one had the distinction of being unique: Hutch's. Like the other eateries, Hutch's served patrons from the mall. Here a hungry patron could buy a double cheeseburger for just a little over twice what she would pay elsewhere. Decorated like a Southern roadside café, the environment drew as many people as the food.

Waitresses dressed like carhops from the forties and fifties. They served up heart-damaging food and did so with attitude.

Judith pulled her silver Lexus SC convertible into the first open parking stall she found, exited, and walked into the restaurant. It took several steps before she realized that she moved with her head down and eyes fixed on the concrete walk. She forced her head and eyes up, reached for the door, and walked into the unknown.

Inside, the Andrews Sisters were singing something about a bugle boy in the army. The aroma of french fries, burgers, and grilled-cheese sandwiches attacked her nostrils. Noises of people about the business of visiting with friends and coworkers reflected off the tile floor and Formica tabletops. The decor was a mix of postwar simplicity and midcentury modern. Judith decided that the theme was mixed but it worked well.

Just inside the door stood a podium with a sign that read: PLEASE WAIT TO BE SEATED.

Judith waited, but her eyes worked the room, searching for whomever it was that she was supposed to meet. Should she allow herself to be seated? What if he had already arrived and the hostess seated her on the wrong side of the restaurant?

Her heart fluttered as she studied the customers. A few looked her way but immediately returned their attention to their companions. None made eye contact; none motioned to her.

"Just one, ma'am?"

A young woman, maybe twenty-two, stepped to the podium and removed a menu. Judith hated the question, "Just one?" It implied that something was missing if you dined alone. She had been just one for half a decade now, but had yet to adjust to the idea.

"I'm meeting someone here."

The hostess reached for another menu. "Is he here yet? Or is it a she?"

Judith had to think for a moment. What had the caller said? "A man will meet you ..."

"A gentleman. We haven't met yet so I don't know what he looks like."

"Would you prefer to wait or should I seat you?"

How should I know? The caller didn't say. "Go ahead and seat me. Do you have anything ... a little more private?"

"No, ma'am. What you see is what you get."

"I understand." *I suppose a clandestine meeting is best held in a public place.*

The hostess pivoted and marched to the back of the restaurant, seating Judith in a corner booth with a view to the chugging traffic of Fourth Street. Menus were placed. "Enjoy your lunch." She started to leave when Judith stopped her. She remembered something.

"I need to order."

"Before your party arrives?"

"Yes. I'm ... on a tight schedule today."

"I'll get your waitress."

Judith thanked her and wriggled farther into the booth until she reached the best level of comfort she could hope for. She set her handbag on the table and tried to calm herself.

In the time from her arrival at her office until she left to make her way to Hutch's, Judith pretended to work but her mind rehashed the phone call countless times. In an effort to assume some control of the situation she exited her office, which she now assumed was infested with electronic listening devices, and prepared to quiz Terri. She stopped short realizing that anyone who could bug her office could bug Terri's as well.

"Marlin called again," Terri began. "I put him off best I could but he seemed really irritated—"

"Walk with me." Judith didn't wait for an answer. She marched through the door, into the wide hall by the elevators.

"Where are we going?"

"The bathroom."

It took a second for Terri to respond. "Is something wrong with yours? Should I call a plumber?" Judith had a private restroom as did Terri. Other employees on this floor shared a restroom. Executives had an executive toilet to call their own.

"Nothing's wrong with my bathroom."

"Then why—"

"Terri. Shut up."

"Yes, ma'am."

Fifteen steps later, Judith pushed through the door into a wide room filled with partitioned stalls, sinks, and white floor tile.

Judith pushed open each stall door and peered inside. Satisfied that theirs were the only ears in the room, she faced Terri.

"There were three packages on my desk this morning, one was marked 'private.' Where did that come from?"

Nonplussed, Terri replied, "I don't know. It didn't have a return address."

"I know that. What I mean is: who delivered it?"

"UPS, I assume. Is there something wrong?"

Judith ignored the question. "The UPS man brought all three packages to you?"

"No. Not really. I ran late this morning." She looked as if she were confessing a crime. Terri usually arrived before eight and spent the hour straightening Judith's desk, laying out needed files, and fielding calls from early risers and East Coast associates. "When I got here, the packages were on my desk. The delivery guy has left stuff on my desk before when I've been gone so it didn't strike me as odd."

"There was no UPS sticker on the third package."

"I don't understand. What's wrong?"

Judith fought off a frown. "You did nothing wrong. I'm just curious."

Terri looked around the room but didn't say what Judith knew was on her mind. Meeting in the restroom was an unusual place to ask questions about a package.

"So you didn't see the UPS guy?" Judith asked.

"No. Like I said, I found all three packages on my desk when I got in."

If the package had gone through the UPS system, then it should bear the company's familiar sticker. Someone had either slipped the package into the UPS delivery or deposited the envelope on Terri's desk before she arrived for work.

"Was your office locked when you arrived this morning?"

"Of course ... but ..." Judith could see Terri's mind trying to put the pieces together. "How did the delivery guy get into my office?"

"Could he have left it last night while you were out on an errand?"

"I would have noticed. I stayed late and only left my desk once to use the restroom, but there were no packages when I got back."

Judith's mind raced with questions that had no ready answers. One thing she grew certain of—she was not dealing with a prankster.

After returning to her office, Judith waited as the minutes dripped by. At 10:45, she left her office for Hutch's.

The waitress, a slightly older, slightly larger, slightly surly woman with bright red hair took a position near the table. "Welcome to Hutch's, is this your first time with us?" She asked the question like she had asked it a hundred times a day, which she probably had.

"Yes. This is my first time. I'd like a bowl of chili."

"You look familiar to me. Are you sure this is your first time here?"

"I look familiar to many people. I have one of those faces."

"No, that's not it. Haven't I seen you on television?"

Of course she had, but Judith didn't want one of those "aren't you somebody famous" moments. "Water. I'd also like a glass of water with lemon, no ice."

The waitress studied her for a moment, looked down at the extra menu then shrugged. "Anything else?"

"No."

"Cheese and onions on the chili?"

"Um, no."

The waitress left and Judith resumed her gaze out the window. A tapping sound got her attention and she realized the noise came from her own fingers as they drummed the tabletop. She folded her hands in her lap.

The waitress returned with a large, steaming bowl of dark chili and set it on the table along with a glass of water. The bowl rested on a saucer and two packages of crackers were wedged along the rim.

"Anything else?"

Judith told the waitress no. Alone again, she stared at the bowl, picked up the spoon but couldn't bring herself to eat. She pushed the concoction around as if waiting for it to cool. There had been nothing in the strange message that said she had to eat the chili.

"You must be the one."

She jumped at the sound of the voice. Standing next to the table was a thin, handsome man in blue jeans and a black T-shirt. His blond-brown hair was parted along the side and reached the tops of his ears. His eyes were blue and a day's growth of stubble covered his cheeks, jaw, and chin. He didn't smile.

"The one what?" Judith knew the answer but wanted to be sure the man beside her was the contact she had been ordered to wait for.

"You're the only woman eating chili." He slipped into the booth.

"It's not by choice." Her words were hard and icy.

Before the man could speak again the waitress appeared. "May I get you something to drink?"

"No," the man said. "Nothing to eat either."

"Okay, if you say so." The waitress paused and looked at Judith again. "Wait. I got it. You're that Judy Finder person. You used to have a television show or something."

"Judith Find and I still do."

"See, I *did* know you."

"You're very perceptive." Judith set the spoon down.

"Hey, I don't suppose you have a picture or something. The owner likes to put up pictures of famous people who eat here."

"Not with me. When I get back to the office, I'll make sure one is sent."

That pleased the woman and, to Judith's relief, she left.

As soon as the server moved out of earshot, Judith leaned forward and said in a harsh whisper, "I don't know what you're trying to pull, mister, but I'm not going to put up with it. If you think you can extort—"

"Whoa." He held up his hands. "You got the wrong guy. I'm the victim here."

"You're the victim? Not likely."

"I'm not the bad guy. I got a call and was told to meet a woman here. The only information was that you'd be eating a bowl of chili. Although I don't know why. That stuff looks awful."

"You got a call?"

He nodded. "On a cell phone, and not my cell phone, I might add."

"Let me guess. Somehow you came into the possession of a strange cell phone. It rang. You answered and a strange voice started telling you what to do."

"I guess we have something in common. The phone was in a padded envelope."

"Was it delivered to your office?"

"I don't have an office. I work from my home. The package was on my doorstep. I found it when I left to grab coffee this morning. If I hadn't been going out, I might not have seen it for hours."

"You go out every morning?"

"Well, yeah. I suppose I do. You're saying the caller knew that?"

"Most likely he did."

"How do you know it's a he?"

"You couldn't tell by the voice? It was definitely a man's voice."

"Michael – 16."

"Excuse me?"

"First things first. It's awkward to carry on a conversation without names." He smiled and Judith sensed his confidence. It made her uneasy. "My name is Luke Becker and you are?"

Judith always felt a little offended when others didn't recognize her. She had been on television for years and her face had appeared in magazine ads, articles, and news reports. Sometimes it took folks a while to put name to face but most at least showed some recognition.

"Judith Find. Just like I told the waitress."

"I wasn't listening to her. Judith Find," he repeated. "Sounds familiar."

"I'm CEO of Find, Inc."

"The home decorating business? Now I know why your name is familiar. I almost bought stock in your company."

"Almost?"

"That's what I do now. I play the stock market."

She started to ask why he didn't invest but thought better of it. It didn't matter in this context.

"You were saying something about the voice. You said Michael–16." She pushed the chili away.

"It's a synthetic voice created by AT&T. Several companies make them. It's a voice used with TTS software—"

"TTS?"

"Text-to-speech. It's software that reads computer documents. Type a letter, highlight the text, click on a button, and your computer reads it to you. It's great if you have poor eyesight or if you just prefer to consume documents audibly."

"I figured I was talking to a machine. When interrupted it started over."

"I got the same thing. I've heard the voice many times. I have it on my computer. It's easy to get off the Internet."

"So are you saying someone had their computer read a message to us?"

"Basically. I noticed that it responded to certain voice commands. That's not unusual. Certain businesses like banks use the same procedure. You call the bank and speak your account number. The computer recognizes the numbers and takes you to the next step."

"What did the voice tell you to do?"

"To come to this place and find a woman eating a bowl of chili."

"And?"

He looked to the street, breaking eye contact. "There was a threat."

"To expose a secret you have?"

"How'd you know ...? Oh, you got the same thing."

Judith gave a nod. Since she didn't want to talk about her secret, she didn't ask about his. "There was another part to the message."

"He will die?" Luke returned her gaze.

"That's it. But *who* will die?" She lowered her voice.

"I have no idea."

She started to ask another question when a teenage boy in baggy pants, a black shirt with some logo she didn't recognize, and a baseball cap turned sideways on his head approached. He carried a package.

"Hey, lady. Your name Find?"

"Yes."

"This is for you." He held out the package.

"Where did you get this?" Judith asked.

He didn't answer.

Luke raised a hand then reached for his wallet. He pulled out a twenty and placed it on the table. "The lady asked you a question."

The youth shrugged. "Some guy came up to me in the mall and offered me fifty bucks to bring that to you."

"What did he look like?" Luke pressed.

"He was about my age. He said some guy gave him fifty to get someone like me to make the delivery."

Judith knew their tormentor could have done the same thing several times, creating a chain of innocent messengers. It would be impossible to trace the trail. Luke must have come to the same conclusion because he handed the twenty to the kid, who immediately left.

Judith picked up the package. It had her name on it as well as Luke's.

She ripped it open and looked inside.

three

W ell, what's in it?" Luke's eyes were glued to the envelope in Judith's hands.

Judith tried to ignore the heated battle between fear and anger raging inside her. She glanced in and saw a lone piece of white paper. She removed it and laid it on the table.

"It's a map," Judith said. Straight lines formed white streets that contrasted with gray areas. In the center of the map was a green square with a name printed across it.

"Yeah, I can see that." Luke pulled it close and studied it. "Golden Oak Park on the corner of Sixth and Golden Oak Road. Ever been there?"

Judith reached across the table and took the paper. "No, but the map makes it clear how to get there. It isn't far. Five or ten minutes maybe." There was a note at the bottom: *Golden Oak Park. 11:25. Visitor's side.*

"The first part is clear enough, but I don't understand 'visitor's side.'"

"The park must have a baseball field. If so, 'visitor's side' might refer to the visiting team's dugout. It's probably nothing more than a simple bench in a public park." Luke looked at his watch. "We don't have much time."

"Maybe we shouldn't go. Meeting in a public place like a restaurant is bad enough. Going to a place with fewer people might be dangerous."

"How do you know there will be fewer people at the park?"

Judith frowned. "It's the middle of a work day which means it's also the middle of a school day. Maybe there will be a few moms with toddlers, but they won't be much help if things go bad."

"I'm going." Luke stood.

"That must be some secret you have." Judith pulled a ten-dollar bill from her purse and dropped it on the table next to the uneaten chili.

The phone in her handbag sounded and Judith jumped. Several patrons looked her way, then, immune to the ringing of ever-present cell phones, returned their attention to their food. Judith snatched the phone from her purse and glanced at the display. She scowled.

"It's not ..."

"No, it's not." With the push of a button, Judith silenced the phone and replaced it in her handbag. She looked at Luke. "My stepson."

"You don't want to talk to him?"

"Not lately, I don't. Let him talk to the message manager." She led the way through the eatery.

Once outside she stepped to her vehicle.

"Wait a sec." Luke moved to her side. "Let's take my car."

"Why?"

"Because I want us to be able to talk freely."

"We can't talk in my car?"

Luke looked at the Lexus. "It's not about the car ... Look. Earlier you asked if the cell phone I received came to my office."

"Right; and you said you didn't have an office and were a day trader."

"Not a day trader ... Never mind that. The package was in your office, right? Not outside?"

"Correct."

"Someone had to arrange for that. Did he seem to know more about your office than you would expect?"

Judith thought of the fireplace. "Yes. I even wondered if there were cameras or listening devices."

"For now, we had better assume that there are. Where do you park at work?"

"At the front of the building."

"Is your spot marked?"

Judith felt a touch of embarrassment. "Yes. You're thinking someone could have done something to my car." She looked at her vehicle.

"I don't know, but anyone can walk into the parking lot, right?"

"I suppose."

"I keep my car locked in my garage. It's less likely that someone could tamper with it."

"But not impossible."

"No, not impossible. But they would have to be good—CIA, NSA good, if you know what I mean."

"But you said you went out most mornings."

"I go to a Starbucks. I park where I can see my car and anyone who approaches it. Is there someone you can call to pick up the car?"

"My assistant. I'll leave a key with the hostess."

"That's a good idea."

Judith studied the man named Luke Becker again. She didn't believe much in intuition, but she had sensed no danger from him. Still, he was a stranger. To trust or not to trust? "Okay. Where did you park?"

"Right where I could keep it in view."

Luke pulled the steel blue Volvo C70 onto Fourth Street. He drove fast and made his turns with sharp jerks of the steering wheel.

"I bet you have a glove compartment filled with speeding tickets."

Luke released a polite laugh. "I'm not speeding."

"It feels like it."

"You're in good hands."

Judith looked at Luke. A thin smile dressed his face but it didn't look genuine. From the moment she had met him, he had been calm and confident, but his forehead wore more wrinkles than it should and his eyes narrowed repeatedly. He was worried and doing his best not to let it show.

"It should be on our left," Judith said. They had traveled north on Archibald Avenue then west on Sixth Street. The park filled the southeast corner.

Luke kept driving.

"You missed it."

"No, I didn't." He drove several blocks, found a convenient place to pull a U-turn, then headed back toward the park. "I'm going to make a right and drive past the park again. I want to see who and what's there before I pull in."

"You are a cautious man, Luke Becker."

"I'm more than cautious. I'm paranoid."

Judith expected a dismissive laugh, the kind of a chuckle someone makes when exaggerating a truth. It didn't come.

Slowing as anyone would when entering a residential side street, Luke gazed through his window at the park. Judith did the same, seeing a gray-black stretch of macadam that made up the parking lot. She guessed it could hold maybe thirty cars. A small building with a pitched roof rested just beyond the parking lot. Restrooms, she assumed. Beyond the building was a basketball court and beyond that a baseball field. She also noticed a play yard with a jungle gym. A mother watched as her two young children scampered on the bars.

"See, there are children here. You said they'd all be in school." Luke drove down the street.

"They look like they're kindergarten age. Some schools run half-day kindergarten programs."

"Oh."

"I take it you don't have kids." Judith turned as much as her seat would allow and stared back at the park. She saw no one else on the grounds.

"Never married." Luke turned the vehicle around. "I only saw one car in the lot, a minivan. It must belong to the woman with the kids."

"Makes sense."

This time, Luke pulled onto the lot and parked on the south side. A row of houses lined the property to the right. Across the street was a large undeveloped lot.

Judith started to exit but Luke caught her arm.

"Just wait."

His eyes darted around, studying the homes, the parking lot, and the few buildings on the lot. Judith yanked her arm away.

"Okay," Luke said. "Let's do this quickly but try and act natural."

"I'm a natural at being natural." Judith opened the door and slipped from the car. The air felt warm, and a slight breeze brought the perfume of green grass to her nose. The sounds of children playing at the other end of the park carried toward them.

A concrete walk led past a planted area and toward the baseball field. Side by side, they walked past the basketball court and followed the path to another walkway that led to the field. Luke had guessed correctly: an aluminum bench rested on metal legs just behind a chain-link fence. A matching bench was situated along the first base side.

"Which is the visiting team's bench?"

"Typically, it's the third-base side." He pointed. "Not a fan of baseball?"

"Can't say that I am. You?"

"Baseball is a metaphor for life."

Judith had a feeling that she would regret the question. She had known men who loved nothing more than touting the philosophical benefits of America's beloved sport. No monologue came. Luke continued down the walk, his eyes fixed to the bench at the south side of the backstop. His stride had lengthened, and Judith had to take a few fast steps to keep up.

The field sat empty, and she could smell the grass of the outfield, which looked recently mowed. Dirt, raked and compacted, made up the infield.

When they arrived at the bench, Luke looked around again as if he could feel spying eyes fixed on them. Judith did the same but saw nothing. The bench and a chain-link enclosure defined the dugout. There was no protective structure.

Judith followed Luke as he walked along the front of the bench, his eyes fixed to the long seat. Judith saw it at the same time as Luke. A dark brown shape protruded from the underside of the bench. Luke bent, reached, and pulled the envelope free.

He sat. Judith joined him.

The envelope rested on Luke's lap. Three, two-inch long and one-inch wide white rectangles were stuck to the surface. Double-sided tape. Whoever placed the envelope had used the tape to affix the package to the underside of the bench.

Judith could see no markings on the surface. No address. No instructions. "Anyone could have come by and found this. It seems a careless way to deliver a message."

Luke disagreed. "You'd have to be looking for it, and as you said, the park is probably empty at this time of day on a weekday. That and ..."

"And what?"

"I'm guessing that someone stood guard until we got here. If our mystery man had an operative watching us at the restaurant, then he could have been alerted when we left. The package doesn't have any dust on it and it doesn't look weathered. I'll bet your next week's salary that it hasn't been here for more than thirty minutes."

"Bet your own money. Are you going to open it?"

"Patience, lady. How do you know it's not filled with some toxic substance?"

"Too elaborate. If he wanted us dead there are a hundred better ways to do it. Open it or give it to me." Judith's patience dissolved like sugar in hot water.

Luke didn't immediately comply. Instead, he fondled the package, pressing at its corners and middle. He stopped at a spot just down from the center. He found something.

"It's not very big." He ran his fingers along the edge of whatever hid in the package. "Certainly not a cell phone." He set the package on end and ripped the sealed edge open, leaving the excised portion hanging from one corner. Judith could see a thin layer of plastic bubble wrap that provided the envelope's padding.

Luke peeked in but said nothing. His brow furrowed and his eyes narrowed.

"Are you trying to be a drama queen? What's in it?"

Reaching in, Luke removed a silver, narrow, thin device. It looked familiar to Judith.

"Is that a—"

"A USB flash drive. A SanDisk Cruzer Titanium to be exact."

"How can you know that?"

"It's printed on the side. It holds a gig of info."

They gazed at the object. "It's one of those portable hard drive things you use with a computer, right?"

"Not a hard drive, a flash drive, but that doesn't matter. Yes, it's used to back up files."

"So there are computer files on it?"

"Probably. Only one way to find out." He stood and started back to the car.

Judith followed on his heels, wondering if Luke was right about someone watching them.

four

The bookstore seemed crowded to Judith even though the clock had yet to reach 1:00. The seductive aroma of books and coffee filled the Barnes & Noble. They had arrived five minutes earlier after taking the most circuitous route from the park Judith had ever traveled. Luke explained that he wanted to know if they were being followed so what should have been less than a fifteen-minute drive up Archibald Avenue to Foothill Boulevard had turned into a forty-five-minute trek through a half dozen side streets, a dozen U-turns, and a short trip up the I-15 and back south again. Normally a comfortable traveler, Judith's stomach began to complain about Luke's driving. She breathed a sigh of relief when they pulled into the parking lot of the B&N.

"Why here?"

"Because it's public, because it has more than one exit, because it's noisy, and because people in bookstores don't bother other people in bookstores."

She wasn't sure she believed the last part. When they exited Luke's Volvo, he walked to the trunk and removed a computer bag.

"Have computer, will travel?" Judith quipped.

"Never leave home without it."

"Always ready to trade a little stock, is that it?"

"Partly."

He led the way through the parking lot and into the store. In the corner stood a coffee shop. Luke plowed through the other patrons and took up residence at a table in the corner. He sat with the wall to his back. "Vanilla latte, extra shot."

Judith blinked several times. "Excuse me?"

"We have to blend in. They serve coffee here so we should be drinking coffee."

"And you want me to fetch it for you?"

"Yeah, that'd be great, thanks."

She wondered if the flush she felt was noticeable. "Did we get married while we were out? I think I may have missed that."

"Oh, stop. This isn't a sexist thing. I have to crank up the computer. You can sit and watch me, or you can contribute to the cause and pick up a couple of coffees. You want me to pay for it?"

"I think I can handle it."

The line moved quickly, and Judith returned in less than five minutes with Luke's latte in one hand and a mocha in the other. The latter she considered a concession to the stress of the day.

"You didn't start without me, did you?" She set Luke's coffee next to the computer. He took it and sipped.

"No. Come sit next to me." He pulled a chair to his right. She hesitated. "Do you want to see this with your own eyes or would you prefer I describe everything to you?"

Judith moved to the chair and sat shoulder to shoulder with Luke. On the table rested Luke's HP laptop; the screen showed a small photo of Theodore Roosevelt, mouth open, jaw tight, teeth bared, and pince-nez eyeglasses perched on his nose. The quote read, "With self-discipline, all things are possible. Without it, even the simplest goal can seem like the impossible dream."

"Teddy Roosevelt?"

"He preferred TR, and yes, I'm a fan." Luke inserted the memory device from the envelope into a USB port on the side of the laptop. A moment later, a window opened listing all the files on the flash memory.

Judith bent closer. "A single document file and a photo file. Which should we open first?"

"I'm having second thoughts." Luke took his hands from the keyboard and leaned back. "I don't know what's in those files. There could be something that would destroy all the information on my computer."

"I'll buy you a new one," Judith snapped. "Why go this far only to back out now?"

"I have a lot of work on this machine. For all I know, there's a worm or virus in those files that will snatch every-thing and send it to someone over the Internet."

"Are you connected to the Net?"

"I don't have to be. The right malware program could log itself on. I mean, we're dealing with a pretty sophisticated guy here. The cell phones, the computerized voice, the use of who-knows-what-kind of surveillance."

"Look, Luke, I'm no computer genius, but I use one every day. Designs come to me in computer files. My business is fully wired, so I know a couple of things. First, you're not on the Net right now. I imagine this place has a wireless hook-up, but you'd have to sign in to use it, right? There's a cost to using the service."

"True."

Judith continued. "Besides, I'll bet you can turn off the wireless device in your computer with that button." She pointed at a button near the base of the screen with a glowing antenna icon. "Nothing can get out if the wireless is turned off. And you seem far too—" she started to say *paranoid* but instead finished with—"cautious to not have everything of importance backed up. Am I right?"

He nodded but said nothing.

"Okay, let's get down to brass tacks, Luke. You're not worried about someone sabotaging your computer; you're concerned that the file on the screen has your secret in it."

"Aren't you worried about the same thing?"

"Yes, but what are our choices? So far we've assumed that whoever is pulling our strings knows our secrets, so if we don't follow through, word will get out anyway. He'll see to it. Not to mention that a life is at stake."

"We think there's a life at stake. We have no proof of that."

"Yet here we sit." She placed a hand on his arm. "Proof or disproof may be in those files."

Luke smiled.

"That's a switch. What's got you grinning?"

"I once read that Noel Coward sent telegrams to a group of well-known members of London society. The telegram read, 'I know what you did. If I were you, I'd leave town.' They all left. It was a joke, but apparently, they all had guilty consciences."

"Everyone feels guilty about something," Judith said.

"Yeah, but not everyone stands to have their secret told to the world."

"Just open the file."

Luke straightened, returned his hands to the keyboard, and selected the document file.

"Uh-oh," Luke said.

On the screen was a small window that read, "Please Log In."

Nonplussed, Judith said, "It wants a password?"

"It seems so."

"Did the caller give you a password?"

"No," Luke admitted. He punched a single key several times. "It seems the password is six digits long."

"That could be anything. There must be hundreds of possible combinations."

"More like millions."

"Why would he hide the info behind a password?"

Luke sighed. "Maybe he's being cautious. Hiding this under the ballpark bench left a couple of variables open. There would be a short time between when the package was left and we arrived, otherwise we might have seen who left it."

"And during those few minutes someone could have stumbled upon the envelope." Judith thought for a moment. "He's thought of everything. At least if someone had gotten hold of it, they wouldn't be able to crack the password. Of course, now we have the same problem."

"It would be something that we know," Luke said. "Something that we could figure out but no one else could." He rubbed his chin. "When you got your call, did the voice mention any names or numbers?"

"No ... wait. Yes. A date. February 27."

"2-2-7? What about a year?"

"No mention of a year."

"But you know the year, don't you?"

Judith paused. Of course she knew the year of her secret. She would have preferred to have forgotten it, but that wasn't going to happen. "1984."

"2-2-7-1-9-8-4. No good. That's seven numbers."

"Drop the nineteen."

"Then that leaves only five numbers. Well ... maybe this way: 022784." He entered the numbers. An error message told them the password was invalid.

"What about you?" Judith gazed at Luke. "You said the caller knew your secret. Did he use a date with you?"

"Yes." The admission came slowly. "May 30."

"Try it."

Luke combined the numbers and typed 530227. Again an error message.

"What time did you get your call?" Judith pressed.

"I don't remember. Maybe 9:45, or something like that."

Judith thought. "Mine came a little earlier. About 9:30. Put my date first."

Again Luke's fingers pressed keys: 227530. He hit the Enter key.

The file opened.

Judith's phone rang.

five

Judith almost came out of her seat. Her heart galloped. She let it ring two more times before she had calmed herself enough to look at the caller ID display. It was Terri's office phone number. "My administrative assistant," Judith explained and snapped open the phone. "Yes, Terri."

"You've been avoiding me."

It wasn't Terri. The voice belonged to Marlin Find, stepson and royal pain. "I've been busy."

"With what? I called your cell phone earlier. I left a message for you to call me. You didn't."

"So you thought you'd use Terri's phone?"

"I figured you'd at least answer a call from her."

"What do you want, Marlin?"

Judith caught Luke looking at her. She lowered her voice.

"We need to talk about the upcoming board meeting. Have you read my memos?"

"Yes."

"You haven't responded." His words were terse and bore an edge.

"You already know how I feel about your suggestions. You're not ready."

"I'm more than ready."

"Not to be president of the firm. I'm keeping that job." She turned in her seat so that her back was to Luke.

"Under my proposal, you'd still be chairman of the board and the public image of the company. I just want to take the burden of the day-to-day work off your shoulders."

Judith felt anger rising in her like magma in a volcano. "The answer is no."

"I have support on the board." She could hear the smile in his voice. "It's just a matter of time."

"When push comes to shove, your supporters will see what you're really after and side with me."

"Gee, *Mom*, you sound like you don't trust me."

"Trust is earned, Marlin."

"When will you be back in the office?"

"When I'm good and ready." She hung up.

"Ah, family," Luke said. "Warms the heart, doesn't it?"

"Depends on the family," Judith snapped and turned her attention back to the document. Simple in appearance, the Word page contained a list of information:

Name: Abel Palek

Gender: Male

DOB: April 30, 2000

Current age: 8 years

Place of birth: Torrey Pines, California

Last residence: 1351 Tennyson Drive, Fresno,
    California

Disappeared: May 9, 2008

Last seen: Fresno, California, May 9, 2008

Instructions: Talk to no one. Do not go to the police
    or any police agency. If you do, he will die.

Incentive: February 27, 1984; May 30, 1985.

"Interesting," Luke said. "No mention of the parents."

"Maybe the boy is an orphan." Judith studied the first part of the document again. "What kind of name is Palek?"

"I don't have a clue. Abel is Jewish. That part is easy."

"He's been missing since May 9. That's last Friday. The whole weekend has passed."

Luke bit his upper lip. "A man can travel a very long distance in two days. And that's just by car. If the abductor took the boy on an airline, they could be anywhere in the world."

"This doesn't make sense." Judith slumped back in her chair. "Why us? The police have better resources than we do and if the kidnapper ..." she lowered her voice. "If the kidnapper took the kid across state lines, then the Feds get involved. Right?"

"Right."

"So why us? We're not private detectives. At least I'm not." She looked at him.

"I told you, I trade stocks."

"But you seem to have a knack for all this computer stuff."

He nodded. "I admit it. I'm a geek. So what?"

"What about the other file?"

He leaned closer to the monitor as if by doing so, new facts would emerge. Judith could still hear the artificial voice of the phone call.

"Let me try something."

Judith watched as Luke moved the cursor to the menu bar of the program and clicked on File. He then selected Properties. A window with five tabs along the top popped up.

"What is that?" she asked.

"It's a summary of the document's properties. When you install a program like Windows, it asks for certain information: name, company name, and the like. When you create a document it applies that information as well as tracks the number of words, the size of the file, when it was created, and so on."

This time, Judith leaned closer. "I see the window but I don't see any information."

Luke clicked through the tabs. "I don't know how he did it, but he's wiped all that information clean. This guy is good."

"Good isn't the word that comes to my mind. Open the other file."

"I can tell by the icon that it's a photo." He double-clicked on the file and a picture program opened. It held three photos.

The first picture filled the screen. A young woman with long black hair that hung to the middle of her back exited a glass door. Her head was tilted down but not enough to hide her face. She looked drawn and worn. "Do you know ...?"

Luke looked at Judith then back at the photo, a motion he repeated several times.

"Yes, that's me—a long time ago. A lifetime ago." Judith forced herself to take in the image. The picture drew old and forced-forgotten images to the forefront of her mind. The coffee in her stomach turned acidic. She moved her eyes from the screen to Luke. She couldn't read his expression. Whatever he felt, he kept to himself.

"Do you recognize the place?"

Judith nodded.

"Did you know that someone was taking your photo?"

"No. I've only been to that place once."

"What place?"

Judith didn't answer. Luke wasn't forthcoming, and she felt no obligation to be so herself.

"I understand." He returned his attention to the computer and clicked the arrow that would open the next photo. Judith thought she detected a slight hesitation.

The next photo was a color image of a young man with thick, shaggy hair that covered his ears and a thin beard that gripped his cheeks and chin. The background was blurred but Judith could make out a few buildings and other people. The man in the picture stood in a busy place.

"You?" Judith asked.

"Yeah. Every girl's dream, right?" His chuckle held no mirth. Then, as if talking to himself, he mumbled, "I've never seen this before. The indistinct background makes me think the photographer used a telephoto lens."

"Can you tell where you were?"

He shook his head. "Not enough visual clues. My best guess is that it was during my graduate days. If so, then those blurry buildings belong to UC Berkley."

"How old were you then?"

"Twenty-five. I'm forty-eight now, so that's about twenty-three years ago—"

"Nineteen eighty-five, just like in the document we just read. My picture was taken when I was twenty-one. I was twenty-one in 1984." She could see Luke doing the mental math. "I'm forty-five. Don't strain your brain."

He smiled. "Sensitive about your age?"

"No. I am what I am."

"Now you sound like Popeye."

"Just open the last photo."

Luke did and the sight of it made Judith gasp. Before her appeared the image of a black-haired boy. Thin, like most eight-year-olds, he sat on a gray rug with a white vein pattern. He wore khaki pants cut off just below the knee and a green T-shirt. He sat cross-legged looking at the camera. His feet were clad in athletic shoes.

"That ... that must be him." Luke's words barely crossed the distance to Judith.

Judith swallowed hard before attempting to speak. "Luke, what ... what's wrong with his eyes?"

six

 arlin Find paced his empty office oblivious to the passing of time. Judith—*Mom*—had once again gotten under his skin, and he was doing a masterful job of cultivating the anger. She never should have spoken to him the way she did; never avoided his calls. But she had and she was doing it more and more.

It wouldn't be so bad if she kept her disdain of him private, but he knew, *just knew*, that others were starting to talk behind his back. The fact that his father had left the business to her and not him wounded him a hundred times a day. Find, Inc., should be his, not hers. He was flesh and blood with the old man, all she had was a marriage certificate.

He stopped his pacing, forced himself to take several deep breaths, and ran a hand over his head. His hair was brown, short on the sides, long on the top. The hair felt stiff; it was caked in gel. The longer hair on top added an inch to his height. He wanted every inch he could get.

Compensation. That had been much of his life. Compensating for low grades, compensating for being shorter than most men, compensating for being second place to the woman who moved in when he was fifteen. At ten years younger than his father, his new stepmother was only fifteen years older than Marlin. He had never accepted her. Oh, she had tried to draw him in, a ploy as transparent as glass, but Marlin never fell for it.

At home, he had played the game. Not wanting to upset his father, who had a temper he wasn't afraid to show, Marlin had played polite and obedient, and gagged on every moment of it.

Now Dad was gone, buried on the hillside of the most prestigious cemetery in Southern California. He had earned that final dignity. Although a father at twenty, his dad had worked his way from finish carpenter to founder and owner of one of the most competitive and respected interior supply companies. During that time, perhaps because of the sacrificial hours he worked to make something out of nothing, Marlin's mother left with another man. His father once told him he had hired a private detective to find her. The man did, in Brazil, living in a small home and addicted to some kind of drug.

He never heard from her again. Marlin didn't care. The woman left when he was still a toddler. What kind of mother does that?

He grew up with no maternal influence. One mother had dumped him; the other had stolen his inheritance. Within a year of the marriage, she-who-would-steal-all had become the new figurehead for the company. His father had said many times, "Judith has the looks and personality to put the likes of Martha Stewart in her place." In quiet moments, young Marlin wondered if that was the reason for the marriage. Did his father need a pretty face to take the firm to the next level? Maybe he never loved her.

That thought made him feel good.

His day neared. It came closer with each sweep of the second hand around the face of the clock. Marlin resumed his pacing. Vice president wasn't enough. Not by a long shot. He needed to be in control; control of everything. And only one woman stood in his way.

For now.

The last thought brought him some peace.

He had done his planning. He had counted his supporters. He had done favors by the score, and people, including several board members, owed him big time. He had to wait for just the right time, and that time would come at next week's board meeting.

seven

The video editing room had an acrid, electronic smell to it. More than once, Karen Rose had suggested the need for better ventilation, but none of her immediate superiors listened. So once again, she sat in an overused-beyond-its-years secretary's chair that groaned and squeaked with every move she made. "Get it done and get it out," she said to herself. The video recorders and computers hummed, filling the small space with white noise that most ceased to hear five minutes after they entered the room.

The equipment was a mix of new and old. Channel 2 news was a competitor in the volatile television news market but not a wealthy one. While some stations had state-of-the-art computers and software, KTOT—known to disgruntled employees as K-ROT—had to make do with videotape decks that should have been scrapped five years ago. Frugality was the wind that drove this news ship—and it was running the organization aground. KTOT's competitors in the Los Angeles market made stars of their news team, but not KTOT. Being part of the LA market gave it some credibility but those on the inside knew that reporters came to KTOT to pad their résumés and to stay only long enough to be picked up by some other station. Karen had often wondered if Lawrence Media, which owned the station, kept it for its tax-loss potential. That had to be it. Karen Rose worked for a station designed to be nothing more than a write-off on some executive's ledger book.

Still, she came to work every day, investigated news stories, wrote copy, and did all the duties common to a television reporter. She also waited. Waited for her cell phone to ring or an email to arrive from another station offering her a better job. She had been waiting two years.

Turning her attention back to editing the videotape, her image, microphone close to her mouth, was motionless before her. Just thirty-two, she felt she looked older by half a decade. The woman who looked back at her wore neat brown hair to the shoulder and pale lipstick and displayed hazel eyes under gracefully arched eyebrows. Her gray, off-the-rack business jacket, matching slacks, and white blouse gave her an air of professionalism. Karen acknowledged that she was not a stunning beauty, but she was also far from being the wicked witch of the west. She was good enough to be in front of the camera, but lacked the eye-candy appeal that had become the hallmark of twenty-first century newscasting.

She made the final digital cut, ejected the videotape, and exited the dim, claustrophobic space. As the door closed behind her, she took a deep cleansing breath, attempting to evict the stale smell of the video bay.

"Is that the school graffiti piece?"

Karen looked up as her news director, Dwayne Hastings, approached. He stopped a respectful three feet away. "Yeah. A story on graffiti in LA; that'll make the ratings spike. Sure you don't want to save it for sweeps week?"

"Sarcasm is an ugly adornment," Dwayne said. He stood six-two, was trim, and still had the piercing blue eyes that had made him the best known news anchor in northern California. San Francisco had been his throne and for ten years, he sat upon it with regal flair. That ended when the alcoholism he had hidden so well became known in the worst possible way. Driving drunk, Dwayne Hastings lost control of his car and slipped over the center line of a two-lane road. He lived, the mother of two in the other car didn't. Lots of money paid to a high-price attorney kept him out of jail, but his days before the camera were over. Only KTOT would let him work in the industry and at half of what he earned before.

Karen had seen tapes of his on-air work and knew that Dwayne had changed his looks. No longer needing to keep a youthful appearance, he let the natural gray of his hair grow out and now sported a trim mustache and soul patch. It looked good on him. Although age had caught up, he was still a striking man—a striking figure whose eyes had lost the luster of life.

"Sorry, Dwayne. I guess I woke up on the wrong side of the web this morning."

He gave a nod of understanding. They both stood with their professional feet mired in the tar of KTOT. "How come you're doing the editing? Where's Cindy?"

Cindy Chu served as senior cameraperson—although she preferred "camera tech." A bright and pleasant woman who had no problem lugging out-of-date video cams around, Cindy was Karen's first choice for work and friendship.

"She dashed home. Her son forgot his lunch. She's making an emergency peanut butter and jelly delivery. She should be back any minute."

Dwayne nodded. He never complained or chastised someone for taking time to meet a family need. Most KTOT employees attributed his patience to the fact that his alcoholism had cost him his family and deprived another of a mother.

"How you coming on the Women in Industry series?"

Another sore spot. Karen considered such assignments as fluff pieces. Very few viewers would tune in to see how some rich woman is making out in the business world.

"It's going. I have my first interview this afternoon."

"Who's up first?" Dwayne had given her several names but left it up to her to refine the roll if she found someone more interesting.

"Judith Find of Find, Inc."

"Ah, the new Martha Stewart. Good choice. I met her once at some charitable get-together. She's sharp."

"I plan to ask some hard questions." Karen waited for the response.

"As you should. Just stay away from slander and libel." He gave a chuckle then turned serious. "Do your best on this assignment, Karen. I know you want out of this cul-de-sac of journalism. I understand. You deserve a break and I may have a way of helping."

Suspicion bubbled up in her. "What do you mean?"

"I've made a call to an old friend. I don't have many friends left, but this guy owes me. I saved his bacon once. Only he and I know what happened and that's the way it's going to stay. Anyway, he's in Seattle. Not the world's largest market, but it's far from being the smallest and the station is a network affiliate. It would be a great next step."

This was out of character. "I thought you wanted to keep the team together."

"I do. At least until I retire, but you deserve a little help. So do me proud on this and I'll make certain the right eyes see it."

"I ... I don't know what to say. Is something going on that I should know about?"

"Be sure you take Cindy with you. She's the best cameraperson we have."

Dwayne walked away leaving Karen to wonder why he so adroitly evaded her question.

eight

Judith closed her cell phone, ending the call.

"Well?" Luke directed the Volvo along the right lane of Interstate 10. They had been driving the freeways, going in circles discussing what to do. As they drove, Judith sat in the passenger seat, Luke's laptop resting on her legs. At times, the daylight glare made the screen difficult to read but Judith learned that she could shield parts of the monitor with her hand, the shadow making the image visible.

"Thirty minutes. The jet has to be fueled and the pilot needs to file a flight plan."

"Any way to keep him from doing that? A flight plan is a map to our destination."

"I think it's an FAA requirement. I'd be asking him to do something illegal and that could cost him his livelihood. Besides, merely asking would raise all kinds of flags in his mind."

"Asking to leave as soon as possible doesn't?"

"Executive pilots are used to sudden requests for transportation. That's what they get paid for."

"Okay. I guess you're right. So we have to kill about thirty minutes."

"In this traffic, it might take you half an hour to turn around and travel back to the airport."

"I hate wasting time." Luke frowned and checked the rearview mirror for what must have been the hundredth time since they left Barnes & Noble.

"We could use the time to talk ourselves out of this nonsense."

"It may be nonsense but it's pretty serious nonsense."

Judith knew what Luke meant. Whoever was orchestrating this had pictures of them from decades before and the dates of their secrets. She knew what she had done and had hoped that it would never come to the surface again. She had spent decades training her mind to avoid any hint of the event; now some stranger had her number and was using it to force her to do what she would never do under any other circumstances.

"I thought we were agreed." Luke's words had taken an edge. "We see this through until we find a way out, if there is a way out."

Judith gazed out the window, a dim reflection of her face revealed the stress she felt. How could any of this happen? How could someone know what she did decades ago and then wave it in her face? And why such an odd request? Find and rescue a boy she'd never met. There had been no mention of blackmail money but the Puppeteer was blackmailing them all the same.

"I didn't mean to snap at you," Luke said. "Did I hurt your feelings?"

Judith looked at the handsome man behind the wheel, then smirked. "It will take more than that to hurt my feelings. I developed emotional calluses a long time ago."

"Still, we're stuck in this together. We probably would never have met if life continued on as it was, and here we are, chugging along the freeway at a breakneck speed of twenty miles an hour."

"I'm thankful for the slower pace. You drive like a New York cabbie."

"I'll take that as a compliment."

"I didn't mean it as a compliment."

"That's okay. I'm an expert at adjusting reality to fit my needs."

"I keep coming back to the 'why us' question. Why a day trader and a businesswoman?"

"There's that word again—day trader. I hate that word."

"Trading stocks yourself instead of using a broker is the definition of a day trader."

He shook his head. "Listen, Ms. Businesswoman, I don't use a broker because I'm smarter than they are, have better insights, know my chosen industry more completely than they do, and have better connections. Why should I pay a commission to someone to do what I can do myself?"

Judith closed the notebook. Reading in the car made her queasy. "Okay, I'll yield the point but your protestation does nothing to shed light on the question."

"Maybe it has nothing to do with what we do now but what we have done in the past. Clearly, we can be blackmailed. Maybe we've been chosen because we both have something to hide."

"Makes sense, at least as much as any of this makes sense." Once again, she thought of asking Luke to drop her by the office and dealing with the fallout the best she could. But then she thought of the missing boy—Abel Palek? She owed him nothing. He was no kin. Yet no matter how many times she told herself such things, the boy with the strange eyes invaded her thinking.

Judith wondered about the youngster. If he were truly abducted, if his life were in some danger, then wouldn't someone know of it and call the police? The mystery man who had drafted them so easily with a threatening phone call and pictures he should not have had tracked them down and found a way to press them into service. He seemed a man of great resources and as such, wouldn't he be the better one to track a missing child?

Judith's head hurt from the unanswerable questions. She did not have enough information to make a reasonable guess at the machinations that put her in the car of a stranger.

"We'd better head for the airport."

"We're shooting in the dark." Judith bit her lip. "What can we hope to find by flying to Fresno?"

"It's the only hard fact we have. The document offered precious little."

"And why is that, Luke? Did it contain so little information because the writer had no other facts or—"

"Or are we being led like a dog on a leash? Yeah, I thought of that too. If that is true, we may learn the next thing we need to know in Fresno."

The dog on a leash image upset Judith. It was not only possible but likely that they were being worked by the caller. Dubbing him the Puppeteer made even more sense. He pulled the strings and they danced.

Judith flipped open her cell phone.

"Who you calling?" Luke seemed concerned.

"Terri, my assistant. I want to make sure she got my car and to let her know that I won't be in this afternoon."

"Are you sure that's wise?"

"I was only warned not to tell anyone what I was being pressed to do. I have appointments that need to be canceled." She hit the speed dial and waited for the ring. Nothing happened. Odd. She closed the phone and repeated the previous steps. This time she heard a ring which ended a second later as a mechanical voice answered.

"I'm sorry but your call cannot be completed. Your account has been suspended. Please dial ..."

"Unbelievable." She snapped the phone shut.

"What?"

"My account has been cut off." She looked at the phone in disbelief.

"Forgot to pay the bill?"

"Of course not. We spend thousands a year on cell phones for our execs and key personnel. Someone is going to get an earful from me." She dialed the two digit number plus pound that would connect her to customer service. The verbal battle began. When it was over, Judith felt more confused than before.

"From what I heard, that didn't go the way you wanted." Luke slowed the car as the traffic continued to coagulate around slow-moving big rigs.

"They said they haven't been paid in three months. I know that's not true. Our CFO oversees an experienced team of accountants. Such a thing can't happen."

"Try my phone."

"You didn't want me to try the call in the first place. Why the change of heart?"

"Just do it."

Judith took Luke's phone. It was one of the newer hybrids combining a cell phone with a handheld PC. It took her a moment to figure out how to dial through a screen instead of with buttons. She raised the phone to her ear.

"I'm sorry but your call cannot be completed—"

She switched the phone off. "Same thing. But you already knew that, didn't you?"

"I didn't know it, but I suspected it. You don't seem the kind of CEO that tolerates shoddy behavior from your employees. My guess is that our friendly Puppeteer has pulled a few more strings."

"Can he do that?"

Luke cut a glance her way.

"Okay, okay, obviously he can. What I mean to ask is *how* can he do that?"

"No way to know that. Maybe he owns the cell phone company, maybe he owns *someone* in the company; he could have bought someone off or blackmailed a key person like he's blackmailing us. We know the guy has some technical skill or people working for him who do; perhaps he hacked the system. Right now, all we have is guesswork."

Judith gazed at the traffic. Hundreds of people surrounded her. Every day she passed thousands of people on the freeways, side streets, in buildings and restaurants, whom she did not know. Any one of them could be a saint and any one a killer. None wore signs that revealed their heart and intent. Everyone kept their thoughts, desires, and sins behind a mask of flesh. She knew this well. She did it every day.

"Do you think he's watching us right now?"

"I've been trying to monitor the traffic. It's why I've been spending so much time in the slow lane. Most California drivers are too impatient to stay in this lane. So far I haven't been able to identify anyone on our trail. Of course, that doesn't mean anything."

"Why not?"

"A professional could follow us and we'd never know it. This guy has resources. If he wanted us followed he'd use a team, not just one man or woman. They'd take turns keeping an eye on us."

"It concerns me that you know this stuff."

"I told you, I'm paranoid."

"Any doubt of that is gone. You have paranoid down pat."

His laugh was forced. "If you're not paranoid, Judith, then you haven't been paying attention. My biggest failing in life is that I haven't been paranoid enough."

The sense of discomfort welling up in Judith made her wonder if mistrust was contagious. After all that had happened this morning, paranoia was no longer an irrational fear. In fact, it might be the most rational emotion she could have.

Luke directed the Volvo from the freeway and aimed for the Ontario International Airport.

nine

Where is she?" Marlin Find entered the room like a runaway ship enters port.

Terri jumped. "You scared me."

"I asked you a question, woman." Terri could see the red of Marlin's face creeping up his forehead. He was a hurricane in an expensive suit.

Terri stood. "I can only give you the same answer as before: I don't know. And the name is Terri, not woman."

The last statement took Marlin by surprise. Normally passive in personality, Terri never spoke harshly to those higher up the food chain than she.

"What's my last name?" Marlin finally managed. The red of his face moved toward crimson.

"What?"

"My last name."

Terri suspected a trick. "Find."

A cold, threatening smirk crossed Marlin's face. "As in Find, Inc.?"

"Yes, Mr. Find, as in Find, Inc."

"If you value your job you'll lose the attitude."

Terri struggled to keep her mouth shut. Something was wrong and she knew it. Judith had left in a hurry, left her car at Hutch's which Terri had to pick up, and now had been out of touch for a couple of hours. Marlin's entrance and anger had thrown a new type of fear in the stew of emotions churning in her. The wise course would be to remain quiet and see what the oaf had to say. Instead ...

"My boss is Judith. As it turns out, her last name is Find as well. Come to think of it, she's your boss too, isn't she?"

Marlin's jaw tightened. "Have you or have you not been in contact with my stepmother?"

"I had a call about two hours ago. Nothing since. I tried calling her but couldn't get through."

"Do you know why you couldn't get through? Because our cell phone account is in the tank. My cell phone doesn't work and neither does anyone else's. That's a bit strange don't you think?"

Terri didn't answer. Of course it was strange. Worse, it wrung a large measure of fear from her. She retrieved her purse, snatched her company cell phone, and dialed her desk number. Instead of ringing she got a message that the call could not be completed. She closed the flip phone.

"Can you tell me what is going on?" Marlin crossed his arms.

"I don't deal with the cell phones."

"I mean about Judith. Where is she? Why can't we reach her? Is there something going on I need to know about?"

Terri lowered her head and then shook it. "I don't know anything, but I'm getting worried. Very worried."

"If you ask me, it's your boss who should be worried."

Terri didn't have the stomach to argue. Anything she said might encourage the leech to stay. "If she calls, I'll tell her you're looking for her."

"And you had better call me right away. I want to know the moment she makes contact."

Terri made no commitment. "Is there anything else, Mr. Find?"

"Just remember your place in this firm. Better yet, remember my place. Now, if you'll excuse me, I have to go fix this cell phone problem. Before this is all over, I may have to have all the books audited. No telling what other bills have gone unpaid."

Terri felt relief as Marlin marched from the office. She was sure he felt that he had put her in her place, but all he had done was increased her resentment of him.

Judith had been gone a short time by most measures. A couple of hours was nothing in a full work day, but Judith never went anywhere without letting Terri know her destination, and when she was gone, she checked in frequently.

Terri had no facts for this, but she knew, just knew, that her boss, her friend, was in deep trouble and there was nothing she could do about it. She began to pray.

ten

The aircraft rested on the tarmac just outside the private rental hanger. The sleek, white-and-blue paint scheme never failed to impress Judith. She flew in the Cessna Citation Sovereign about three times a month. Other Find, Inc., execs used it as frequently to woo major distributors, wine and dine key clients, reward designers and suppliers. Nothing made an executive feel more important than being given a ride in a multimillion-dollar aircraft.

Luke parked in a small lot adjacent to the hangar, repacked his computer in its case, locked the car, and stared at it for a moment. Judith now knew enough of the man to know that he was worried that someone would tamper with his car. There was no way to keep an eye on the vehicle while flying at several hundred miles per hour. She thought she saw him sigh as he approached her and the two pilots who waited at the steps that led to the jet.

"Saying good-bye to your baby?" Judith asked.

"You know what I was doing." He studied the aircraft then the two pilots.

"This is Captain Tim Nelson our pilot and Larry Takita his first officer."

The pilot stood tall and trim. The gray tint in his hair spoke of a man of advancing years. Still he held himself with a military bearing. Larry Takita looked to be in his late twenties. He bore the attractive, smooth features of Japanese men.

Both men nodded at Luke. Both wore white shirts and blue pants, uniforms of the modern pilot.

"It's a pleasure to have you aboard with us today, Mr. Becker." The captain extended his hand and Luke took it and gave it a brief shake.

Luke looked at Judith and she answered before he could ask. "Many times. There are two crews for this flight. This crew is assigned to me, the CFO, CIO, and senior VPs."

"Is there a problem?" Nelson asked, eyeing Luke.

Judith gave her best smile. "No, Captain. Mr. Becker is a nervous flier."

"I understand." Nelson could have been a diplomat, Judith decided. "We expect no problems on the flight. The bird is fresh from a full service and the weather is clear. We'll have you up and back on the ground safely before you know it."

"Did you know that most airline disasters occur after routine maintenance? Some mechanic forgets a screw for this or a bolt for that and the next thing you know the impellers break loose of the engine cowling and come ripping into the cabin." Luke didn't wait for the answer. He fast-stepped up the stairs.

The captain turned to Judith and raised an eyebrow. Judith just shrugged.

Fifteen minutes later they were in the air and banking in a wide arc to the north. Judith watched the ground recede. Below she could see the I-10 and I-15 freeways, the San Gabriel Mountains green with spring rains. Large buildings shrunk to tiny boxes. Wisps of clouds decorated the air.

The cabin could seat eight passengers in two groups of four. The seats were soft, with white and brown leather. A green, custom weave carpet covered the deck, and unlike the plain white interior of most aircraft, the bulkheads were covered in a blue and white vinyl decorative covering. Judith's design tastes were not limited to homes and commercial buildings.

They remained silent as the craft climbed through the air. Some air turbulence over the mountains made the small jet bounce, but the rough ride ended a minute or two later.

Luke broke the silence. "Ever been to Fresno?"

Judith said, "No. I've flown over it a few times but have never had a reason to go there."

"Me either." He seemed distracted.

"What's on your mind?"

Luke fidgeted and looked out the window.

"I was only joking when I called you a nervous flier," Judith confessed.

"A joke to you; a fact for me. I hate flying."

Judith gave a reassuring smile. "I'm starting to sense that. Bad experience?"

He nodded. "A commuter flight out of Asheville to Atlanta. We hit cruising speed and altitude. The pilot switched off the seat belt sign. I unfastened my belt. Ten minutes later we hit a pocket of bad air. The plane dropped a thousand feet before leveling off. The sudden drop sent me flying from my seat. I smacked my head on the overhead luggage rack. I gave up flying."

"Yet here you are."

"Not by choice." He frowned. "I don't suppose this thing has a printer in it."

"It does." Judith reached down and to her right and pulled a thin mahogany table with a thick bar-top finish from a recess in the bulkhead. The table pivoted into place and a metal knee bracket locked it into place.

"Clever." Luke reached for his computer.

"One doesn't spend millions for an aircraft like this with-out getting the kind of necessities business execs need. There's a USB cable to your left. Pull it from its holder and plug it into your computer."

"All the luxury a corporate warrior could want." The sar-casm was clear.

"A company jet is not just luxury, Luke. When you pay an exec mid to high six figures, you don't want him cooling his heels in some airport lobby waiting on the mercy of the air-lines to get him back and forth to meetings. More than that—and you of all people should appreciate this—is the security issue. The jet allows us to keep execs safe and the material they carry safe. It's an ugly world out there."

"You're preaching to the choir about the ugliness of the world." He set his computer on the table. "I don't see the printer."

"It's up by the galley. It would just be in the way in the cabin. It's a color ink-jet. Will that work for you?"

"Perfect. This will take a moment."

"We've got less than an hour before we arrive in Fresno. I wonder ..."

"What?" Luke leaned back as he waited for the computer to boot up.

"Our cell phones have been cut off but—" She nodded to a green telephone handset that sat snug in a cradle in the bulkhead.

Luke pursed his lips. "It might. Is it on the same cell car-rier as your phone?"

"No. I'm going to try."

"I wouldn't. Even if our—employer—has thought of that or couldn't cut it off, he would certainly have your company phone tapped, or have bugs placed in your office and that of your assistant."

"If I don't call in, my assistant will slowly go nuts. Sooner or later, she's going to call the police assuming I'm hurt or have been abducted."

"I think he wants us cut off from everyone."

"Frankly, I don't much care what he wants. He's not our friend, Luke; he's our problem. I'll do what I have to do to protect myself. I've gone this far because I have yet to figure a way out of this, but I will not be his puppet."

"We are already his puppets. That began when we answered the phone."

"So you plan to just go along like a sheep following some sadistic shepherd?"

"Don't start with me. This morning I was a happy recluse sitting at my computer reading blogs and juggling investments. Now I'm a refugee fleeing my past and on a mission to save a boy who might not even exist. For now we move with caution."

"We do? You calling the shots now?"

"What?"

Judith knew from his expression that he understood her. "What is it with men? Do you think this is some movie where a man and woman are teamed up and the man makes all the hard decisions because the woman is just too frail or stupid to make the right choices?"

"I said nothing like that. Sheesh, get over yourself, woman. It's your life, your jet, your phone, do what you want. Do you want me to step outside while you call?"

Judith started to snap back but the image of Luke stepping outside a jet traveling four hundred miles an hour and thirty thousand feet above the earth tickled her. She swallowed the laugh but couldn't hide the smile. She grabbed the phone before Luke could comment and dialed her office number.

Seconds ticked by at glacial speed. Judith was about to hang up when the crackly ringing gave way to a familiar voice.

"Find, Inc., Judith Find's office, this is Terri, how may I help you?"

"Terri. It's Judith."

"Ms. Find? I've been worried."

Ms. Find? She only called Judith that in the presence of others. Someone must be in the front office with her. "Terri. I had to make a sudden trip and won't be in the office this afternoon—"

A loud pop stabbed Judith's ear and she almost dropped the phone. The pain faded in the thundering pounding of her heart as she heard Terri scream.

The line died.

eleven

We have to turn around!" Judith released her seat belt and shot to her feet, then thought about what she was doing. She could contact the captain through the handpiece she held a moment ago. That was one of the reasons it was there. She reseated herself and reached for the phone.

A hand stopped her.

"Wait," Luke said. "Tell me what happened."

"I have to tell the pilot to turn us around."

"In a second; first tell me what happened."

Judith felt fury rise in her. She didn't like explaining her-self under normal conditions; stress made her all the more obstinate. She jerked her hand away. "I'm telling you something's wrong."

"I'm not arguing with you. I'm trying to understand."

She clenched her jaw then let it relax. Reason pushed and shoved against the fear that clouded her judgment. "I heard something. A loud pop, then Terri screamed."

"A loud pop? Like a gunshot?" Luke leaned forward.

"No. It sounded electrical, like a short in the phone."

Luke pressed her. "What kind of scream?"

"What do you mean what kind of scream? How many screams are there?"

"Come on, you know the answer to that. There are scores of screams. Did she scream like something surprised her or like someone with a bloody axe just walked in the room?"

Judith thought, the sound of Terri's voice still ricocheting in her mind. "Surprise, I guess."

"Not terror, but surprise?"

"I guess. I don't know. How am I supposed to know the difference?"

"Okay, something startled her but didn't terrorize her. That's good." Luke's eyes darted from side to side and his brow furrowed.

"We don't know that. I'm guessing." Judith reached for the phone again, picked up the handset but didn't dial. "You don't think we should turn around?"

"No. It would be counterproductive for us and for the Puppeteer."

"Why should I care? If Terri's in danger, I should be there."

"Really. Let's see: if we turn around, we could be back on the ground in thirty or forty minutes assuming we can land right away. By the time you get to the car and drive to your office another twenty or thirty minutes will have elapsed. Figure an hour."

"If that's what it takes."

"I can understand the desire to go back, Judith, but have you thought that you might be doing her a greater disservice than aid?"

Judith tilted her head. "A disservice?"

"Yes. What just happened? You called your office, you connected, and then something happened on the other end. Part of our marching orders was not to contact others. This guy means business. I doubt he's going to tolerate much rebellion on our part." He leaned back. "Remember I said that he might have your offices bugged or your phones tapped. You told me he knew what your office looked like. Someone must have spent some time in there and they may have planted spy cameras, listening devices, and who knows what else."

Judith reset the phone. "How could he know ... You mean that he or one of his minions was listening in when I called and did something?"

"Exactly. I'm guessing they planted a device in the phone to deliver a shock, or sound, or even destroy the electronics of the phone. It could be one of a hundred things."

"But why?"

"To keep you incognito. Most likely it was a message to you. Who knows what the next message will be like? It could be worse."

"And so by going back, you're saying I could be further endangering Terri?"

"I'm afraid so."

"But you're just speculating." The fury roiled in Judith.

"That's true. I could be all wet. Are you willing to take the chance that I'm wrong?"

Judith thought for a moment, letting her gaze roam out the window. She felt so alone, her mind as inconsequential as the few gossamer strips of clouds beneath them.

"No."

Terri examined her left hand. It bore a red stripe across the palm. For a moment she thought she saw a blister rising, but none appeared. Her left ear hurt, her knees felt weak, and her stomach flopped like a fish on a wood dock.

"Are you okay?" Marlin reentered the office through the same door he had fled a few seconds before.

"I . . . think so. I feel a little funny. Maybe I should see a doctor."

"Of course, of course. Was that Judith on the phone?"

"What?"

"Focus, girl. Was that Judith on the phone?"

Terri wondered how long the jail sentence was for stabbing an obnoxious clown with a letter opener. For a few seconds, Terri was ready to pay the price. "Yes."

"What did she say?"

"Nothing. Well, nothing I could hear." She looked at the pieces of the phone on her desk. "How can a phone fracture like that?"

"I don't know. Are you sure she didn't say anything?"

Terri reached for the letter opener with her undamaged right hand, took it, then used it to push the phone's receiver toward Marlin. "Here. Why don't you call her yourself?"

Marlin looked at the phone. "No, thanks."

Terri put down the letter opener and opened her handbag. She removed a compact and popped it open, using the mirror to look at her ear. Other than a slight reddening, it seemed fine. Returning the compact, she examined her hand. The red mark was already fading and would probably be gone by the time she could be seen by a doctor at any urgent care.

She looked at Marlin.

Marlin looked at her.

Finally, Terri spoke. "We should do something. I'm calling the police."

"For a technical failure?"

"Technical failure? Look, I'm a little too rattled to play good-employee-bad-boss. So get as angry as you like, but this is not technical failure. When was the last time you heard of a phone zapping its user and blowing itself apart?"

"It didn't really blow up. It just sort of fell to pieces."

"With all due respect, Mr. Find, you didn't stay around long enough to see what happened. It went off and you disappeared."

"A reflex action. You'd have done the same."

She moved into Judith's office, Marlin close behind. "Call it what you will, it was abnormal. I'm calling the police."

"We don't need the negative publicity. I forbid you to call."

She stopped at Judith's desk and looked at the phone. She hesitated. She looked up in time to see Marlin smile.

"I see you're coming around. Do not make that call."

"I'm not coming around." She walked past him, through her office, and to the elevator. She punched the call button.

"What are you doing?"

"I think I'll use the pay phone in the lobby. Whoever rigged my phone may have rigged Judith ... Ms. Find's."

Marlin seized her arm. It felt like a vise had closed on her flesh. She refused to wince or reveal any sign of pain.

"Let go of me or the phone will not be the only thing lying in pieces up here."

"You think I'm afraid of you?" He laughed.

"Can you say assault and battery? If you fear bad press about the police investigating my phone, imagine what the press will do with a story about the senior VP of Find, Inc., abusing a female employee. It might even have an effect on stock prices. Who knows?"

"You wouldn't do that."

"Try me."

The elevator arrived. Terri stared into the cold eyes of Marlin. He relented, releasing her. Without a word she stepped into the elevator and let its doors shut. The look on Marlin's face chilled her.

As the elevator descended, a wave of nausea rolled through her. She had never stood up to someone as rich and powerful as Marlin Find. In truth, she had parroted what she had seen Judith do a few times. Courage was not her strong suit.

She thought of the phone.

She thought of Judith's call.

Soon a blizzard of fear drove the nausea away.

Terri began to cry.

twelve

Judith struggled to focus. Terri's startled scream still reso-
nated in her mind. Luke had printed several documents:
the boy's picture, the Word document, an Internet-generated
map of the house they planned to visit in Fresno, and the
photos of themselves from years before.

"There has to be something we're not seeing." Luke shifted
the papers on the small desk as if by rearranging them he
would see them with new insight.

"I can't get past his eyes. Surely someone has been playing with the photo in the computer." Judith picked up the
color print of the boy named Abel Palek and saw the same
dark hair, the same fair complexion, the same serious look,
and the same lavender eyes.

Lavender eyes. It made no sense. Judith had nothing more
than high school biology but she was pretty sure purple eyes
were unnatural. She had read novels where the author had
described a character, usually the beautiful protagonist, as
having violet eyes, but these were as purple as lilacs. "Maybe
he's wearing contacts?"

"Maybe. I don't think it's possible for a human to have
purple irises."

"Why would someone fit a boy with colored contact
lenses?"

"Maybe he has a vision problem and the purple tint protects his retina. Maybe ... maybe ... I got nothing." Luke
leaned back and rubbed his eyes. "We'll be landing soon and
I hoped to have more info than we do."

"If the Puppeteer wants us to find the boy, then why give us so little information?" Something else about the photo puzzled her.

"Perhaps it's all he has."

Judith didn't agree. "He has too many resources. If he knows so much about us that he knows the secrets that would make us his marionettes, then how can he be so ignorant about this?"

"I don't have a clue."

Clue? Was that it?

Judith shoved the photo across the table. "Can you zoom in on this?"

"You mean zoom in on some part of it? I can with the computer, but looking closer at his eyes isn't going to help."

"I don't want to see his eyes. I want to see the floor."

"You're not serious."

"I am. Just show me some of your computer kung-fu or whatever it is you do and give me a close-up of the floor."

Luke leaned over the table again and started tapping keys. In a few moments he had the picture on the screen displayed by photo software. He turned it so Judith could see. He moved the cursor to the toolbar and tapped the icon of a magnifying glass. "Say when." He tapped the icon again and the picture grew larger.

Judith leaned in. "There's something familiar about the floor."

"It just looks like a wood floor; maybe one of those laminate jobs—"

"That's it!" Judith pulled the computer closer and took over the keyboard. She worked with computers every day. This wasn't complicated. She zoomed in closer and closer. "This photo is unusually clear."

"It's a big file. Almost two megabytes."

"I don't believe it." Judith raised a hand to her mouth. "What are the odds?"

"What do you see that I don't?"

Judith turned the laptop so Luke could see it. "You hit the nail on the head when you mentioned laminate."

"I don't follow."

"How do I explain this? There are different types of wood flooring and different ways of installing them. For example, a true wood floor is a series of narrow planks connected by a tongue and groove edge. The wood is glued if it's being installed over a concrete substrate or toenailed if placed over a subfloor. Because the planks are true wood all the way through, it's an expensive way to go but the floor usually lasts longer and is easier to repair.

"Most laminate flooring consists of a thin layer of decorative wood—say red oak—over a fabricated substrate. Those floors are usually installed by floating the floor over the subfloor."

"Floating?"

"The flooring snaps together. It isn't nailed or glued. It allows the floor to expand and contract."

"I don't see why any of that is important."

"The floor in this picture is a laminate. The style is called Blocked Maple. I know because I designed it."

"You designed the image used on the floor?"

"Not personally. We have a design department and sometimes we use outside designers. They approach us and if we like what they have, we make suggestions, buy the rights to the image, and farm it out for production. We handle the marketing."

"And you recognize the pattern."

"It's as unique as a photo of your mother. You look at something long enough and it gets burned into your memory. This pattern was designed and photographed by a guy named Stewart Blink."

"Stewart Blink. That's his real name?"

"I doubt it. Some of these artist types like to remake themselves."

"I never thought of a floor designer as being an artist."

Judith smiled. "You need to broaden your horizons, Mr. Day Trader."

Luke sighed but didn't object to the dig. "How does any of this help us?"

"It helps us because that particular design flopped big time. I lost a truckload of money on that design. No one knows why, but it took off like a herd of turtles."

"You have a way with words, lady. I'll give you that. Still, I don't see—"

"I think I can track the few sales we had. It won't be easy, but a few calls might narrow the field for us."

"You're saying that we might be able to find the address where the boy is being held?"

"Not just by that." Judith looked at the image again. "I also recognize the Persian rug."

"You're kidding, right?"

"Not at all. Remember, this is what I do. My company specializes in interior design products. We're one of the top players in the field and we're not a one-pony show. We design and manufacture everything from paint to light fixtures. It's a multibillion-dollar business and we make our money by being informed and putting out the best product. Two years ago, we retained an overseas company to manufacture a line of Persian inspired rugs."

"And you know for a fact that that rug is one of yours?"

"I do."

The pilot's voice came from the overhead speakers, announcing their descent into Fresno. The table had to be stowed and the computer put away. Both were done reluctantly.

"Here's the thing." Judith stacked the printouts. "I might, and emphasize the word *might*, be able to track where the flooring went and compare it to where that style of carpet was sold. It's possible that the numbers will be too large, but we won't know unless we try."

"You keep that kind of data? You know who bought what?"

"No, we don't, but the retailers do a pretty good job. I'll start by seeing what outlets sold that type of flooring. It went out in trial, which means there were a limited number of retailers stocking the item. The rug may be more difficult but it might work."

Luke narrowed his eyes.

"What?"

"I'm trying to calculate the odds that two products from your company would appear in a photo of a missing boy you've been asked to find."

That had crossed Judith's mind as well. The odds were astronomical and that made it all the more frightening.

thirteen

I assure you, Officer, it's nothing more than a malfunction in the phone." Terri could see the tension on Marlin's face.

"I plan to call the manufacturer and give him a piece of my mind."

Better keep what you have left. Terri stood to one side, rubbing the palm of her left hand. It had ceased to hurt and the redness had almost faded completely.

The focus of Marlin's attention was a trim, black man in a black suit coat over a gray dress shirt with a maroon silk tie and charcoal colored trousers. Terri noted his shoes were shined, his tie hung straight, and the coat looked expensive. A definite clotheshorse, she decided.

"We're already here, Mr. Find. We might as well take a look. I'd hate to think that I called out a county bomb expert and not put him to good use. I'm sure you understand."

"But ..." He trailed off.

Marlin could be obnoxious but he wasn't stupid. This battle was lost to him. He had no choice but to play along. He turned his heated gaze to Terri. It was going to be a rough time after the cops left. She hoped Judith would be back soon. Terri could use her protection.

The bomb squad, three men with electronic equipment Terri didn't recognize, made their way to the elevator. They had cleared the room, examined Terri's damaged phone, and checked Judith's desk phone. In both, they found a device that couldn't be classified as a bomb, but didn't belong in any business phone. The detective thanked the men and released them.

Detective Wilson served the City of Ontario, but all matters dealing with explosives fell to the county sheriff's office. Only after the office had been declared safe had Terri, Marlin, and everyone else on the floor been allowed to return.

Wilson looked at Terri and his eyes drifted to her hands. "Are you sure you don't want to see a doctor?"

Terri stopped fidgeting. "Um, no, I'm fine. Just a little unsettled by all of this. The paramedic said I was okay."

The last hour had been filled with excitement. Terri had used the pay phone in the first floor lobby to call the police. Once the dispatcher heard the phrase, "phone blew up," she dispatched not only the police but fire and paramedic units. The entire building was cleared and the county bomb squad went into action. Every phone on the floor had been examined but only Terri's and Judith's had been tampered with. Bomb sniffing dogs had searched every floor.

Things were returning to normal but Terri knew the talk would continue for weeks.

"Now that we know that there are no bombs in the building," Marlin said, "maybe we can all get back to work."

"I am working," Wilson said.

"Of course. I didn't mean you. I meant my employees."

"I need you and Ms. Penn a little longer."

Terri watched Marlin work his jaw as if to object but he said nothing. To protest too much might make him look like he was covering something up.

"Do either of you know of any reason someone would plant electronic devices in Ms. Penn's and Ms. Find's phone?"

"No," Terri said. "And I'm worried about her. She went to an unscheduled meeting this morning and hasn't returned. I was talking to her when the phone did what it did."

Wilson nodded. "I have a crime scene investigation team coming over. They'll take the phones and dust for prints. I'm afraid they're going to leave a mess." He looked around the office, clearly impressed by the luxury and design. "Pity."

"I understand," Terri said.

"You said you were talking to Ms. Find on the phone when it shocked you."

"It rang, I answered, then zap. I got shocked." She rubbed her palm again.

"Where is Ms. Find now?" Wilson stepped to Terri's desk and examined the phone again.

"Like I said, I don't know." Terri tried to prevent the stress she felt from coloring her tone and words but the effort was useless. "She got a package she didn't expect. Something was wrong. She quizzed me about it before she left. I didn't know what to tell her."

"Does she normally get packages?"

"All the time. Three or four a day. Usually from designers and the like."

"But something was different about this one?"

Terri nodded. "We don't know where it came from or how it got here. That's why I'm so concerned about her. And when the phone went ballistic I got even more worried."

The forehead of the detective furrowed. "Tell me more about the package."

"I don't see what a package has to do with all this," Marlin said. "And we know Judith is fine because she called in before the telephone mishap."

"I'm suspicious by nature, Mr. Find," Wilson said. "You share a last name with Ms. Find. What's your relationship to her?"

"I'm her stepson, as if any of that is your business."

If the jab bothered the detective he didn't let it show. His patience with Marlin impressed Terri, but she wished the officer would put him in his place.

"You're not worried about your mother?" Wilson asked.

"I'm certain she is well. She has a very independent streak."

"Ms. Penn, you said that Ms. Find was upset about the package?"

"I don't think upset is the right word. She's not the kind to be intimidated, but I know she was puzzled and maybe even a little put out. In the bathroom she said—"

"In the bathroom?" Wilson raised an eyebrow.

"Yes, sir. That was weird. She insisted that we meet in the ladies' room."

"Why would she do that?"

"She didn't say. I asked, but she told me to hush and follow her, which I did." Terri felt stupid for not having pressed the issue.

"Does she often tell you to hush?"

"No. I can't remember her ever saying that to me. It made me think something was really wrong."

"I can imagine. Then what happened?" Wilson took no notes but Terri was certain he was memorizing every word.

"She asked about the package. We discussed how it could have gotten on my desk. You see, I left last night and I always lock my office. When I came in, there were three packages on my desk."

"And you don't know how they got there?"

"Detective, the woman is just an administrative aide. Surely she just forgot to lock the door and the UPS guy set the packages there."

"I *locked* the door last night." Terri had given up hiding her emotions.

Wilson raised a hand. "Mr. Find, your office is on this floor, correct?"

"Yes."

"Why don't you wait for me there? I need to ask Ms. Penn a few more questions."

"But—"

"I appreciate your help, Mr. Find. Thank you."

The words carried an unspoken message. Marlin took his time leaving, like a child hoping a father would change his mind about exiling a child to his bedroom. No change of mind came.

Alone with the detective, Terri relaxed some but her stomach still twisted and churned.

Without a word, Wilson walked into Judith's office and began looking around. He stood in the middle of the expansive office, slowly turning, his eyes moving as if they were video cameras capturing every detail. "It's a nice room."

Terri tilted her head. The words were true but spoken in a way that made her think the detective's thoughts rested elsewhere. "Ms. Find is very proud of it."

Wilson strolled from the center of the room to the desk, to the fireplace, to the artwork that hung on the walls, back to the seating area. His steps were leisurely. He returned to the desk and paused behind it. He stopped and stared at a spot low on the wall. Terri moved closer and followed the detective's gaze. He stared at an electrical outlet on the wall. It looked like every other outlet in the office—except this one tilted slightly to the right, so little that Terri would never have noticed it had the detective not been staring at it. She also saw a slight scratch in the paint.

He turned. "Ms. Penn. I'm afraid I'm going to have to ask you to accompany me to the station. I have more questions for you."

"What? But what if Ms. Find comes back?"

"You may leave her a note, but I must insist. Come with me."

He took her by the elbow and led her from the room.

fourteen

Terri almost melted in relief when Detective Wilson told her that he had no intention of taking her to the police station.

When she confessed her confusion, he led her to a quiet corner of the first floor lobby. Outside, beyond the glass wall of the reception area, the last fire truck pulled away. Two patrol cars were parked by the walk that led from the parking lot to the front of the building. A uniformed officer chatted with a news reporter, a woman who held a microphone in front of the cop who seemed to be enjoying the attention. A cameraman stood a few feet away. It took a moment before Terri realized that it wasn't a cameraman but a camerawoman. The sight of them reminded her of an appointment that Judith had made for that afternoon. She wondered if the reporter in the lot was the same that was supposed to be in Judith's office. Terri wondered what they were saying.

"I think your company may have a problem. You saw the electrical outlet?"

"Yes, but I don't know why an outlet is so important."

"You noticed the faceplate was crooked and that someone scratched the paint. That was the only mark I could see on the walls."

"Ms. Find is picky about such things." Terri still struggled to follow the detective's logic.

"Why do you suppose your boss took you to the ladies' room to ask you about the package?"

"I don't know. This whole thing is out of character for her."

Wilson frowned and looked like a man trying to explain calculus to a preschooler. "Let me cut to the chase. I think someone has bugged your boss's office and yours as well. I can't be certain without removing the cover, but there may be a listening device behind the outlet faceplate. Your boss figured that out somehow. It must have something to do with that mysterious package. Did she tell you what was in it?"

"No."

"There may be video surveillance going on. I don't know much about your industry. Is it competitive?"

"Well, yes. Of course. Very much so."

"Is it the kind of business that attracts industrial spying?"

"I suppose so. I know the executives have to sign nondisclosure agreements, go through background checks. Judith ... Ms. Find is very secretive about new products and designs. Do you think one of our competitors planted the listening device?"

"I'm just guessing at this point."

Terri bit her lip. "What do I do? And what about Judith? How do we find her?"

"She made an effort to contact you. It's a shame you couldn't hear what it was she had to say."

"I'm really worried. Are you going to put out a missing person's report or whatever you call it?"

"She's only been gone a few hours. She may not be missing, but I promise to stay on this. For now, I want you to go to lunch, take a walk, hit the gym, do something that will eat up a couple of hours before you go back to work. I want the spies to think you went to the station with me." He pulled a card from his wallet. "Call me if Ms. Find comes back or contacts you. My pager number is on there. It pages my cell phone. Call it anytime and I'll return your call."

"How can I work knowing that someone is listening to everything I say?"

"I'm going have our tech guys come over. They work with our crime scene techs. They'll sweep the area and seize any spy devices. That will tip our hand that we know about them, but that's probably already been done. Can't unwind the clock."

Terri felt pulled down by the quicksand of worry and fear, but she was determined to do exactly as told.

Karen Rose turned from the sheriff's deputy and faced the camera. "For the employees of Find, Inc., and the dedicated police and fire personnel of Ontario there is a great sense of relief that what was thought to have been a bomb turned out to be nothing more than a faulty phone. This is Karen Rose reporting from the parking lot of Find, Inc." She continued to stare into the lens for several seconds then lowered the microphone.

"Not bad," Cindy Chu said, relaxing and pointing the business end of the camera down. "Serendipity, baby. Talk about being in the right place at the right time."

"Too bad it was nothing but a cranky phone."

"You're not saying that you wanted there to be real bombs in the building, are you?" Cindy unloaded the camera from her shoulder.

"You know better than that." Karen began to loop the mike cable. "I don't want disasters to happen; I just want to be there when they do. That's the news business."

"Do you think the interview is still on? Or are we going to have to settle for this story?"

Karen started to reply when she noticed a woman approaching. Her eyes were fixed on Karen but her steps were timid. "I wonder what all this is about."

"Excuse me," the woman said. Karen figured her to be close to fifty and she had an air of authority about her. "You're with KTOT?"

With the call letters painted in bright yellow on the side of the blue news van Karen knew the question was rhetorical, a way of starting a conversation.

"Yes," Karen said. "I'm Karen Rose. How can I help you?" The woman's voice seemed familiar.

"We've spoken. I'm Terri Penn, Ms. Find's administrative assistant."

"Yes, I recall. We spoke on the phone. You helped arrange the interview."

"That's me. I'm afraid the interview is off for the day. I'm sure you understand."

"Actually, this would be the perfect time for the interview. We could show how a woman executive of Ms. Find's stature deals with an emergency like this."

"I'm afraid that won't be possible," Terri said. She started to turn.

"Wait a minute. We had a deal. It costs the station a lot of money to send me and a camera tech out. You can't just brush us off."

Karen watched Ms. Find's administrative assistant frown. There was something else in her face; something that said a dark secret was hidden behind the mask. "I apologize for the inconvenience, but you did get a story. Granted it wasn't planned, but you were here at just the right time. I don't see any other television media. Do you? It looks to me like you got a scoop."

She may look a tad mousey but there's a little hint of fire in her. "Is Ms. Find here?"

"No."

Unlike buildings in major cities, the Find, Inc., building didn't have basement parking. Karen returned her gaze to something she had seen earlier: a series of parking stalls with aluminum poles. One post bore a small sign that read: J. FIND. In the stall sat a late model silver Lexus.

"Isn't that her car?" Karen nodded in the direction of the vehicle.

"I parked it there."

"You drive your boss's car, or are you just using her parking place?"

"Ms. Find is not in the building. The appointment you had with her must be postponed. Please call again and I'll see when Ms. Find can fit you in."

"Wait—"

Terri Penn didn't wait; she didn't look back.

"Weird," Cindy said. "Of course, they just had a bomb scare. I suppose I would shy away from the media too if I was a bigwig like Judith Find."

"Yeah, maybe." Karen wasn't convinced. Her reportorial instincts were chiming like Big Ben. "There's something wrong with the picture."

"Like what?"

"Like why Find's right-hand woman is leaving the building when everyone else is going in. I'd think that there'd be a ton of calls to make, people to direct and the like."

"The deputy told us the incident happened on the top floor. Maybe the lady was involved and just needs a little time to herself."

"Maybe." Karen stood with the mike cable in her hand, mired in one of those moments field reporters often faced: walk away or barge in. She needed a story—a big story to show her skills to the bigger markets. Being timid might be the sure way to spend her entire career at KTOT.

Conflicting thoughts covered her mind like ocean foam on the beach. She watched as Terri Penn moved past the car in Judith Find's slot, walked another fifty or so feet and slipped into a blue Volkswagen Jetta. The engine started and the car drove slowly away. As soon as it had left the parking lot, Karen said, "Get the camera."

"I just packed it."

"Stop complaining, Cindy, and grab the camera. We're going to interview Ms. Find."

"But she's not here."

"So says her guard dog, but I know when I'm being lied to. She's here and if she isn't, something else is afoot. Let's go find out what it is."

"Okay, lady, but if you get in a fistfight with some bruising security guard, you're on your own."

"You'd probably ask him out."

"Maybe. At least I'll know that he has sound judgment."

The lobby was wide and as ornate as one would expect for a business based on interior design. Sandstone tile complete with fish fossils covered the floor; plants and small trees— real, not silk, Karen determined—filled every corner. A sitting area boasted sofas, heavily cushioned chairs, and tables made from expensive-looking wood. Karen knew nothing of interior design but she was pretty sure this stuff didn't come from the local furniture store.

A curved reception desk stood at the gateway to the eleva-tors. A twenty-something blonde with just the right amount of makeup on just the right kind of face wearing just the right kind of women's business attire sat behind the smooth, mahogany desk. She looked a little flushed, something to be expected of a person who had just endured a bomb scare. Learning that it was nothing more than a phone mishap would take some time to seep into the mind and to settle a pounding heart.

Karen approached and offered her biggest smile. "Wow, what a morning," she said glancing at the name plate on the desk.

"You can say that again." The receptionist's voice was clear and lilting. "I've never been so scared."

"Good thing it turned out to be a false alarm."

The girl knew how to be friendly. "Don't I know you?"

Good, a viewer. "I'm Karen Rose with KTOT News and this is Cindy Chu, ace camerawoman. You must be Darla Alli-son. I was told you'd be the first person I would see."

"That's it. I've seen you on television. It is like so cool to meet you." She stopped suddenly and reined in her youth speak. "Are you here because of the scare?"

"We did a piece on that, but we have an appointment with Ms. Find. It was set for earlier, but with everything that happened we had to wait."

"Of course." She looked at the computer monitor and typed in a name. "I have to verify the appointment. No one is allowed on the top floor without permission."

"Certainly. I understand. You can't be too careful these days. We have the same rule at the station." They didn't but Karen thought a little common ground might go a long way. She waited as Darla punched in the name. Her fingers flew over the keys—clearly a woman who had done this countless times.

Karen learned a long time ago that time passes slower for the devious. She feared that Terri Penn had canceled the appointment but hoped that she had forgotten in all the excitement. Cindy cleared her throat nervously.

"Here it is." Darla opened a drawer in front of her and removed a plastic card with a magnetic strip. She swiped it through a device next to the computer monitor that reminded her of a debit card reader in a fast-food joint. Darla watched the screen for a moment then smiled. She handed the plastic card to Karen. "Use the elevator closest to the lobby. Once inside, you'll see a slot just above the floor buttons. Slip this in face up and remove it. The elevator will take you directly to the executive floor."

"Thank you. You've been a big help."

"It is a pleasure meeting you." She smiled unveiling a row of perfect teeth that must have cost her parents a fortune.

Ten steps later, Karen and Cindy entered the elevator and watched as the doors closed.

fifteen

Judith's father had been a big fan of Buddy Rich and Gene Krupa. Hardly a week went by in which she wasn't exposed to the aggressive rhythms of the big band drummers. She thought of them as she stood at the door waiting for someone to answer the bell. She thought of them because neither man at their best could match the pounding of her heart.

She couldn't find the right word to describe the situation: surreal, abstract, confusing, enigmatic. She settled on *madness*. What better word would convey the nonsensical behavior of flying in a corporate jet from Ontario to Fresno so she could stand on the porch of a 1920s bungalow home to ask questions of whoever lived here about the abduction of a boy? Yup, madness was the word of choice.

"Nice place." Luke rocked on his heels, his hands behind his back as if waiting in line at a Taco Bell. "Well kept. Someone put a lot of time into this house."

Small talk, the result of nerves. Apparently he didn't feel any more at ease than she did.

"Arts and Crafts style if I'm not mistaken."

"California bungalow. It was a popular style until the Second World War. Should we ring again?"

Luke knocked on the aluminum screen door. It rattled loudly.

"Ease up, Conan. We want them to answer the door, not run out the back."

"I didn't knock that hard."

Judith decided he was right, but it still sounded like he had shaken the foundation. Her nerves were getting the best of her. "Maybe no one is home—"

The door opened a crack. "Who are you?" A woman's voice. Judith could see enough gray in the dark hair and wrinkles around the one eye that peered at them through the narrow opening to know that a woman on the north side of prime barred the door. The eye was bloodshot.

"My name is Judith Find and this is Luke Becker. We were hoping we could—"

"Judith Find? The television lady?"

"I've done some television and commercials for our products."

"I'm not interested in buying anything." The woman started to close the door.

"We're not selling anything," Luke interjected.

"This isn't a good time." Again the door began to close.

"We know. That's why we're here." Judith took a quick breath before letting the next words tumble from her mouth. "We're here about Abel."

The door closed.

"What now, fearless leader?" Judith asked Luke.

Luke extended his hand to bang on the screen door again, when the sound of the chain lock being unlatched worked its way past the jamb. Slowly the door opened again, this time more than a crack. The woman stood on the other side of the screen. "Do you know where he is?"

"No, ma'am, not yet." Judith could hear the hurt in her voice. The timbre testified of a throat raw with weeping.

"You're not with the police. What do you want?"

"Only to help." Judith hoped her sincerity could make it past the screen. The woman was Judith's height; her hair mussed and unattended to. She wore a thin pink robe over a flannel gown. Judith could see no makeup and didn't expect to. Before her stood a woman displaying every sign of depression: lifeless eyes, downturned mouth, slumped posture. The woman was in mourning for the loss of someone dear.

As Judith studied the woman, the woman studied her and did so in a way that made her feel naked before the grieving woman's eyes.

To his credit, Luke said nothing. Better to let woman bond with woman. Judith appreciated his discipline. "May we come in?"

The woman turned and walked into the dark house leaving the door open. Judith looked at Luke who offered only a shrug. Judith pulled open the screen door and stepped in, holding the door just long enough for Luke to take hold of it. Once inside, she closed the door. It seemed the polite thing to do.

The interior showed the same concern for maintenance as the outside. Judith immediately looked at the floor and saw hardwood strips laid in the traditional staggered pattern. Unlike the picture, this flooring was oak and looked original to the house.

The woman had moved to a sofa that looked freshly plucked out of the 1950s. A rocking chair was nearby as well as a love seat that matched the sofa's flowery upholstery. The home was clean and orderly except the area around the couch. A small, walnut coffee table with turned spindle legs held several dirty glass tumblers, one empty box of tissue and one box that appeared half full. Clumps of wadded white tissue lay on the table and a few on the floor where they had fallen. A bed pillow rested against one arm of the sofa and a wool blanket at the other. The woman had been sleeping here.

"If you don't know where Abel is and you're not with the police, then why should I speak with you?"

"We're trying to help," Judith said.

"How can you help? You sell furniture or something, don't you?"

"Interior products," Judith corrected. "But I'm not here because of my business. We're trying to find Abel."

"Are you with them?" She spat out the last word like a person spits out a rancid piece of meat.

"Who do you mean?"

"You know."

"Ma'am," Luke began, "we're not with anybody but ourselves. All we want to do is ask a few questions."

"Then how do you know about Abel? He's special. The world doesn't know about him. You must be with them. What did you do with my boy?" Tears flooded her eyes and she reached for a tissue. It struck Judith as a well-practiced motion.

Judith spoke in low tones. "Ma'am ... I'm sorry, I don't know what to call you."

She examined Judith through wet eyes. Events had almost crushed the woman but she still showed the signs of a mother's strength. "You really are her, aren't you? The lady I see in the television commercials."

"Yes, ma'am. I really am Judith Find. What's your name?" Judith recalled the computer document that listed the abducted boy's name as Abel Palek, but she had a feeling that this woman was not the boy's mother. She certainly didn't have his purple eyes.

"Ida Palek. My husband is ... was, Ed Palek."

"Was?"

"He died two weeks ago. I buried him two days before ... before ..." The stern shell she had been showing gave way.

Judith and Luke exchanged glances. It communicated well enough. "I'm so sorry, Mrs. Palek." *Husband dies and two days later an abduction takes place in your home.* Judith felt sick but she knew what to do: she let the woman cry. When her Allen died, she did her share of weeping. There were days when she thought she'd be crying the rest of her life, but time changed that. Now she hurt without the tears.

Judith reached out and touched Ida's knee. "I lost a husband. I know it hurts."

"You're not going to tell me that the hurt will go away, are you? Everyone kept saying that. 'Give it time,' my friends said, 'then things will get better. The hurt will stop.' I don't believe them."

"I wouldn't tell you that." She leaned back. "The pain changes. It becomes manageable. Life resumes, but there will always be the pain of the loss."

Ida dabbed at her eyes. "How did your husband die?"

"Aneurism on the descending aorta. It gave way. One minute Allen was alive; the next he was dead in his office. The doctors said, short of having him on the operating table at the time of the event, nothing could be done."

Ida nodded in understanding. "Coronary. Ed went to bed one night and never woke up."

Mist invaded Judith's eyes. She had told the truth about the pain never fully going away.

A few moments later, Ida spoke. "I don't know what to do, what to think, who to trust. I'm afraid to leave my home in case Abel returns."

"And the police have no leads?" Luke asked.

"Police? I can't call the police. They warned me not to. I know what those people are like."

"What people, Ida?" Judith waited. Ida's head lowered.

"I can't talk to you about it. I'm not supposed to discuss it with anyone. That was part of the deal."

"Excuse me for being blunt, Mrs. Palek," Luke said, inching to the edge of his seat. "It seems to me they broke the deal when they took Abel."

"Do you think they will hurt him?" Judith asked.

"No. I don't think so. He's too important. Too expensive."

"Expensive?"

She blanched. "I've said too much. If you don't know where he is, you shouldn't be here."

"You had better tell her," Luke said.

"Tell me what?"

Judith took a breath. "I don't know how to explain this, but this morning both Luke and I received a message saying that we should find Abel ... and that he might be in danger."

Judith thought Ida would melt into the pattern of the sofa. "I still don't understand. Why you? Who called? Do they know where Abel is?"

"I'm afraid I don't know. We were told not to go to the police; that doing so might endanger Abel's life. So we haven't. Later we received some computer files—Luke, let me have the printouts."

"They're in the rental car. I'll have to go get them." Luke rose and hustled out the front door.

"Is he your new husband?" Ida wondered.

Judith almost laughed. "No. We just met this morning."

She looked puzzled. "Yet you've teamed up to find a boy you don't know?" The mask of puzzlement turned to suspicion.

"I know it's too much to believe. I hardly believe it myself." Judith decided not to reveal the rest of the incentive—keeping a secret hidden she long believed was dead.

Luke felt a sense of relief as he stepped from the house and onto the porch. The house seemed oppressive, dark, and truth be told, he didn't know how to deal with weeping women. It wasn't that he had a heart of coal, he told himself, but that he was born a male and most men found tear-bearing women a frightening mystery.

Wasting no time, Luke descended the few steps that bridged the distance from walkway to porch deck, walked to the curb where he had parked the rental, popped the trunk, and removed his laptop bag, slipping the strap over his shoulder.

As he pushed the trunk of the sedan closed, a movement caught his eye. Ida Palek's home rested in a cozy, tree-lined neighborhood, a gentrified community manicured and maintained less and less by an aging population and more and more by young, double-income families trying to get a foothold in the housing market by buying older homes.

The curbs were clear of parked cars except one two houses down and across the street. Glare on the windshield masked the occupant, but Luke could see that someone sat behind the wheel. He wasn't sure what motion had grabbed his attention, but Luke knew it was some kind of movement, like a man quickly setting something down.

Luke looked at Ida's house then back to the car—a straight line of sight. While some men might deny their neuroses, Luke embraced his. A long train of possibilities rumbled through his mind. None of them good. Had he been listening to them? Following them? Was he waiting for back up?

Of course, he may be a part-time father picking up a child for his share of custody. Then again . . .

Luke decided to take a chance. Readjusting the strap of the computer bag, he stepped into the street and marched to the car, his eyes glued to the driver.

Every step seemed a mile's journey, but Luke pressed on against the tide of fear that urged him to flee. After five steps down the street he could better see the man: sandy, short-clipped hair, square jaw, weasel eyes. The last part was a prejudged opinion of Luke's, who already knew he didn't like the guy in the car.

The driver's side window was open and Luke approached like he had no cares. The man shuffled things on the seat as Luke neared, clearly hiding something.

"Excuse me, pal." Luke stepped as close to the door as possible to prevent the man from opening it. He laid a hand over the slot that held the retracted window placing his hand on the door lock. He pressed the lock down. "I'm here visiting my Aunt Ida and I want to take her someplace special for dinner, but since this is my first time to Fresno, I don't know where the good places are. Can you recommend a spot?"

Luke looked past the man and saw a large, aluminum case on the passenger seat, the kind used to hold electronic or camera equipment. This guy wasn't waiting for his child.

"Sorry. I don't eat out much." His voice was an octave higher than Luke expected. The man wore a tan sport coat over a black colorless shirt. Luke took note of the large bulge on the left side. The guy was packing.

"Really? Dining out is one of life's great pleasures. Sure you don't have a favorite restaurant?"

"Beat it, buddy. I told you I don't eat out."

Luke took a step back and raised his hands as if surrendering. "Okay, okay. Take it easy. It's only a question."

Turning, Luke walked away, his back to the man in the car. With every step, his spine tingled like spiders had taken up residence just under his skin. Luke waited for the burning sensation of being shot in the back. It never came. He trotted up the stairs and back into the house.

Closing the door, he raised a finger to his lips. A television rested on the far wall of the living room opposite the sofa. He turned it on and raised the volume.

"What are you doing?" Judith asked.

Again, Luke raised a finger to his lips. He crossed the room, placed his mouth by Judith's ear, and said, "We have to go—right now."

sixteen

Ida was confused and frightened. Judith couldn't blame her. A pair of strangers had come to her home and in less than twenty minutes insisted that she flee with them out the back door. At first, she insisted on getting dressed, but Luke insisted that any delay could be disastrous. Two minutes later, Ida had shown them the back door which they used.

Carrying a wad of Ida's clothing under one arm and a pair of size six shoes in her hand, Judith led the other two out the back door, through the rear yard, and to a gate that led to Ida's neighbors—people she said would be gone this time of day.

"I don't want to seem ungrateful, but why is there a gate to your neighbor's yard?" Luke brought up the rear.

"We're friends," Ida said just above a whisper. "We used to barbecue together. They both work. No one is home."

The conversation ended there. Judith opened the gate and stepped through, hoping the Joneses or whatever their names were didn't have a dog. They didn't. What they did have was a garden shed—more importantly, an unlocked shed. Luke pointed to it and the three slipped inside.

The shed smelled of fertilizer, the gas and oil of a lawn-mower and the stale air of a poorly ventilated space no larger than a walk-in closet in a midsized home.

"Okay, Ida, change as quickly as you can. Running around in a gown and robe might attract attention."

"Um, Luke ..." Judith said.

"Come on, come on. I think we're in trouble here."

Ida didn't move.

"For being such a bright man, Luke, you can certainly be as dumb as a brick."

Luke looked puzzled. "What?"

"I think Ida might like a little privacy."

Judith watched Luke rub his face. "Okay, okay. But hurry. You stay with her." Luke slipped outside.

"I don't want to leave." Ida's voice reminded Judith of a frightened child. The poor woman had been through a meat grinder, no, was *still* in the meat grinder and now stood in a shed lit only by the light creeping in through the crack in the door.

"I know you don't, Ida, but something is terribly wrong. I trust Luke." Judith began to sort through the clothing they had snatched before exiting the house. She hoped they had grabbed everything. In her hands were a pullover sweater, a pair of elastic band casual pants, white socks, and a pair of New Balance shoes.

Ida changed and Judith poked her head out the shed door. "Luke?"

"Yeah." He appeared from the side yard. "You ready?"

"I guess so. Ida is reluctant to leave."

"It doesn't matter. We have to go. It's unsafe for her to stay there. I'm an idiot. I should have thought of it earlier."

Judith stepped out, Ida followed reluctantly. "Thought of what?"

"Not now. I'll explain later. Let's just get out of here."

"But the car is in front of Ida's house. How are we going to get it?"

"We're not. That's what they're expecting." Luke started back for the side yard.

"So help me, Luke, if all this is the result of your uncontrolled paranoia, I'm going to sic the FBI, CIA, and NAS on you."

"NSA not NAS, and they already know about me."

The side yard led to the front of the house. Luke went through first, then motioned for the others to follow. The sidewalk was too narrow to allow them to walk three abreast. Judith chose to stay by Ida's side letting Luke follow a few paces behind, something he said allowed him to keep a better lookout.

Without turning around, Judith asked, "So what's the plan now?"

Luke's reply came quickly. "I think we should get back to the airport. We'll be much safer there. We can regroup and plan a better strategy. We passed a strip mall on the way in. It's only a few blocks. We can walk there and phone a cab, but we need to hurry."

"Are you sure you're not just overreacting?"

"Let's see: A man sits in a car a few doors down—a rental car I might add—has a kit of electronic or photo equipment on the front seat and carries a gun in a shoulder holster, and he happens to be there the hour we arrive in Fresno. I'd call that suspicious."

"How do you know all that?"

"I went over and talked to him. People who do surveillance never do that."

Judith looked over her shoulder and caught him smiling with self-satisfaction. It irritated her.

"You walked up and spoke to him? Just crossed the street and said, 'Howdy'?"

"It was the only way I could confirm my suspicion."

"Did you see the photo equipment or the electronic gadgets?"

"No, they were in an aluminum case." Luke's words had a sandpaper feel to them.

"How about the gun? Did you *actually* see the gun?"

"No. He had it hidden under his coat."

Judith felt uncomfortable and angry. All of this could be Luke's overactive paranoia. She stopped and faced him.

"Keep moving," he said.

"No. I think you just scared ten years off my life and for no good reason. Everything you've described can be explained in other ways. A man sits in a rental car. Well, you didn't see him until you went to *our* rental car to retrieve those printouts. He has an aluminum case on the front seat. So what? For all you know he has loan documents in there."

"It wasn't that kind of case." The smile had vanished.

"The point is you didn't confirm anything."

Judith saw anger flare in Luke's eyes. He opened his mouth to speak but the words never came.

She felt it before the sound of it registered. The ground lurched and vibrated. A millisecond later the roar of an explosion assaulted her ears. She jumped then covered her head.

It ended as fast as it had come.

Silence inundated the area, broken only by the sound of birds leaving the branches of the trees as fast as they could.

"What was that?" Judith's ears were ringing. She turned in the direction of the sound. Black smoke and dust rose in the air.

"My house!"

Judith had expected a scream, but instead it came as a whimper.

Ida started back toward her home but Luke intercepted her, placed his arm on her shoulder, and said in soft but firm words, "You can't go back. It's not safe. We must keep moving."

"My pictures, my papers, my ..." Her voice thinned to nothing.

Judith started toward her, to comfort her, to take her in her arms and give the poor woman a chance to weep.

"Not here," Luke said. "We're being watched." He nodded across the street. A mother holding an infant stepped from the house and gazed to the column of smoke rising a short distance away. Another mother holding the hand of a screaming toddler stepped to her porch.

"Let's just continue walking. Calmly. Normally."

"Her house just blew up, Luke, there's nothing normal about that." Judith's heart rattled in her chest.

"I didn't say it was but the less attention we draw to ourselves the better."

With his arm around Ida, Luke led the way. Judith followed a few paces behind and wondered how much worse things could get.

seventeen

I'm telling you, Dwayne, something is up at Find, Inc., and I don't mean draperies." Karen Rose leaned forward in the leather guest chair as if being closer to her boss's desk made her words more believable.

"You were told that Find wasn't in the office yet you connived your way past the receptionist and on to the executive floor. Is that right?"

"I prefer to think that I finessed my way in."

"Nonetheless, you used guile." He shook his head then smiled. "That's what I like about you."

"Well, it didn't do me any good. The only person we spoke to was Find's stepson, Marlin Find. He's the senior VP or something like that. Once he learned we weren't there to interview him, he started to show us the door. To make him feel a little better, we taped a few minutes of him telling us how well the emergency policies he instituted had worked. I'm just guessing here, but I don't think they have an emergency policy. I asked the receptionist on the way out and she said she never heard of one."

"So the guy's a blowhard." Dwayne Hastings looked a year older than when she saw him this morning. Once an eager newsman, he had grown weary of the game and could no longer keep his disdain a secret.

"Yeah. You know the type. My point is, something odd is going on over there, but I don't know what."

"What evidence do you have?"

"Find's assistant ..." She paused as she tried to recall the name. "Terri Finn ... no Penn—Terri Penn. The woman looked ready to crawl out of her skin. And the phone blowing up—"

"You said it didn't really blow up."

"True. It just sort of fractured. I saw it before having to do a soft shoe with Find's stepson."

Dwayne rubbed his chin. "I don't know, Karen. That's not much. We certainly can't run anything other than the false alarm angle."

"There's more. Just as we were leaving, the county crime scene department shows up. I recognized one of the techs from the High Tech detail. I did a piece on them about six months back."

"I remember. It was my idea."

Karen smiled. "Of course it was. All the good ideas are yours."

"That's my girl. What do you glean from the fact that someone from the High Tech detail came to the scene?"

"You don't send someone like that out without cause. I think there's something more going on with the phone and with Judith Find."

"Do you think she was hurt by the trick phone?"

Karen leaned back. "Maybe. They could have snuck her out or something."

"Did you—"

"Call the hospitals? I did that while Cindy drove us back. No good."

"What you're telling me is that you're running on gut instinct."

"For now."

"Okay, stay on it. This station could stand to scoop the competition for a change. Just don't get so involved I can't use you for other things."

"I assume you have identification?"

He looked at the cop and smiled. Of course he had identification. He had lots of it, much of it with various three-letter combinations from the government's alphabet soup. Those he kept hidden away. For today's activities, he produced an ID card issued by the State of California Bureau of Security and Investigative Services showing his legal standing as a private investigator.

"Sam Pennington, P.I." The cop, a kid who couldn't be over twenty-five and still looked like he was waiting for his first shave, studied the picture then compared it to the real thing. *Go ahead, ask for my driver's license.*

Satisfied, the officer handed the ID back. "Tell me again."

"Sure. I'm supposed to be tailing a wayward husband and snapping a few photos — I know, I know, it's lousy work and a long way from my detective days in Dallas."

"You worked for the Dallas PD?"

"Yup. I started in Mesa, Arizona. I grew up near there, but had a chance to move to the big city. R and H for three years."

"Robbery/Homicide? That's good work."

"It was until I messed up my back taking a perp down. He didn't like the idea of going back to jail, something he should have thought of before he offed a convenience store clerk. He decided to run; I decided to pursue. He earned a lifetime bed in the pen and I earned a tweaked back and dislocated shoulder."

"Ouch."

"The shoulder healed fine but it took a couple of years of therapy and two surgeries before I could sit long enough to hold down a job."

"So you lived on disability and later started a career as a P.I."

"That's the story. It ain't glamorous, but it pays my Netflix bills."

The cop chuckled. "Do I want to know what kind of movies you watch?"

"Probably not." They shared a brief laugh.

Then the officer turned serious. It doesn't do to laugh at the site of a burning home. "Okay, I gotta get this straight for my report. You were tailing a cheating husband."

"Waiting for him is more like it." He leaned against the car and pulled a pack of cigarettes from his coat pocket. "Do you mind?"

"Actually, I do. I hate cigarette smoke."

Pennington nodded. "Understood. I hate these things too but I can't seem to get the monkey off my back. They're not kidding when they call it an addiction." He returned the pack to his coat and continued.

"Thanks."

"Anyway, this is a new case for me. Pretty routine, really. A woman thinks her man is sleeping around and comes to me for proof one way or the other. She gave me this street as a place where the mistress might live. I get a description of the car and a picture of the man. Following is too risky, too easy to be noticed. So I came here to stake the place out."

"Did he come by?"

"Nah. I think the wife is missing a cog or something, if you catch my drift." The cop said he did. "So I'm sitting here waiting and watching when I see that car over there pull in front of the house ... or what used to be the house."

"Did you see who got out?"

"Absolutely. A man and a woman. Both go to the front door and someone lets them in. Maybe ten, fifteen minutes later, the guy comes, goes to the car, pops the trunk, and pulls out what looks like a computer bag. At least I thought it was a computer bag."

"You think maybe there was a bomb in it?"

"I can't swear to that, Officer. I didn't get to see inside the thing." He looked at the house. "Then something strange happens. The man spies me and looks real worried, like he thinks I've been watching him, but instead of going back into the house, he walks over to me."

"You're still in your car at the time?"

"Yup. Hadn't budged in over two hours. My back is telling me all about it." For affect, he reached a hand behind him and rubbed the small of his back. "So, he comes over and leans in my open window." Pennington decided not to mention that the man touched his car. The cops would want to fingerprint everything and that couldn't be good for him. "Now I'm spooked. I thought I was dealing with some kinda nutcase. He looks me over and eyeballs my photo case. I wonder if he's going to rob me but instead he asks about finding a decent restaurant. He wants to take his Aunt Edna or Ida or something out and could I tell him of a good place."

"What'd you tell him?"

"I told him I didn't know of any places. I just wanted him out of my window. He had me trapped. I feel kinda stupid about that. I shoulda seen it coming."

"Then he went back to the house?"

"Exactly. He crosses the street again, jogs up the stairs, and disappears inside. Ten minutes later, kaaboom! There's an explosion, the windows blow out of the house, and it starts burning." He paused for effect. "Do you think they were still in there?"

"Don't know, Mr. Pennington. The fire department will have to figure that out. How can I reach you?"

Pennington made up a cell phone number. "There's one more thing: I recognized the woman."

"You're kidding."

Pennington shook his head. "I've been trying to think of her name since the explosion, and then it hit me." Again he paused for effect. "I've been seeing this girl and on nights we don't go out, I sit around her place and watch the tube. She likes all those home improvement shows, you know, the ones with all the interior designers?"

The officer said he knew.

"Well, because my girl likes to watch the shows, I have to watch the shows. Truth is, they're not that bad. Well, the woman I saw go in the house is the same woman I've seen on some of the commercials. Her name is Judy Find ... no, that's not right."

"Judith Find?"

"Yeah, that's it. I take it you've seen her."

"I'm married to a woman who likes those same kinds of shows. Martha Stewart and Judith Find, the two biggies."

"Except this Find lady is more into interior design and furnishings, things like that."

"Are you certain it was her?"

"As sure as a man can be."

The officer nodded, lost in thought. It wasn't every day that a nationally recognized figure is associated with a possible bombing.

The officer thanked Pennington, shook his hand as one cop to another, and excused himself. Pennington knew that a more senior officer would be over to talk to him and he'd have to run through the same story. He'd tell it the same way. Cops were morons.

Mostly he had told the truth. That was the best way to lie. The more truth in the mix, the easier the lie went down.

Firemen doused the flames in short order but most of the damage had been done. The shell of what had once been a home was all that remained. The fire had done its job. If only he had been able to set off the device before Ida Palek and her visitors had escaped.

More work remained to do.

He hated it when things didn't go according to plan.

eighteen

Ida sat in the business jet's leather seat shaking and rocking like a metronome. When Judith first met the woman she noticed her red and swollen eyes—that condition had worsened. Awash with pity, Judith sat in the seat closest to the woman and wondered what to say. What opening lines could be used with a woman who two weeks ago lost a husband unexpectedly, then had a child kidnapped from her home, only to have two strangers come by and ask for answers she couldn't know, then hear the sound and see the smoke of an explosion that surely devastated her house.

Instead of words, Judith reached across the narrow aisle and laid her hand on the woman's arm. "Can I get you anything?"

Ida didn't respond. She rocked. She quaked. She stared straight ahead.

Looking forward, Judith watched as Luke spoke to the pilots. They nodded and he came back to where Judith and Ida sat. He hunkered down on one knee. "I think it's best if we get going soon. I'm not sure what happened at the house, but I know it means nothing good for us."

"Couldn't it have just been an accident? A fluke?" Judith already knew the answer was no.

"We're alive," Luke said looking at Ida. "That's what matters. Staying alive and finding Abel."

"Why would someone do that?" Ida asked. The question came with childlike innocence.

"I don't have many answers, Ida." Luke looked exhausted. He had saved them from serious injury, probably saved their lives, and it had taken its toll on him. After the explosion, Luke led them to the strip mall and made a call for a cab which brought them back to the Fresno Yosemite International Airport.

Ida gave no sign of hearing the words.

"Ida, look at me." Luke touched her knee. "Ida, I need your attention."

As though climbing out of a hypnotic trance, Ida turned her face to Luke. To Judith she looked like a porcelain doll with too many years of hard play on her.

"Ida, I know you don't know us, but we are your friends. What has happened is horrible. We can't bring back your house. We can't bring back your husband. What we can do—at least what we can try to do—is help find Abel. To do that, we will need your help. Do you understand?"

She nodded without conviction.

Luke continued. "We are alive. You must focus on that and on helping us locate Abel. Can you do that?"

"I don't know. I'm so confused."

"We know you are," Judith said. "You are not alone."

Ida dissolved into tears.

Luke rose and stepped to the front of the plane motioning for Judith to follow.

"I'm going to get you some tissue. Would you like water or juice?"

Ida didn't respond. Judith moved forward to the small galley behind the cockpit.

He whispered. "What are we going to do with her? She's a wreck."

"You'd be a wreck too if you endured all she has. Give her time; she has to let all that out before she can reason clearly." She opened a small refrigerator and removed a bottle of water. She then picked up a couple of napkins. The galley didn't have the tissue she promised.

"I asked the pilots to take us to San Diego."

"What? Why did you do that?"

"Remember the document. The only other physical location we have is Torrey Pines. That's in San Diego County."

"As I recall, all we have is the name of the town and the fact that it was the boy's birthplace."

"True, but I'm betting on your ability to use those sales and distribution records."

Before the plane had landed in Fresno, Judith placed a call using the business jet's phone. The very act of making the call had frightened her. The scream from Terri still rang clear in her ears. She could never forgive herself if she caused her assistant pain, but she was the best one to get the job done.

At first she tried Terri's cell phone. Like all key personnel, the company provided her with the phone. Unhindered communication remained one of the key business principles for Find, Inc. It began with her husband and she continued the practice.

The moment she dialed the number she received an automated voice informing her that the party could not be reached. Judith felt no surprise. Her phone service had been decommissioned; she assumed it might be true for every phone on the account. But Judith had an ace in the hole—Terri carried more than one cell phone, a practice she began when her aging mother began to call during business hours to ask her daughter to pick up milk or the latest *TV Guide.* In her eighties, she could no longer comprehend that her daughter went to work and attended meetings with the president of the company. The second cell phone could be silenced, granting Terri the power of answering only when appropriate.

The second call went through and Judith learned that Terri was out of the office while the crime scene techs examined the scene.

"The detective thinks that your office is bugged." Terri sounded frightened. Judith thought she had a right to be.

"I know this is weird, Terri. I don't pretend to understand all that is going on, but I need your help."

"You know I'll do whatever I can. Where are you?"

"I can't tell you that; I can't even tell you why. Don't ask questions, Terri. It might make things worse."

"I don't understand."

"Neither do I but that's the way it is. I need some research done and you're the best person in the company to do it. But here's the thing: You have to do it on the sly. Don't tell anyone what you're up to. Don't talk to the police about it."

"This doesn't sound right, Judith." She could hear the stress in Terri's voice.

"I know. Believe me, I know. Given those constraints, are you still willing to help?"

There was a pause. "Yes, of course."

"Okay, here goes. Do you remember the Bertinelli rugs we experimented with about eighteen months ago?"

"I do. I remember thinking how odd it was to hire an Italian company to make Persian rugs."

Judith had taken Terri with her to Italy to approve designs, tour the factory, and ink the deal. The trip brought fond memories.

"One of the rugs in the design series had a narrow beige border with a field of gray patterns. I think it was the second in the series."

"It was."

"Good. Now, do you remember the laminate flooring we did two years ago? The Stewart Blink design?"

"It's hard to forget. It didn't do all that well."

Judith gave a mirthless chortle. "You're being kind. I'm still answering questions about how much we lost on that pattern. Here's what I want you to do. I need to know if there's a house out there with both the rug and flooring."

Another pause. "You want me to find a single address that has both the rug and the flooring in common?"

"I know I'm asking a lot."

The sound of Terri's long exhalation carried over the miles. Judith gave her time to think.

"The flooring went out under trial, so the number of retail stores is limited to maybe fifty or so. As I recall, we tested in the western states only: California, Arizona, and ..."

"Washington and Oregon. That's it."

"I suppose I can find out which stores returned the flooring and how much. That will tell me how much they sold. Same thing with the rugs, although some may still be hanging in stores. When do you need this?"

"Yesterday."

"I'll head back to the office now. I might have to invade someone else's space if the crime scene people aren't done spreading fingerprint dust everywhere."

The thought of black smudges all over her walls and furniture made Judith shiver. "Find out who's on vacation and borrow their work space. It might be safer anyway." She assumed Terri understood the reference to the listening devices.

"How do I get hold of you?"

"You don't. I'll be out of touch for a few hours. I'll call you when I can."

"I understand."

"Terri? You're the best."

"That's what I keep telling people."

nineteen

Karen Rose stepped into Dwayne Hastings's office. He had buzzed her on the intercom and demanded that she come to his office immediately. It was the first and only such demand Karen had received.

"You wanted to see me, boss?" The office was clean to a fault. Most men in Dwayne's position would have stacks of file folders, news scripts, newspapers, "While You Were Out" slips, and a dozen other must-have-close-at-hand piles. Dwayne's desk, a red-oak chunk of woodworking that could double as a bomb shelter had a single pad of paper, a ballpoint pen, and a phone. His computer sat on a bureau behind him.

The starkness of the office didn't surprise Karen, she had been in the office before, but she did notice that the phone had been pulled closer to the center of the desk. Dwayne stared at the phone and spoke into the air, the handset resting in its cradle.

"Here she is now." Dwayne motioned for Karen to enter. He mouthed, "Close the door," to her.

"Okay," a voice said. Dwayne had the caller on the speaker phone. So this was to be a conference call.

Karen shut the door and took a seat in one of the worn guest chairs across from her editor.

"Karen, I have Bob Hazen on the line. He's with an affiliate station in Fresno. He's doing us a big favor."

"Oh? Hello, Bob."

"Hey, Kelly."

"It's Karen."

"Sorry, my bad." The voice sounded tinny and came with more white noise than Karen liked, but she could hear well enough. The station really needed new phones. She was certain that wouldn't happen any time soon.

Dwight smiled. "Tell her what you got."

"Okay, but this makes us square, Dwayne. Agreed?"

"Agreed. You don't owe me."

"Not now I don't," Bob said then added, "I want video of your report with a tag referencing this station."

"Gladly." Dwayne's smile broadened.

Karen gave him a quizzical look.

Bob's voice floated from the speaker. "Okay, here's the deal. Less than an hour ago there was an explosion in the east part of town. I've emailed the address and community name. You should have that by now."

"I got it," Dwayne said.

"This is an older neighborhood; filled with residents that have lived in those homes for better than thirty years and young couples just starting out. It's a quiet place with almost no crime." He cleared his throat. "About two o'clock, police and fire responded to an explosion and fire. The house was gutted and there's no sign of the owner, one Mrs. Ida Palek. I did a little checking on her. She became a widow two weeks ago. No one knows where she is."

"The house just went up?" Karen asked.

"That's how the fire chief described it. At first they thought it might be from a broken gas line, but when I was doing the shoot, the arson guys showed up. That means the chief saw something that didn't add up."

"Can we get that video?" Karen felt the rush of an interesting story, but she felt there was more coming. Dwayne wouldn't have demanded her presence for a fire in another city, especially not a single family residence. Houses burned down all the time. One in Fresno would have no interest for San Bernardino County residents.

"I'll post it on an in-house–only part of our station's website. You can download it from there. I'll send you the URL."

Karen looked at Dwayne who still wore a grin. "Okay, so you have a house go up in flames and an explosion—"

"And a missing owner," Dwayne added.

Karen continued. "Okay … and a missing owner. What does that have to do with me?"

"First," Bob said, "because there is an eyewitness and that eyewitness fingered someone who owns a business in your town. So I wanted Dwayne to send someone out and try to get an interview. You know, share the story."

"We have lots of …" Alarms went off in Karen's mind. "You don't mean—"

"Imagine my surprise when I learned that you had just been out to Find, Inc. There's nothing more powerful in the news business than serendipity."

"Hang on a sec." Karen stood. A gallon of adrenaline had just entered her veins. "You're telling me that you have an eyewitness who saw Judith Find near the house."

"Not near—*in the house.*"

"Are you saying she's dead?" Karen worked at keeping her reportorial detachment in place.

"No. No bodies found in what's left of the house. The eyewitness saw her and someone else go into the house."

"And the eyewitness is certain that he saw ... or is it 'she' saw?"

"He."

"This guy is certain that it was Judith Find?" Karen began to pace, her mind spinning like an out-of-control carousel.

"She's a public figure. As I understand it, he recognized her from television."

Karen could almost sense Bob's satisfaction. Reporters loved this kind of stuff. "Did you talk to the eyewitness?"

"I'm afraid not; he was gone when we got there. I have his name and one of my crew is trying to track him down."

Karen looked at Dwayne. She started to ask if Dwayne had told Bob about the excitement at Find, Inc., but decided against it. If she knew her boss, he had withheld that tidbit.

"So when do you want the feed?" Dwayne asked.

"ASAP."

Dwayne leaned over the desk. "We're on it. I'll shoot you an email when I get your footage."

"Okay, but don't drag your feet on this, Dwayne."

"You got it, pal. Thanks for remembering an old friend."

"Just paying a debt, Dwayne. Just paying a debt."

"Understood." Dwayne switched off the phone.

"This is incredible." Karen flopped back in the seat.

"I thought you might like it. Now get out of my office and get some footage from Find, Inc. Make it good. We have a scoop, let's not flush it."

She stood and started for the door. "On my way." Karen stopped. "By the way, just what did you do for this guy that earned such a decent payback?"

"It was years ago. We were both still field reporters. We were down a cameraman on an especially busy news day. I knew enough about the equipment to operate it. In his zeal to get to the scene of a story he smashed up the news van. Thing wouldn't budge. We had to be towed. My reputation had already dropped in the can, so I took the blame. Fortunately, no one else was involved so the police weren't called to the scene. My drinking was pretty well known at the station then."

"You took the fall for the guy? Dwayne, that's nuts."

"Yeah, I know. Here's the irony. I had been drinking that day. If I hadn't, I would never have volunteered to be the scapegoat."

Judith thought about what he said. "This had better be everything he says it is, or otherwise he hasn't come close to paying you back."

"It doesn't matter. What is, is. Now get out of my office."

Detective Ben Wilson had just reached his desk in the Archibald Avenue headquarters building when the phone rang. He snapped up the phone and identified himself.

He listened then said, "You've got to be kidding. Fresno?"

Five minutes later, he was back in the car heading to the building he had left only a few hours before. This time his task was not to investigate a phone, but a person.

twenty

The business jet made a smooth descent and landed at Lindberg Field near the heart of San Diego. Warm air and a clear blue sky greeted Judith. She had been to San Diego many times and come to love its unique lifestyle, blending the laid-back approach of Southern California's most southern residents with the bustle of the big city. Most metro areas were just cities, but like Chicago, New York, and San Francisco, San Diego had personality. For the briefest moment she allowed herself the deception that she was here on vacation. The fantasy burst a moment later when Luke and Ida emerged. Ida made uncertain steps on the air-stairs but negotiated them without stumbling.

Ida had occupied much of Judith's thinking over the last hour of the short flight from Fresno. What was she to do with the woman? They couldn't take her with them. Judith had no idea what they were going to face and having a third person along might irritate the Puppeteer even more. Sending her back to Fresno could only endanger the poor, bedraggled woman. Her home didn't explode by accident. Luke had been right in hustling them from the house. It had saved their lives.

And what if they did find the boy? Would Ida allow him to be turned over to the Puppeteer? Not likely.

True as all of that was, Judith could not bring herself to just leave the woman to roam the large and confusing terminals of Lindberg Field.

"We should get into the building," Luke said. "I don't like standing in the open."

"You know, this airport has an FBO. We don't have to go into the main terminal."

"FBO?" It was clear Luke was distracted. "Oh, fixed base operation. Yeah, I know. Your pilot said the same thing when I told him we wanted to exit as near the public terminal as possible."

"And why is that?"

Luke cut a glance her way. "Because there is anonymity in crowds. It's easier to hide in a group."

Despite it having saved their lives, Judith grew more impatient with Luke's paranoia. She didn't argue. They moved toward the concrete walls of the terminal. Judith led the way, Luke and Ida walked close behind.

Inside, the hubbub of travelers—grumpy with delays in security checkpoints, uncomfortable chairs, and employees (who looked at them but never truly saw humans, just customers)—stood next to walls, worked on laptop computers, and read magazines and books, waiting to board their flight.

The crowd made Judith nervous. A thousand strangers surrounded her; any one of them could be in league with the Puppeteer or with whoever decided to destroy Ida's home while the three of them were still in it.

"What now?" Ida asked.

Judith glanced over her shoulder then slowed so she could walk next to the woman. During the flight, Ida's emotional state had settled. Her eyes were still rimmed in red, but the weeping had stopped. In fact, it had stopped so suddenly that Judith worried the woman had slipped into some emotional coma.

"Are you hungry? Need to use the bathroom?"

"I'm fine. I just don't know what to do. What do you plan to do with me?"

"Ida, we haven't abducted you." The question wounded Judith. "We brought you along because we feared for your life."

"Are you going to let me go with you to find Abel?"

Straight to the heart of things. Judith didn't know how to respond. *How do I answer a question like that?*

"You're not going to return him to me, are you?" Ida pressed.

Judith stammered and Luke came to her aide. "I can promise you, Ida, we mean Abel no harm. To be honest, we don't even know why we've been chosen to find him. I know it's hard to trust strangers—it's almost impossible for me—but we need you to trust us."

"Why?"

Luke frowned. "Ida. We didn't blow up your house. Someone else did. Someone wants you dead because you know too much, and I don't think they're going to give up just because they failed the first time ... We need a better place to talk."

"You're not going to find much privacy around here," Judith said.

"Antarctica may be the last place on earth with any real privacy. We'll just have to make do."

Judith watched as Luke glanced around. He began by staring at the ceiling and it took a moment for her to realize that he was looking for and identifying video cameras. "Follow me."

They moved through the crowds like salmon moving upstream. Their only advantage was that they carried no luggage, which made things a little easier. They passed a Starbucks kiosk surrounded by customers in need of caffeine; several fast food establishments, all tied to some major food chain; and two bookstores filled with the latest *New York Times* bestsellers.

Near the center of the terminal they found a sport's bar called the End Zone and Luke worked his way in. A twenty-something woman with straight blonde hair with red highlights that reminded Judith of a redwood plank greeted them.

Patrons took up about half the seats and booths. Televisions were situated around the facility with various sports programs. One showed CNN's "The Situation Room." Wolf Blitzer held court.

"Good afternoon," Luke said. "Do you have anything in one of the back corners?" She gave him a strange look. "I need a break from the crowds."

"Ain't that the truth," the young woman said. "It gets on my nerves, too. This way please."

One minute later they settled in a booth in the most distant corner of the facility. A waitress arrived and dropped off three menus. Before she could leave, Luke said, "Wait a sec." He removed his wallet, drew a twenty from it, and set it on the end of the table. "I wonder if it's possible to get the music turned up a little." He didn't explain his reasons to the waitress and she asked no questions. The twenty had done all the talking necessary. A few moments later the background music—music from the seventies—rose in volume.

"You are one weird man, Luke Becker." Judith shook her head in disbelief.

"If you only knew." He picked up the menu. "Everyone order something."

"I'm not hungry," Ida said.

"Of course you are." Luke opened her menu. "Unless you'd like to stand out to everyone who walks by."

The corners of Ida's mouth turned down but she looked at the menu. Luke's eyes went elsewhere, scanning the ceiling and walls.

"Did you know that some California restaurants are equipped to eavesdrop on their customers? They even post a warning on their doors."

"No, I didn't know that and I'm not sure I'd care if I did."

"You should. Nearly nine hundred million dollars is spent on eavesdropping equipment every year in the U.S. Still, this is the best we're going to be able to do. They can't monitor every eating establishment in the airport."

The waitress returned, eager to be of help, and Judith was sure, eager to earn another large tip. Luke ordered a turkey sandwich, Ida a salad, and Judith opted for soup. Nerves had made her stomach uncooperative.

Alone once again, Luke asked Ida, "Do you feel up to answering questions?"

"I don't know that I should."

"I can appreciate your confusion and mistrust, but we need to know more about you and your son. Back at your home you said something about not talking to the police; that it was part of a deal. What deal?"

"I'm not supposed to talk about it."

Luke's face darkened. "Ida, someone has taken Abel and destroyed your house with the intent of killing you."

"I don't know why they would do that. I've done everything I was supposed to do." Judith could hear the tears in her voice.

"Stay strong, Ida. I can't speak for them—whoever 'them' is, but it looks to me like someone is trying to cover their trail. If so, then something or someone has them frightened. Blowing up the house was a desperate act."

Judith wondered if it would have happened if she and Luke hadn't shown up on Ida's doorstep. She chastised herself. It didn't matter now. *What's done is done. Focus on the present.*

Ida looked to Judith but said nothing. Still, Judith knew she wanted direction. Judith took her hand and gave a gentle squeeze. "We've given you no reason to trust us, Ida. We know that. In some ways, we're victims too. I want to help. Luke wants to help. But we need as much information as possible. What did you mean when you spoke of 'the deal'?"

"Abel isn't really my son."

Despite her earlier suspicions, the words stung Judith. "What?"

"Ed and I couldn't have children. Actually, it was Ed. His body produced an antibody that made him infertile. He felt horrible about it. Men are that way. He felt like he had failed as a husband and as a man. Infertility isn't that rare, really. About 25 percent of men have a problem. Knowing that didn't help him. He didn't care about other men, just his failing."

"Then how—"

"I'm a surrogate."

The table fell silent, the void filled with the noise from the televisions and the patrons whiling away their time before boarding whatever airline awaited them.

"So, that means ..." Luke seemed reluctant to say it.

Ida spared him. "It means that Abel is the product of ART."

"Art who?" Luke wondered.

"Not Art the name," Judith corrected. "A-R-T: assisted reproductive technology." Ida looked at her and had the same stunned expression as Luke. Judith spoke softly. "I can't bear children. Allen and I considered fertility treatment, but it never worked out."

"It sounds like you got an education." Luke shifted in his seat.

"That's all I got." Judith turned to Ida. "Go on."

"Then you'll understand why I went through everything I did. In vitro fertilization isn't new and not even unusual anymore. The first IVF child was born to a British couple in 1978, thirty years ago. Our problem was money. The procedures cost between eight to ten thousand dollars per cycle. My husband didn't make much money. Our whole married life we lived from paycheck to paycheck. We ran up credit cards and took a second mortgage on the house, but traditional IVF and GIFT procedures didn't work."

"Is 'gift' another acronym? I thought I'd ask before displaying my ignorance again."

"Gamete Intrafallopian Transfer," Judith explained. "It's not used often, maybe 2 percent of ART procedures. Something like three hundred GIFT babies are born in the U.S. every year. U-S stands for—"

"I know what U.S. stands for, Judith. I'm only moderately stupid."

Judith smiled, but it didn't last long. Maintaining humor was impossible. To Ida she asked, "ZIFT?"

Ida nodded.

"Translation, please." Luke rubbed his eyes.

Ida waited for Judith to explain.

"Zygote Intrafallopian Transfer. Instead of implanting gametes from both parents in the woman's fallopian tube for fertilization, the fertilization takes place in vitro and the zygote—you know what a zygote is?"

Luke nodded. "I stayed awake in college. A zygote is a fertilized ovum."

"Right. In a ZIFT procedure, the zygote is implanted in the mother."

"And this is the procedure you underwent?" Luke asked Ida.

"Yes."

Judith felt confused. "If my memory is right, ZIFT treatments are as expensive as GIFT."

"In my case, it was several thousand more." Ida drew a finger below her eyes. "We were tapped."

"Then how did you afford another procedure?" Judith asked softly, trying not to tip her over the emotional precipice.

She lowered her head and stared at the table. As she opened her mouth to speak the waitress arrived with the food. Ida froze. Once the plates were set and the waitress gave Luke her biggest you're-my-favorite-customer grin, they were alone in the corner booth again.

Ida picked up her fork and pushed a cherry tomato around the edge of the salad. "We had given up all hope when I got a call. A man said that my doctor had recommended me to a special program. They claimed to have made great strides in the field of fertility treatment. I had a moment of joy but then explained that we could no longer afford the procedure." She set the fork down. "He said everything would be free. All I had to do was allow them to follow the child's development."

"And you agreed?" Luke tried to look neutral but Judith detected his abhorrence. The man was nothing if not consistent.

"My husband and I talked it over and decided that the opportunity was too good to turn down."

"So you called them back?"

She shook her head. "They insisted that they be the ones to call. The man explained that there were many women in my situation and if word got out that a certain number of procedures were being done for free they would be inundated with tearful pleas. Complete secrecy was the price we'd have to pay."

"And that didn't set off alarms in your mind?"

"Shut up, Luke," Judith snapped. No man could fully understand what women like Ida—like her—went through.

"I'm just saying that such behavior on the part of a stranger is indicative of ... of ... What are you looking at?"

Judith's eyes were fixed to the one television showing news. "I think we may have a problem."

Luke turned and groaned.

On the screen played video footage of what had once been Ida's house. The bar had the volume down so as not to interfere with the other stations, but Judith was certain she heard her name.

twenty-one

So?" Detective Ben Wilson raised an eyebrow to add the question mark to his unfinished inquiry. He stood near the executive elevator with a youthful man showing a head of disheveled brown hair, clear eyes, and a day's stubble on his chin. He wore a vest that identified him as a member of the forensics unit.

"All clear. We found a bug in the phone of the main office as well as one behind the electrical outlet plate near the desk and one by the fireplace. There was also a small spy camera—actually a wireless, two-point-four gigahertz, hi-res, four hundred lines, three-point-six millimeter, seventy degree angle lens, delivered over seven hundred feet L.O.S.—"

"Dirk?"

"Yeah?"

"Faster and funnier."

Dirk Markos blinked as if processing the comment. "Oh. Sorry. It's a wireless camera that can deliver a decent signal up to seven hundred feet line of sight if there aren't too many walls around."

"So someone was watching and listening to Ms. Find?"

"No doubt about that. The microphones and camera are top of the line."

"Seven hundred feet means the spy could be anywhere in the building."

"It's worse than that. The seven-hundred-foot range is line-of-sight so its practical distance is less. If our peeper is located on the floor below and behind closed doors, then the signal would be even less. I figured that someone might not want to be on the same floor as the person he or she is watching, so I took a look around for a repeater."

"You mean a transmitter that increases the distance?" Wilson saw where the forensics tech was going.

"Right, this little baby sees what it sees and transmits it to a receiver which has more juice. The problem with these little guys is that the battery runs down in about six hours or so. Some will run longer but they don't have to broadcast far and for an extended time. My guess is that this camera is a cut above the stuff you get off the Internet but it still is confined to the laws of physics."

"This leads where?"

"I found a repeater in Mr. Find's office."

Wilson had been a cop too long to be surprised by much, but that caught him off guard. "That a fact? His office is right next to Ms. Find's."

"It could be coincidence." Dirk smiled.

"Yeah, right. Coincidence. We know how often that happens. I think I'll have a little talk with Mr. Find. Tell me about the secretary's phone."

"Senior administrative assistant. I made that mistake when she came by."

"She came by? I told her to take a long lunch and give you guys time to do your work."

"She didn't interfere, just picked up a couple of files she said she needed and then left. Anyway, I located the device that did the damage. It's mostly electronic smoke and mirrors designed to make noise and deliver a slight shock to the user. I've never seen anything quite like it. I need to study it more, but my best guess right now is that it was supposed to fry the phone's electronics, which it did, but with greater force than intended."

"How do you know what was intended?"

The tech shrugged. "I don't know it; I suspect it. If the perp wanted to do real damage it would have been easy enough to do. He could have blown the woman's ear off. For now, I'm assuming it was meant to be some kind of warning."

"A warning about what?"

"Beats me, Detective."

Wilson could see the fury building in Marlin Find. His jaw tightened so much that the detective expected to hear teeth crack. The slick-dressed executive sat in his high-back leather chair that Wilson was sure would cost him a week's salary and he squeezed the armrests. Wilson could see the man's muscles work under the shirt. Find might be a little short but he certainly seemed in shape, not that that frightened him. Over the course of his career he had arrested gang members and thugs who lived only to pump iron and sell drugs.

Find was not a man like that. Wilson had sized the man up: he was full of anger, enjoyed throwing his weight around, but could be cowed easily enough. He had dealt with his kind before—the executive who could make an employee cry but couldn't hold his own in a real confrontation.

"I don't mind telling you, Detective, that I don't like what you're suggesting." He shifted in the chair, his head held high as if he were the captain of an aircraft carrier. Wilson sat in a chair opposite the desk, a chair Find had taken pains to describe as "designed for this specific office, blending teak and leather like never before." He sounded like a catalog.

"And I don't mind telling you, Mr. Find, that I don't care what you like. Now, we can make this a contest of wills or you can climb down off your high horse and answer a few questions."

"I don't have to answer your questions. I'm not under arrest."

"Would you like to be?"

It always happened this way. First, the interviewee was all goodness and light, willing to help in any way, then a question upset them—maybe because it got too close to the truth—so they put on their best I'm-so-offended-that-you'd-suggest-such-a-thing act, which was then followed by anger and resistance. Find went to phase three more quickly than most.

"I don't respond well to threats, Detective."

"That's why I don't make threats." He let the verbal bomb land. The question was whether Find would call his bluff. He had no reason to arrest the young exec.

"I don't know how that transmitter got in my office. I am not now nor have I ever spied on my stepmother."

The word mother seemed to hang in his throat. "Who else has access to your office?"

"No one."

"Not even Ms. Find?"

"Not even her."

"Do you clean the office yourself?"

"Of course not. Well, there is the cleaning staff. They have a key." Some of the wind left his sails. "But they're just janitors."

"Just janitors, eh?" Wilson hated arrogance in all forms. Career prejudice irked him.

"You know what I mean. The device your man found is rather technical. Not the kind of thing you'd expect a janitor to deal with."

Wilson sighed and rubbed his eyes for effect. "I worked my way through college cleaning offices."

"Well ... I didn't mean ... of course you were gaining experience ..."

Best to let him squirm a little. It took effort not to smile at Find's discomfort. A moment later, Wilson asked, "Do you know how most high-tech crimes are committed? They're done by someone on the inside of the firm. Either an employee gets paid off, blackmailed, or initiates the crime himself. Let me ask you this: if the janitorial staff were to walk in here right now, could you identify the real ones from any imposters?"

Find frowned. "I doubt it."

"You doubt it?"

"No, Detective, I wouldn't be able to identify them."

"Well, I'm just a dumb cop, but if this were my business, I'd keep track of such things."

Find squirmed but said nothing.

"Two things. First, we have learned that your stepmother's office was bugged with wireless microphones and a camera. The repeater was found in your office."

"I'm telling you I didn't put it there. I didn't know a thing about it until one of your people came in and did what he called a sweep. That's when I first learned of the device."

Wilson looked in the direction of a contemporary chrome and glass television stand that held a large, thin, plasma television. The device had been plugged into a wall socket behind the DVR and other electronic equipment. It would have been impossible to see.

"Any idea who might want to spy on Ms. Find?"

"We have lots of competitors, most of whom we've left in the dust over the last four years. Our stock has tripled, our name ID is through the roof, and we have one of the most coveted brand names of any business. So take your pick. I can name two dozen companies that would like to see us go under."

"You have that many competitors?"

"Of course." Find leaned forward. "Look Detective, Find, Inc., is multifaceted. Our products cover flooring, wallpaper, designer light fixtures, outdoor furniture, paints, fabrics — anything and everything that touches on interior design. So there are several companies that make paint, but our brand outsells them because of the Find name."

"And because your stepmother is so well known."

He bristled. "It might seem like that to someone unfamiliar with large business operations like this one, but her figurehead status is just that. We're the leader because we provide the best product."

The time had come to spring the question he had been holding like an ace up his sleeve. "What can you tell me about the explosion in Fresno?"

"I don't know how the phone ... What?"

"The house in Fresno. The one that exploded and your stepmother was seen entering."

The color drained from Find's face. "You mean ...?"

"No. I'm sorry." He wasn't. Wilson wanted to gauge the reaction. "No bodies found. Just a burned-out house Ms. Find was seen entering."

"In Fresno? How did she ...? Oh." He snapped up the phone and punched a button. His assistant answered. "I want you to find out where the jet is. Immediately. Call me right back." He crammed the receiver back in the cradle.

"I take it this is all news to you."

"Take it any way you want." He shot to his feet and paced behind his desk. "Fresno? What's in Fresno? She said nothing to me."

"The police in Fresno want to talk to her."

"What is going on here? First the cell phone thing, then Terri's mishap, now you're telling me the offices have been bugged—"

"Just Ms. Find's offices on this floor."

"That's enough." He began to swear.

"What about the cell phones?"

"None of them are working. Apparently our illustrious leader hasn't been paying the bills."

"Is that like her?"

For a moment, Wilson thought Find was going to say yes, but he didn't. "No. She's pretty good about such things."

"She pays the bills herself, does she?"

Find shook his head. "No, we have accountants and a CFO who take care of such details, but I spoke to them. He doesn't understand what the problem is. Nonetheless, the ultimate responsibility rests with her."

The phone rang and Find seized it like a cat attacking a mouse. "What? When? Where is it now? Well find out." Again the receiver hit the cradle. "That was my assistant. She determined the corporate jet left early this afternoon for a destination unknown. Well, I guess we know."

"Is there a way to find out where the jet is right now?"

"Who knows?"

"I wonder if they filed a flight plan."

"Probably." Find returned to his seat. He seemed calmer— maybe too calm. Wilson saw a glint in his eye.

Wilson stood. "I'd appreciate it if you'd keep me informed if she contacts you. I'll let you know if we learn anything else about the electronic surveillance."

"Thank you, Detective."

Before Wilson could reach the door, Marlin said, "I'm sure this is all just a misunderstanding." He could smell the lie. "I need to be prepared. What kind of trouble could my stepmother be in for this explosion thing?"

"That depends on involvement. If she is involved, then I can think of half a dozen felonies the D.A. would toss at her. Of course, she might be the victim. Someone has bugged her office. Whoever did that could be behind the explosion."

"Of course, of course, I'm sure that's what it is."

"Then again ..." Wilson let the words hang.

"What?"

"The homeowner has gone missing. We might be looking at kidnapping. My advice is this: if she contacts you, you had better tell her to get to her lawyer and contact the police."

"If this gets out ..."

"Kinda makes that janitor job look good, doesn't it?"

Oddly, Find seemed to find humor in that.

Two steps outside the door, Detective Ben Wilson began to make phone calls.

The obnoxious detective had finally left his office. Marlin rose, crossed his office, closed the door, then returned to his desk.

He picked up the phone and buzzed his assistant. "I'm going to call for an emergency meeting of the board. Start making calls. Tell them it is a 'must' meeting and that I expect everyone to be there—or at least to be available for a teleconference. I want as many faces as possible. The meeting will start at ... make it four tomorrow afternoon." He listened for a moment. "Yes, something is wrong. Just make the calls."

Marlin leaned back in his chair and for the first time in a frustrating day sensed a cool flow of pleasure.

Maybe, just maybe.

twenty-two

O kay, okay, everyone stay calm." Luke scanned the restaurant.

Judith looked at Ida then back to Luke. "We are calm, Luke. I don't see anyone panicking."

"Sorry. It just seemed the right thing to say."

Judging by the response of the restaurant's patrons, the news story went unnoticed. What few diners watched the overhead televisions had eyes fixed to the ones with sports programming.

"What do we do now?" Ida asked.

Before anyone could answer, the waitress, still inspired by the twenty Luke slipped her, arrived with a broad smile. "Is everything delicious?" She looked at Ida's untouched food. "Is there something wrong with the salad?"

Ida blanched. "No, I just wasn't as hungry as I thought."

"You want me to get you something else?"

We want you to leave us alone. Judith kept the words locked in her mind.

Ida said, "No."

"I know what you mean, honey. I don't like to eat before I fly either."

For a moment, Judith thought Ida was going to correct the waitress but the woman caught herself and offered a simple smile.

The moment the waitress left, Judith relaxed, unaware that she had tensed as much as she had. Was the waitress

141 / alton GANSKY

looking at them differently? Had she seen the newscast or had she been too busy keeping track of customers?

Luke sat in silence, his eyes shut, and his head moving slightly from side to side. She made eye contact with Ida then shrugged. Judith hadn't known Luke long enough to know what the motions meant. She suspected that Luke had fallen deep into thought.

A second later, his eyes snapped open. "This is a problem."

In a less stressful situation Judith might have laughed at the understatement. "Think so? I kinda thought we had problems when someone tried to blow us up."

Luke's mouth dipped. "What I mean is, this has become much more complicated. If the news media has the story, then we can be certain that police agencies everywhere have been notified. We have to assume that since a witness identified you, local police in Ontario are searching for you."

"But we're in San Diego." The fact gave Judith no comfort. The Puppeteer made clear they could not go to the police. They hadn't but now the police were involved, at least in trying to find them.

"That's our only advantage. We need to get the most out of it."

"Oh." Judith had a thought that removed what little appetite she had. Luke tilted his head in an unspoken question. "The jet. If they're looking for me, then what would they do? If they assume that it was really me the witness saw in Fresno, then they'll know I had to get there somehow. My car is at the office. Remember, I had Terri pick it up from Hutch's."

"I remember," Luke said. "And the cops can determine when you were last seen at the office and compare that with when you were seen in Fresno."

"And know that I flew. It won't take them long to figure out the corporation has a business jet."

Luke raised his hands to his face. "Please tell me the pilots didn't file flight plans."

"I'm sure they did. It only takes a few moments. It can even be done verbally."

"What's that mean?" Ida wondered.

Judith answered. "It means that it's only a matter of time before someone figures out that the jet traveled from Ontario to Fresno to San Diego."

"We can't stay here much longer," Luke said.

Judith agreed although a large part of her wanted to walk up to the closest airport security person and lay out the whole story, but she couldn't bring herself to do it. Her future was at stake, then—and it shamed her that the thought came second—there was Abel's safety to consider.

"This changes everything." Luke shifted his weight like a man perched on a pebble-filled cushion. "We had some advantage when we began, but now that the police and others are looking for us, we have to be even more careful about what we do."

"They're not looking for you, Luke. They're looking for *me*. I'm a publicly recognizable figure. That must be why the witness knew who I was. You're not."

"Granted, but it makes no difference. The Puppeteer has handcuffed us together."

"Maybe we should go on separately."

"How? How do we do that? He didn't say it specifically, but I think part of the deal is that we stick together."

"And what about me?" Ida asked.

And what about you, indeed. Judith had no ideas. They couldn't cart an unwilling woman along. They had no idea what lay ahead and based on the narrow escape they just faced, the future might be dangerous. Of course, the demolished house provided proof enough that the woman was in danger. She couldn't go home. What was left?

No one spoke, the question too sticky to dismiss easily.

"I'm going with you." Ida made the pronouncement in solid I've-made-up-my-mind tone.

Luke shook his head. "I don't think that's wise, Ida. We're not sure where we're going or what we'll find. There is too much uncertainty."

"What certainty do I have now? My house is charred rubble, my husband is dead, and my son is missing."

"Still, Ida, it's unwise."

Judith spoke up. "I think she should come with us."

"Are you daft? You know how difficult this is."

"No, I'm not daft." Judith leaned over the table to keep her voice from carrying to the other patrons. "You're not thinking this through. We can't stay here much longer and we haven't learned all that Ida has to say. She may have more information." Judith nudged the woman with her foot. She jerked.

"That's right. I'm not telling you any more unless you let me come along."

Luke started to speak, but Judith cut him off. "Not only that, she can identify you. You introduced yourself to her at her home. If the police get hold of her, they'll have names and descriptions for both of us. If she claims we kidnapped her, then we have bigger problems. If she implicates us in the kidnapping of her son, then the FBI gets involved. Right? The FBI has jurisdiction over child abduction. It's bad enough having local cops from two cities—"

"Three cities," Luke said. "If your pilots filed a flight plan, then they know the jet is here and the locals will be notified by a phone call."

"Okay, three cities."

"But it's hard enough for two people to stay invisible, especially when one has had her face on television for years. Three people might be impossible."

"Think, Luke. If we find Abel, do you think he's going to run into our arms because we look like a nice couple? He's been abducted from his home. He wants to see his mother."

Ida's face set like stone. Judith couldn't tell if she was acting or if a strength and intelligence previously masked by sorrow was now coming to the surface. Either way, she was playing the part well. Judith just hoped she had chosen the right side.

"I know when I'm being worked." Luke's frown turned into a scowl.

Judith answered the scowl with a grin. "You are, but you know that taking Ida is the right decision."

"I don't think she'd turn on us, but you make a good point about Abel responding to his mother better than to us, and about our need to hear the rest of Ida's story." He leaned back and his shoulders rounded. "You win."

Once again, Ida seemed on the verge of tears, but Judith saw something new in the woman: resolve.

"What now?" Ida asked.

"We leave but once outside the restaurant, we split up."

"Split up?"

Luke raised a hand. "Not completely. They're going to be looking for three people, one man and two women. We stick out like coal on snow. You two walk together, I'll stay a few steps behind. We are never to lose sight of one another. And speaking of sticking out, Judith, you need to buy a hat, or scarf or something, and some shades. Disguise yourself the best you can. Don't—I'm serious about this—do not use any credit card or debit card. Got it? They're looking for you and any transaction other than cash can be traced. Do you have any money?"

"Enough."

"Okay. I'm going to get more cash from an ATM machine. No one has identified me yet so I think I can get away with it. Once they do, all my plastic gets tossed."

"Understood." Judith took a deep breath. "Let's go."

Luke threw two twenties on the table and the three walked into the concourse of the airport.

Sam Pennington taxied the Piper Arrow 180 aircraft to the runway and waited the final clearance to take off from the Fresno Chandler Downtown Airport. He had wanted to be in the air sooner, but the local cops and fire investigators had an endless stream of "just one last question." Finally satisfied, they gave him his leave and he returned his rental car and rented the single engine aircraft. At 120 bucks an hour most people would have choked at the expense, but Pennington didn't care. It wasn't his money he was spending.

The tower radioed his clearance and Pennington put the craft into motion. An experienced private pilot, he felt the thrill of acceleration and lift and soon exchanged the view of the ground for the blue of the central California sky. Soon he'd be at altitude and traveling at 130 knots.

His destination had been easy to determine. People like Judith Find didn't travel in commercial airliners. A couple of phone calls and two or three lies got him the information he needed. What he didn't know was why Judith Find had been at his target's house in the first place and who the man with her might be. Pennington liked things clear and in the proper order, but life—especially his life—seldom cooperated.

"In due time," he said to himself and banked the airplane in the direction of San Diego.

It bothered him that they had flown to San Diego. How had they known? How could they know that his employers set up camp in the city? Something was missing. No, not something—someone. Could there be another player? If so, who?

He had a few hours to consider such things and to plan his next step.

Pennington wasn't sure how things would progress but he was certain it wasn't going to be pretty.

twenty-three

Fifteen minutes after they left the restaurant the threesome stood at the curb of the terminal, melded into the mass of humanity moving in and out of the building. Judith and Ida stood twenty feet away from Luke. Judith had taken his advice and purchased a powder blue cap with the words Sea World stitched over the brim and a pair of sunglasses. One look in the mirror had told her she personified a Southern California tourist.

Judith raised a hand and a green-and-white cab pulled to the curb and a tired-looking man exited the driver's seat and moved to the trunk.

"No luggage. We're not in town for long." Judith opened the backseat and Ida slipped in. The driver, a dark-skinned man with a scruffy swath of stubble across his face looked puzzled. "Oh, and there are three of us."

Luke stepped to the open door and waited for Judith to seat herself in the back. He joined her. The driver returned to his spot and closed the door.

"Where to?"

"Can you recommend a good hotel?" Luke asked.

"Sure, there's lots of them around here—"

"In the north county."

"You want me to drive you all the way to the north county? Inland or oceanside?"

"How about someplace in between."

The cabbie thought. "Lot's of people like the Marriott chain. There's also Holiday Inn ..."

"Marriott is good. One of the larger ones."

The cabbie nodded with assurance. "You might want to call ahead and see if they have rooms available. Those places can fill up quick."

Judith cut her eyes to Luke. Neither of their cell phones worked any longer. "I think we're good, but thanks for the suggestion."

"It's your fare, mister." The cab pulled away.

Terri felt as if she had put in a fourteen-hour day and it was only 5:30. Since receiving a call on her private cell phone from Judith, she had worked at a feverish rate to correlate information never meant to be correlated. She had made calls, spoken to shippers, installers, billing, and more. Once she had gathered all the information she could begin to sort through it. Fortunately, she was a whiz with computers. She didn't know how they worked, nor did she care, but she did know how to make them obey.

Most of the employees had left for the day, and the forensics crew had finished their work in her office and Judith's. Terri, however, felt more comfortable in the third-floor conference room, one of the smaller meeting rooms used by midlevel managers. Here she had access to a laptop, the Internet, and thanks to Judith's unflagging trust in her, accounting documents protected by passwords.

At first, the task of finding what homes had purchased both the Persian rug and the Blocked Maple design of laminate flooring seemed impossible but she got a break. The flooring never made it out of the testing phase. Only a few outlets stocked the material. Since it was being tested, the outlets kept close records. There weren't many to keep. Very few people wanted it.

The area rug was a different matter. More of them sold but there was good news on that front as well. Retailers kept close tabs on their stock. With laser scanners and sophisticated database software, most could keep track of buying trends not only of the neighborhood the store served but of the individual buyer. By comparing addresses, Terri found what she was looking for.

There was only one address that fit the bill.

Terri wondered how Judith knew that.

She had nothing to do now but wait for another call.

"Something isn't right." Karen Rose sat in the passenger side of the KTOT news van, staring at the near empty parking lot of Find, Inc. Only a handful of cars were visible, including the Lexus convertible parked in the CEO's spot.

"Reporter's intuition?" Cindy Chu struggled to stretch but the confines of the driver's seat limited her efforts. They had been sitting for forty minutes trying to decide their next move.

"I suppose. You have those times when you've seen things, listened to what people have to say, and still have a feeling that everyone else is wrong."

"All the time. The way I figure it, I'm right and they're wrong."

"That's what I like about you, Cindy—your enormous, blind confidence."

"At least you didn't say arrogance."

"I'd never say anything like that—at least not while I'm confined in a small space with you." Karen opened a file on her lap. The first thing she did after leaving Dwayne's office was scour the Net for any information she could find on Judith Find and Find, Inc. She found lots of information, very little of it useful.

"She's all image."

Cindy looked puzzled. "What?"

Karen held up the printouts. "She's all image. Go to the Find, Inc., website and you get a short bio about Judith, lots of media pictures, some downloadable video, and a billion pages of products. Every other site I went to had nothing but good to say. No dirt. No rumors. No complaints. The company is sound, the stock is solid, profits every quarter. She's spick-and-span; a business Barbie."

"Did you expect her dark secrets to be posted on the web?"

"No, but I expected a little more humanity. With people like Martha Stewart there are those that love her or hate her. With the Find woman, there's almost nothing but fluff."

"Maybe that's a good thing."

Karen closed the folder. "Maybe. Let me ask you something. You're at a house and it blows up but you get away; what's the first thing you'd do?"

Cindy bit her lip as she thought. "I guess that'd depend on whether or not I'm the one who blew it up."

"Why would a wealthy, well-known woman blow up another person's house?"

"Maybe she had some kind of grudge or was being blackmailed."

"Judith Find has millions of dollars."

Cindy shrugged. "So? Millionaires can be blackmailed."

"If you had millions of dollars and were highly recognizable, would you blow up a home? I mean personally?"

"I see what you're getting at. You're saying she'd hire someone to do it."

"Exactly. Her mental elevator would have had to snap for her to personally travel to Fresno and do the deed, especially since she could wave enough money around to capture the attention of every criminal mercenary in three countries."

"But there was a man with her. Maybe he forced her to do the deed. You know, like the rich kid from the newspaper family and that anti-something-or-other group."

"Patty Hearst and the SLA?"

"Yeah, her. Maybe someone found a way to force her to do something she wouldn't normally do."

Karen gave it some thought. "No dice. The SLA wanted attention. No one is claiming responsibility. There's got to be something else."

"Did you check to see if she has a criminal record?"

"Pure as the driven snow as far as I can tell. I checked for articles and other news reports on her but nothing. It's like a PR firm controls the media around her."

"They don't control us."

"And here we sit in an empty parking lot looking at a locked building and a parked car."

"It's a shame the janitorial crew wouldn't let you in." Cindy chuckled. "What kind of world is this when even the maintenance people have unshakable integrity? Don't they know how difficult that makes our jobs?"

Karen reran everything she knew so far and came up with the same mystery and no new answers. "I've got a bad feeling about this, Cindy."

"You think we're going to get in trouble? Sued by a major corporation?"

"No. I think Judith Find is the one in trouble. I don't know what kind or how severe but I'm willing to bet my paycheck the woman is in way over her head."

"You can't broadcast psychic feelings over the television airwaves. The station owners might have something to say about that."

Karen gazed through the window at the empty Lexus. "What have you gotten yourself into, lady?"

twenty-four

Use the phone in the lobby." Luke sounded tired.

"Why?" Judith asked. She *knew* she was tired.

"Because when you use a phone in a hotel room, it's routed through a computer switchboard and recorded, just in case you're making long-distance calls."

It made sense and the fact that it did worried Judith. Was paranoia contagious?

Judith, Luke, and Ida sat in the lobby of the Triton Hotel. The cabbie had dropped them off at the entrance to the Marriott on La Jolla Village Drive and they stepped into the lobby, went to the bar, and sipped sodas for twenty minutes. They then exited the lobby, hailed another cab, and chose a different hotel. Judith needed no explanation. She held the same fear as Luke. The cabbie would return to the airport and the police, if they were on the ball, would interview as many drivers as possible, assuming that they had either rented a car or taken a taxi. Sooner or later, they would connect with the man who drove them to the Marriott. The police would arrive a short time after that. They couldn't stay in the Marriott, and Luke never intended that they would.

The Triton was a new fifteen-story structure in the east part of La Jolla. Judith immediately noticed the smooth design of the exterior that made it noticeable but still gave the impression that it belonged to the terrain. The interior showed the guiding hand of a designer who knew what he or she was doing. Deep cushioned leather sofas and chairs populated a lobby centered around a fireplace with a large, circular copper top. The fireplace was what Judith called "new-unique"—a variation of an older idea. Instead of concrete logs designed to look like wood lapped by natural gas-fed flames, the base of the open pit was white sand from which frolicked yellow flame. Natural gas percolated up through the sand providing fuel to the flames.

They sat around the fire resting and trying to get their bearings.

Luke had secured two rooms, one for Judith and Ida and one for himself. To further throw off anyone trying to track them, he had done the same at the Marriott. He explained that the police or worse, those who had bombed Ida's house, might follow the cabbie's direction to the Marriott, and upon checking with the front desk learn that two women and one man had checked in. The police would flash a badge and show a picture which the desk clerk could confirm. They might check the room or stake it out to see what move the fugitives would take. It could take them all night to realize the rooms were never used.

"I'll be back." Judith rose and made her way to the lobby pay phone and placed a collect call to Terri's private cell phone. Terri picked up on the third ring.

"Are you okay?" No amount of electronics could disguise the woman's concern.

"I'm fine, Terri. How are you holding up?"

"I'm a complete wreck. The police have been back around asking questions about Fresno and that reporter from the television station has been hounding me."

"You haven't been talking to her, have you?"

"Of course not. I've been hiding out in the third-floor conference room."

"A clever choice."

"Is it true, Judith? That you were at a house that blew up? A house in Fresno?"

"Terri ... It's best I not involve you."

"What's going on? I want to help."

Judith could hear tears in her voice and her heart began to ache for her friend and aide. "I know you want to, and you are. You're the best." She heard a sniff.

"I want to do more."

"Now listen to me, Terri. You must not endanger yourself. Don't lie to the police. Don't mislead them. I don't want you getting in trouble with the law."

"But what if they ask me if I've spoken to you?"

"Tell them the truth, I suppose."

"If I do, they'll do something like seize my cell phone or get the phone records and know where you were when we spoke."

"It's a risk I'll have to take. If you start lying to the police you're likely to end up in jail. You have an elderly mother who needs you."

"I know, but ..." She trailed off and Judith heard more sniffing. "Wait, Perry Mason."

"Huh?"

"You know how my mother likes the old Perry Mason television shows with Raymond Burr."

That was true. Terri had mentioned the hours she endured watching the old black-and-white episodes. "I don't follow."

"Anytime Perry had a client who was in trouble and whom he didn't want talking to the police, he would have his secretary Della take the client to some hotel and check her in under her own name. That way, he could hide her but since she was registered under her own name—"

"She wasn't really hiding."

"Mom's been talking about a vacation. Maybe I'll take her on a drive up the coast."

Judith thought for a moment. There was merit to the idea, but while it would keep Terri from being pressed by the police, it would also mean that Judith would have no one at the firm she could contact. Maybe that wouldn't matter. She didn't have many choices. "I'll leave that up to you, Terri. I can't advise you about that."

"I understand." She paused for just a second. "There's something you should know. Mr. Find has called for an emergency board meeting tomorrow. I've been avoiding him, but word travels quickly in these halls."

Anger came to a boil. "That little weasel. Do you know what he's planning to do?"

"No, but I can guess that he's up to no good. The thing with the cell phones, your office being bugged, your sudden disappearance, and the news flashing your picture around about an exploding house—well, my guess is that he's going to try to get more control of things. You know, make you look bad and him good."

"Figures." Judith's mind revved. "I can't come back right now."

"Can he take control?" Terri sounded even more frightened.

"I doubt it. Not tomorrow anyway. If he can sway enough board members, he might get the process started."

"But the board loves you. The business is as strong as ever."

"Maybe the board loves me, but Marlin can be convincing and conniving when he needs to be." Judith sighed. "Okay, I can't deal with that now, and I've talked too long as it is. Did you find out anything about the flooring and rugs?"

"Yes, and I admit that I'm surprised. I wouldn't have bet two nickels that I'd find what I did."

"Which is ..."

"An address in San Diego, it's near La Jolla. Do you know where that is? It's close to the ocean."

"I do know where it is." *I'm closer than you know.* Terri gave her an address on La Jolla Farms Road. Judith thanked her and said she hoped to see her soon.

Emotions played king-of-the-hill in Judith's mind. One-second fury over Marlin's move with the board rose to the top only to be replaced with fear over what Terri may face with the police, only to have a chill of concern for her own situation. When she awoke this morning, she had been in control. Life was good and filled with comfort and purpose, now she was tumbling headlong down a course whose destination she did not know.

She plopped down in the leather chair and stared at the wisps of fire.

"Well?" Luke asked. Ida just stared at Judith in silence.

"She gave me an address on La Jolla Farms Road."

"Let's have it."

"My stepson has called for an emergency board meeting. I think he's pulling something. I should show up. You know, crash the party."

"Tomorrow? Can't happen." Luke offered no words of comfort.

Judith watched the flames lapping at the air, dancing on the snow white sand. "Easy for you to say. You're not the one about to be ousted. That firm is my life. I have no meaning without it."

"Meaning is not found in things." The words came from Ida.

"What's that mean?" Judith spoke more harshly than she intended, and she saw Ida cower. "I'm sorry. I'm just a little on edge. Okay, I'm a lot on edge. I may be losing everything."

"I know the feeling," Ida said. Judith's heart tumbled. "It was something Abel used to say. He always said the strangest things."

"The address," Luke prompted. Judith recited it and Luke pulled his computer from its case. In moments, his fingers were flying over the keys. "The advantage with a large hotel is their wireless service. It's fast and can be accessed from anywhere in the building."

"Joy." Judith had grown too weary to hide the sarcasm. She had lived a week in the last few hours and the stress of it drained her. She laid her head back longing for a nap, no matter how short. Maybe she should go to her room—

"Wow." Luke said.

Judith pulled her mind from the fog. "What?"

"That's not a house, it's a compound." Luke moved to the middle of the sofa. "Gather 'round ladies." Judith moved from the chair to Luke's right. Ida sat on his left.

"What are we looking at?" Judith studied the image. "Satellite photo?" A color photo showing the ocean, a beach, and a cliff with large structures filled the screen. She could easily make out swimming pools, cars, large trees, and even see waves frozen in digital time.

"Exactly. There are several services that provide free photos to the public: Google Earth, Local.live.com are two. Some of the photos are a little dated but not too much."

"That's where my son is?" Ida asked.

"Well, that's where he *was* when the photo was taken."

Sadness washed over her face and Judith reminded herself that she could not understand what the poor woman endured.

Luke's fingers moved along the keyboard. "I'm going to save these images. They might prove useful. Now, let's see if I can't mine a little more info from the Net." A few keystrokes later, Luke sat back looking satisfied.

"Are you going to let us in on your skullduggery or just sit there with that self-satisfied smile?" Judith had been on the move since this morning and sitting around made her nervous. She checked the lobby doors again, just as she had sixty seconds before.

He pointed at the screen. "One of the advantages, and in my view, disadvantages, of the Internet is the availability of personal information. There are many websites that allow reverse lookup. Some you pay for, others are free. I put in the address and got two names: Alex Zarefsky and something called Cal-Genotics."

Ida choked.

twenty-five

I think it's time we heard the rest of your story, Ida." Luke spoke softly. "You know the name?"

She nodded. "Alex Zarefsky . . . Dr. Zarefsky. He's the one . . . he was my doctor."

"For the fertilization treatment?" Judith asked.

"Yes, although I always called him Dr. Alex. He insisted. I don't think he ever told me his last name."

"Then how did you learn it?" Luke closed his laptop.

"I saw it on my chart. His nurse set it down when I was in his office. I remember thinking it was an odd name—Zarefsky."

"Where did you go for the implantation procedure?" Judith said.

"I went to Dr. Alex's . . . I mean Dr. Zarefsky's clinic in Los Angeles."

"He has a clinic in LA but owns a home in San Diego?" Judith asked.

"I guess so. He never told me where he lived. However, I did get the impression that he had more than one clinic."

Luke was on the computer again. "Cal-Genotics has a website."

Judith leaned toward the screen and strained to see the small print. The laptop wasn't designed to be read from the side. "All I can read is their motto: Making Life Happen."

"It's the kind of site maintained by a publicly held corporation." Again he pointed to the screen. "See, it's got the usual basic info plus a section for investors and media." He adjusted the screen to better read the web page, then read aloud. "Our Mission: Cal-Genotics exists to research and provide new solutions in the field of human fertility. We apply a diverse approach blending genetics, bioinfomatics, and biotechnology to discover new and better treatments for infertility."

"Sounds noble," Judith said.

"Yeah? Well, I've researched enough companies to know that a pretty web page does not a profitable company make."

"I wasn't thinking of investing," Judith said.

"Neither am I." Luke moved the cursor around and clicked on the provided links. "They trade on NASDAQ ... at close of trading today a share was worth 43.27, up almost a full point ... volume is just under three million shares."

"What's all that mean?" Ida asked.

Luke answered quickly. "It means that they're doing all right for themselves." He kept working. "I found a link to their management team, and yup, there he is, Dr. Alex Zarefsky, president and CEO, holds a BS degree in biology from Stanford, an MD also from Stanford, and an MBA from Harvard.

The guy gets around." Luke fell silent as he read. "He's the founder of Coast Fertility Care Centers."

"That's the name of the center I went to." Ida's eyes were fixed to the monitor. Judith wondered if Ida could see better than she.

Luke nodded. More tapping. "It looks like he has several clinics. When I was a kid there was a national franchise of dental offices, all under the name of one dentist. I wondered how the poor guy could go to all those offices. Later, I learned he didn't. It was just his name."

"You think that's going on here?" Judith said.

"In a way. He has two clinics on the east coast—Boston and Miami; three on the west coast: two in San Diego and one in Los Angeles." Luke looked to Ida. "You say you dealt with Zarefsky directly?"

"Yes. He did everything. He and his nurses."

Judith began to sort the information in her mind. "Okay, we know Abel had his picture taken at a house in La Jolla, that the house is owned by a Dr. Zarefsky, and that it was he who treated Ida."

"Right," Luke said. "We also know that Zarefsky is tied to a biomedical research firm specializing in infertility problems. What we don't know is if Abel is still at the house and why he was taken in the first place."

Frustration mingled with weariness and Judith wished for her home, her bed, and her comfortable and well-known surroundings. Things seemed surrealistic and not quite right, like an old tape recorder playing an audiotape a touch too slow. The sofa beneath her, the humming of the fan in Luke's laptop, distant voices of other temporary residents in the hotel told her that all remained real. She wished it weren't so.

"How do we get my son?" A new edge had become evident in Ida's voice.

"I have no idea," Luke said. "The house has a cliff to the rear, and best I can tell from this photo, a large wall and gate along the road. Certainly there must be security cameras and probably guards. I can't imagine them taking Abel and not providing some protection. The houses on either side are bound to be as secure. The only possible way in is from the beach side, but that doesn't look likely. The cliff looks too high to climb and even if I were an experienced climber, I'm sure I'd have trouble with the loose soil. It's beach geology. Even if someone like me could make the climb it wouldn't solve the problem of electronic security and guards."

"We can't give up," Ida said. "He needs me. He's just a boy."

"I know." Luke studied the image on the monitor. Perhaps, Judith thought, to avoid making eye contact with a distraught mother.

"I wonder . . ." Judith trailed off.

"What?" Luke and Ida spoke in unison.

"If we can't get in, maybe we can get them to come out."

Luke looked into Judith's eyes and she realized it was the first time he had done so. She felt an odd sensation.

"Judith Find, you are a brilliant woman."

"What have you got on your mind?"

Luke smiled. "Did I see a shopping mall nearby? I'm going out for a bit. I'll be back."

There was little to see. Judith, Luke, and Ida drove along La Jolla Farms Road and passed the house they had seen from the satellite photo downloaded from the Internet. A seven-foot high wall clad in rough, white, Spanish-style stucco ran the length of the front property line. Centered in the wall was an ornate wrought-iron gate backed with a black metal mesh, designed to keep prying eyes from gazing onto the lot and at the house. A black metal box on a steel post sat a few feet in front of the gate and to the left side of the drive—the perfect distance for a person in a car to stop, enter a code, and drive in when the gate opened. The setting sun and encroaching darkness made observation tricky.

"Such is the price of having a mansion on the beach," Judith said. "All these houses are behind locked gates."

"How open is your home?" Luke asked.

"I didn't say they were wrong, just that everything has a price." She and Luke met eyes. Nothing more needed to be said.

"Not too slow." Luke sat in the front passenger seat. He had wanted to be free to observe as much as possible. "We don't want to draw attention to ourselves."

"Everyone is driving slow, Luke. This is tourist territory." In the rearview mirror, Judith could see Ida sitting as close to the door as possible. She gazed through the window at the wall that hid the house where her son was being held. Judith felt certain that if she slowed the car too much, Ida would leap from the moving vehicle and attempt to scale the wall.

Luke, however, had ceased gazing at the barrier. His eyes scanned the road ahead. "Not much room on the sides of the road. We'll just have to make do."

"What now?"

"We put your plan in action. Let's find the nearest pay phone."

Luke took a deep breath and waited. The fact that the phone rang three times before being answered surprised him.

"Nine-one-one, what is the nature of your emergency." The woman sounded bored.

Luke began to pant. "I was ... I mean, gunshots ... La Jolla Farms Road ... I heard screaming too." He gave the address.

"You heard gunshots, sir?"

"That's right. Three, maybe four. I don't know. I was just driving by ... you know ... looking at all the fancy houses when I heard a scream and the bang, bang, bang. You had better hurry. I don't have a good feeling about this."

"I notice you're calling from a pay phone—"

Luke expected that. There's no blocking caller ID with the police. "Yeah, my cell phone is dead. Stupid piece of junk. Dies on me all the time."

"May I have your name, sir?"

"Um, sure ... No. Forget it. I don't want to be involved. I just thought you should know."

"I need your name, sir."

Luke immersed himself in the role even more. "Look, lady. Send someone or don't. It's on your conscience. I've done the right thing." He hung up and returned to the car.

"Do you think it will work?" Judith said as Luke reentered the car.

"It should, but we're not done. It's your turn."

"Mine?"

"The cops are going to call the residence. Someone there will answer and say, 'No, everything is fine.' But if the cops get more than one report of a shooting they'll have to investigate and want to talk to someone face-to-face. We need you to make the same kind of call."

"But if I call from a pay phone it will look suspicious, and you know the state of our cell phones."

Luke reached into his pocket and removed an inexpensive-looking cell phone. "You're going to use this."

"Where did you get that?"

"At the mall. These days a person can get almost anything at a major mall. This is a pay-as-you-go phone. No contract. No credit check. I buy the phone, prepay for a handful of minutes, and we're good to go. Now make the call. Tell them that you were jogging by, but be quick about it. Too much time between calls will look suspicious."

"Then you drive. I don't like talking on these things and driving strange streets at night."

They changed places and Judith dialed the phone.

twenty-six

Judith tensed as Luke pulled to the side of the road yielding to two black-and-white patrol cars barreling past with light bars tossing splotches of blue and red on the terrain. Pulling back onto the road, Luke continued on as they had done before until they had passed Zarefsky's house. Judith looked at the side mirror on the passenger side of the rental car and saw the lights from at least two more police cars. Zarefsky was about to have his evening disrupted.

As they passed, Judith could see the gate opening. "He's letting the police in."

"That's the beauty of living in a litigious society. The police receive an emergency call like the one we gave and if they refuse to show and the call turns out to be real, they get their socks sued off. We gave them enough cause to search the grounds. They don't need a warrant if they have cause to believe a life may be in danger."

"Sometimes you frighten me," Judith said.

"Sometimes I frighten myself, but then again, society scares me more than anything else. I'm going to make a U-turn. I don't have much time."

Luke did and pulled to the west shoulder of the road and stopped in front of another walled property. He reached for the door handle. "Wish me luck."

"Be careful," Judith said.

"Be careful with my son," Ida added.

Judith watched as Luke strode toward the flashing lights fifty yards away and she felt sick.

Luke's heart tapped like a drummer on caffeine. He tried to calm it but despite a mental discipline he had long prided himself on, it continued to pound at an accelerated rate. As he approached, he saw three of the four patrol cars pull through the gate and down the long drive he had seen in the aerial photo. He walked with a casual gait, like a man on a peaceful stroll near the ocean, but he felt no peace. Not a man of great courage, Luke preferred the quiet of his home, his space behind locked doors, viewing the world through computer screen and television. Now here he walked toward what could only be an adventure that turned out badly. Still one foot preceded the other and he moved closer to the open gate, still not fully certain what he would do next.

He thought about how stupid all of this had become. So what if he had a secret? What did he care if people knew? He couldn't care less what others thought of him. He was a man of solitary existence, comfortable with his life and his choices. It would have been easier and probably wiser if he had told the Puppeteer what he could do with his threats.

But he hadn't. And he did care, as much as it galled him to admit it.

Cars on the road slowed as drivers and passengers rubbernecked to see the action taking place on the most exclusive street in San Diego. He guessed their fears. *You work hard, build or inherit some wealth, build a ten- or twenty-million dollar mansion overlooking the ocean, protect it with alarms and high walls, and still the police are needed. Wealth couldn't buy safety, health, or privacy. There is always someone who can find a chink in your armor.* Luke knew that now more than ever.

He paused at the gate and looked for an officer. He didn't know what police procedure would be followed in a case like this. Did they leave a man behind to guard the gate? He saw no one. Down the street he saw a fresh set of emergency lights approaching. Even at a distance he could see that it was an ambulance. A sensible precaution in light of the nature of the call.

Acting like he belonged on the scene, Luke took a deep breath and stepped through the gate.

"Do you trust him?" Ida's voice came in a breathy whisper from the backseat.

"Luke?" Judith gave the question thought. "I guess so. I haven't had any choice so far. I've only known him since ... lunch. That seems so long ago." Since meeting Luke at Hutch's in Ontario, she had traveled by car and plane, escaped an explosion, evaded the police, and now sat at the edge of a street not knowing what to do next. "Crazy, isn't it?"

"I could just walk up to the police and tell them that Abel is my son. They'd give him to me, wouldn't they? Abel would verify it."

"They might but they'd have lots of questions, such as why you haven't reported him missing, and why you didn't go to the police in Fresno after your house was destroyed."

"I could tell them that Abel was just visiting Dr. Zarefsky and that I had come to pick him up."

The idea had crossed Judith's mind but the three of them had been warned not to go to the police or the boy would die. As it was, they were skirting disobedience by faking a shooting call. If Ida had direct contact with the police then things might get worse. It didn't matter now, the die was cast. "I don't think they would buy it. Besides, there seems to be more at work here."

"What do you mean?"

"Well, we've explained how Luke and I have come to be involved—forced to be involved. The man we call the Puppeteer seems to know a lot, things it should be impossible for him to know. He's one factor. Your Dr. Zarefsky is another unknown. Someone has made an attempt on your life already. We have to be careful. We don't know who to trust."

"If Luke gets Abel out, what will you do with him—with us?"

"Do? We have no plans to do anything. We were told that if we didn't do something, he would die. So we're doing something." The harshness of the comment rang in Judith's mind. "I'm sorry. I could have phrased that much better."

Ida said nothing.

Judith wished she hadn't come to work that morning.

Now on the other side of the wall, Luke could see the expansive grounds. He estimated the property covered five acres; trees, shrubbery, and other plantings covered the grounds. He could smell the salt air from the ocean and see half of the sun's orange disk above the horizon. The sound of waves on the shore near the bottom of the distant cliff rumbled through the air.

A desire to flee rose in Luke and he nearly yielded. Nothing about this made sense. He had become certain that at some point since rising from bed, his mind had left him. Maybe that was it. Maybe all of this was a dream and in a moment, the alarm would sound and he would put his warm feet on the soft carpet of his bedroom. No matter how much he wished it so, the current reality overpowered the fantasy.

He wasn't in bed. He wasn't in his home. He stood on the side of a long drive that followed a gentle slope to a massive house with a copper-clad, mansard roof, green from weathering. Three of the police cars were parked on the circular drive, next to the entry, their lights flashing spots on the wall. Headlights added their illumination to the exterior house lamps. Two officers moved slowly along the perimeter of the mansion. Their guns were drawn. The front door stood open and warm, gold light poured from it like water from a fountain.

Although he couldn't see what transpired inside the home, Luke could guess. Whoever was home complained that no shots had been fired and that all this was a load of nonsense.

Nonetheless, the police felt compelled to search. They had to. If they didn't and it came to light later that someone had been wounded or killed, then the officers would be making their living as security guards. They would look in each room, interview every person present, and then, satisfied that they had been the target of a joke, leave, their mood spoiled for the week.

Luke moved from the drive into a small stand of trees. The satellite photo he downloaded of the property flashed in his mind. The arrangement of buildings matched in every detail but one: a new structure, a single story of maybe a thousand square feet, stood near the pool. Guest quarters? Pool cabana? He couldn't tell. It must have been built since the public access photo had been taken. It didn't surprise him.

He moved with prudence. Some considered him paranoid but he viewed himself as wisely cautious. It didn't take paranoia to know that an estate this size had security cameras. His first task was to locate them. His second task was to wait for the opportunity to present itself—whatever that might be.

Moving north, Luke made his way to a hedge that bordered a tennis court and crouched down, peering at the house through a small opening in the plants. To his right stood a large oak tree. Beneath it rested a stone picnic table and two benches, no doubt imported from Europe. Two uniformed officers exited the front door followed by a narrow man in beige slacks and a black sport shirt. Luke couldn't see well from his vantage point but he could make out enough detail to know that the man matched the picture he had seen on the Cal-Genotics web page. He gazed at Dr. Alex Zarefsky whose body language made it clear he was an unhappy man.

"Are you the one they're looking for?"

Luke jumped but managed to stifle a scream. The voice had come from his right and above his head. He looked up into the oak tree. A boy sat on one of the limbs.

"You scared the life out of me," Luke whispered then looked back toward the house. They hadn't been heard.

"Are you?"

"No, son, I'm not."

"Someone said they heard gunshots. I overheard the police say that."

Luke couldn't believe his luck. "You're Abel, aren't you?"

"Able to do what?" The boy kept his voice low.

Luke blinked. "What?"

"You asked if I was able. I can't answer unless I know what it is you want me to do." He smiled. "It's a joke."

"I get it," Luke whispered. "How about this: Abel, are you able to come down out of the tree?"

The boy looked at him in a way that made Luke feel like his soul was under examination. "Okay." With a speed that frightened Luke, the boy scampered quietly from the tree and knelt down by the hedge.

Even in the dimming light, Luke recognized the youngster: same age, same hair, and same lavender eyes. He held out his hand. "Mr. Abel Palek, I presume. I'm Luke Becker and I've come to find you."

Abel shook Luke's hand.

"I've been expecting you," Abel said. "I knew someone would come."

"What are you doing in that tree?" Luke kept his voice low and glanced back at the house. The officers were enduring a tongue-lashing.

"Dr. Z doesn't want anyone to see me. He told me that I should hide if anyone came looking for me."

"But you spoke to me."

"Dr. Z has no truth in him. You do. Is my mother with you?"

Luke wanted to ask what that meant but he didn't have time. "Your mother is waiting for you not far from here. All I have to do is figure out how to get you out without being seen." He let his eyes trace the way he came and back to the still open gate. As he did he noticed a black Mercedes SUV pull into the drive. He caught a glimpse of the driver—the man from Fresno.

Abel grabbed Luke's arm. "He's not a good man. There is evil on him."

"I got the same impression when I first met him. Okay, when he reaches the house, we'll head back up the drive—"

"No. It won't work. They have cameras."

"We don't have much choice, kid."

"I know a way. Follow me."

Sam Pennington stood by his boss as he ranted at the police officers. Pennington said nothing for awhile, then placed a hand on Zarefsky's elbow and squeezed. "Dr. Zarefsky, the officers were only doing as their training dictates."

"They demanded entrance and barged into my home!"

"Of course they did, and had there been someone with a gun on the premises then we'd be thanking them now. It's not their fault that someone turned in a false report." He squeezed Zarefsky's elbow tighter to punctuate his message. "The real crime is the person who made the false report."

Zarefsky stared at Pennington for a moment, and then he nodded. For a genius, Zarefsky could be stupid.

"Maybe I have overreacted." Zarefsky addressed the officers. "I apologize. Of course you were doing your job. I'm ... well, I'm a bit of a privacy nut. Having people making demands of me then searching my home ... Well, I'm sure you understand."

The officers smiled in the way men do when they want to end a conversation and left.

Pennington pulled Zarefsky inside and shut the door. "How long has this been going on?"

"I don't know. The whole thing is stupid."

"No, it's not. It's brilliant. When did the cops arrive?" Pennington moved through a wide foyer, over handmade terrazzo tile, and into the great room. A few steps later he stood before an antique rolltop desk.

"Fifteen minutes tops. They had been here only ten minutes when you arrived.

"I see you had the good sense to lock this down. Where's the key?"

Zarefsky removed a metal key from his pocket. "I thought it best if the cops didn't see the surveillance cameras. If they had, I probably could explain it away. I mean, most of the homes here have some kind of camera system."

"But not like this." He inserted the key, turned it, and lifted the rolltop. Six color monitors filled every inch of the space. Pennington took in their images in a second. "The boy's not in his room."

"He's been told to stay out of sight if people come over." Zarefsky seemed nervous.

"Out of their sight, not ours." Pennington opened a side panel in the desk and pulled a wireless keyboard from the space. He typed in a command and the image from the driveway camera rewound. He stopped, and then ran it forward. A second later he hit pause. The dark image of a man entering through the gate was fixed on the monitor. Pennington swore. "I know him."

"Who is he?"

"He's the guy from Fresno." Pennington swore again.

"The one with that Find woman?"

"Yeah, the one with Judith Find. I've got to give him credit, this approach was sheer genius. I may have underestimated him." He entered the commands to return the image to real time. "He called the cops and gave them a story they'd have to follow. Of course, they come barreling in, distracting you and forcing you to conceal the security system, then he walks in a few minutes later. It's the only way he could get on the grounds."

"But why?"

"For some reason he wants the boy, and if we don't hurry, he's going to get him." Pennington set the keyboard on the top of the desk. "You watch the monitors. Call my cell phone if you see anything. Keep a close eye on the boy's room and the driveway." He glanced at the other monitors but saw nothing. "The cops are gone. Close the gate."

Pennington ran from the house.

twenty-seven

Are you sure you know where you're going?" Luke followed the lad as he moved quickly along the wall at the north property line and toward the cliffs at the rear of the lot.

"Of course, I know. They let me wander the grounds but I can't go out to the street."

"I'm surprised they let you out of the house."

The boy pointed to the pool house. "I stayed there and not in the house. It's got like guest quarters and stuff. They put in a big television and lots of video games—Xbox and everything. I think they just wanted to keep me quiet for a couple of days."

Abel moved through the darkness like a cat; Luke struggled to see but managed to keep up with the boy. Both moved hunched over, like special forces soldiers in the movies.

"Abel!" The voice rolled across the grounds, loud but without alarm.

"Uh-oh. It's him."

"Who?"

"The man. The evil man. He calls himself Mr. Pennington, but I think he's lying about his name. Maybe I should distract him—"

"Not a chance, kid. If I return without you, your mother will fry my liver for lunch."

"Eww."

"Just stop talking and lead on. I'm trusting you."

Abel nodded and continued forward until they reached the cliff's edge. The sound of waves pummeling the beach rose from the sand below. The darkness prevented Luke from seeing how long a drop it was to the beach below but he felt sure that a fall would not turn out good. He hoped that Abel wasn't entertaining the idea of climbing down.

"Be careful," he whispered.

"Abel! Time for dinner." This time the voice carried an edge.

Luke knew dinner had nothing to do with it. With the police gone, they had figured out that Abel wasn't where he was supposed to be. Seconds became crucial.

In an effort to maintain privacy and the separation of estates, the builder had erected a wall that ran from the front of the property to the very edge of the cliff. A simple three-foot high wrought-iron fence that matched the front gate, except for the metal screen meant to keep prying eyes from prying, ran the back of the property—a barrier to prevent someone from slipping over the edge. Abel climbed it in a second. Before Luke could speak, the boy stood on the other side, holding onto the fence with one hand. Luke's heart shuddered.

"Come on," Abel whispered.

Then he disappeared.

Luke sprinted to the fence and looked over, hoping Abel had been able to grab onto something to prevent his fall.

"Over here."

Luke turned his head and saw Abel scampering over the neighbor's back fence; a fence made of anodized metal posts and clear plastic panels. One didn't pay twenty million for a house overlooking the Pacific just to block the view with some opaque structure.

Now Luke understood. He slipped over the metal fence, shinnied to the neighbor's side of the wall and joined Abel in his trespass. In the dim light shed by the neighbor's house, Luke saw Abel smile and wiggle his eyebrows. The boy had adventure in him.

Wordlessly, Abel started along the wall again, this time moving toward the front of the property. In moments, they were hunkered down in a corner of the perimeter wall. Abel leaned forward and whispered in Luke's ear. "Can you lift me to the top of the wall?" Luke nodded. "You'll have to climb it by yourself."

"I can do that."

"He's not calling for me anymore." Abel's breath tickled Luke's ear. "He knows I'm gone. We have to hurry. He'll start searching the neighborhood next." He turned, stood, and Luke placed his hands on the boy's hips and lifted. If he felt nervous about climbing a seven-foot high wall, he didn't show it.

Luke had a greater struggle. Even as a child he showed greater mental agility than physical. It took three tries before Luke made it to the other side and only after leaving several layers of skin on the surface of the wall.

"This way." Luke guided Abel north along the road. A short distance away, he could see the rental car. "That's ours. Your mother is in the backseat—"

Luke's feet left the ground. By no conscious action of his own, he turned and saw the grimacing face of the Fresno man Abel called Mr. Pennington.

"We meet again." He seemed to hiss his words.

Before Luke could raise a hand something hit his head and flecks of light burst in his eyes. The man had delivered a near skull-cracking head-butt. Something thick and warm ran down Luke's face.

The man turned, dragging Luke with him. "You picked the wrong man to mess with, pal." He drew a fist back. Luke tried to raise an arm in his defense but the head-butt left him stunned and slow.

"Hey!"

The attacker turned to the voice and Luke saw a swift, blurred motion. The man screamed and dropped Luke who slumped to his hands and knees. He tried to rise when something heavy rolled over his back. He heard a loud thud and got a glimpse of the attacker's head bouncing off the pavement. He had been pushed over Luke's back.

"Come on. We've got to go." The voice belonged to Judith.

"Woozy ... head hurts ..."

"Pass out on your own time, buddy. We're not waiting on you any longer."

Luke struggled to his feet, aided by desperate hands pulling on his shirt. He staggered toward the car. "I could have handled him."

"That's right, Rocky. You had him right where you wanted him."

"It's not my fault. He hit me." Luke's senses were returning. "Abel?"

"He's in the car."

"Smart kid. He's the one that got us out."

"We're not out yet." Judith helped Luke into the front passenger seat.

"You okay, mister? He hit you real hard."

Luke recognized Abel's voice. "Did he? I don't think I noticed." He touched his forehead. "Great. I'm gonna have a knot the size of a baseball. There goes my rugged good looks."

Judith started the car and made a quick U-turn. "What rugged good looks?"

"Easy. I have a fragile ego." He felt sick. "You slugged that guy?"

"I hate to be the one to tell you this, but I broke your new cell phone."

Luke had to think for a moment before he caught her intent. Then he laughed. Not from the humor of her comment but from the release of fear that had held him in its grip.

From the back came the sound of gentle sobbing and the soft words, "My boy, my precious little boy."

The dark of the night slipped into Luke's mind.

twenty-eight

Need more ice?" Judith took the makeshift icepack from his hand and examined it. She had made the pack by placing ice from the ice machine in the hall in the plastic liner of the ice bucket and wrapping that in a towel from the bathroom. He sat on the bed, she stood next to him.

"I think it's fine."

"Let me see." Luke tilted his head up and Judith gazed down on a growing knot on the right side of his forehead. She looked at his eyes: both pupils were equal. A good sign. "That has to hurt."

"You have no idea. How's the kid?"

"He and Ida are snoozing on the sofa. Both are exhausted, especially Ida. Fear and worry are hard taskmasters. She looks worn out. We should switch rooms with them."

Luke had arranged for two rooms but decided they should stick together. This room on the eleventh floor was a suite with a separate bedroom and living room. A small kitchenette was tucked into one of the corners.

"I don't think we should stay."

Judith handed the cold pack back. "I had a feeling you were going to say that. There are a lot of hotels in the city; we should be safe here."

"Maybe, but I had to show ID to get the rooms since I paid in cash. Someone working the phones could find us pretty easy. It's just a matter of time and discipline. If I were doing it, I'd start with the more expensive hotels within a ten-mile radius."

"Like this one." Judith leaned against the low dresser. "It's a good thing they don't know your name."

"They know yours."

Judith smiled. "Which would be significant if I had used my name to get the rooms, but I didn't."

"That's right. Man, I think that guy knocked what little sense I had right out of my brain."

"Besides, where would we go?" Judith started to pace. "We have Abel now, but I have no idea what to do next."

"Me either." Luke paused. "I don't think I've said thank you. You probably saved my life. I don't know what he intended but I'm certain it wasn't good."

"You're welcome."

"You really hit him with the cell phone?"

"I held it in my fist and gave it all I was worth. I forgot to bring my brass knuckles along."

Luke laughed, then grimaced. "You are one tough date, lady."

"Is your head okay, Mr. Becker?" The young voice startled Judith.

"I thought you were sleeping." Luke sat up. "Ow. I've got a class A headache."

"I just pretended to sleep. My mom is real tired. I can tell. I thought that if I pretended to be asleep she might doze off."

"You amaze me, kid," Luke said. "You got guts and sensitivity."

"I heard you talking. What are you going to do with me?"

Judith stole a glance at Luke, then lowered herself to Abel's level. His lavender eyes fascinated her. "We don't know what to do, sweetheart. We're kind of lost at this point."

He nodded. "You should wait."

"Wait for what, kid?"

"For leadership," Abel said. "When in doubt, the best place to go is nowhere."

"I prefer to be a little more proactive than that," Luke said.

"Waiting is doing something; it's not doing nothing. Wait on the Lord and He will save you." Abel stood in the doorway. "I'm hungry."

Judith felt stunned. "I'm sorry. What did you say?"

"I said, I'm hungry."

"Before that."

"It's from Proverbs. You know. In the Bible."

"You've read the Bible?" Luke wondered.

"Uh-huh, there's one in the other room. May I have a grilled-cheese sandwich?"

Judith said, "I'll call room service. I'll get something for everyone." She shot a quizzical look at Luke. When talking to Abel she couldn't tell if she were speaking to a child or a very small man. "Let's go in the other room and let Mr. Becker rest."

"Okay, but what about the others?"

"Do you mean the men who took you?" The child had a right to feel insecure, Judith thought.

"No. The other children. The ones like me."

Luke stood. "There's more like you?"

"Lots more."

"Hold still."

"I don't want to hold still, Doc. I'm losing time." Pennington shifted on the barstool. He was seated at Alex Zarefsky's breakfast bar.

"You were out for several minutes. Follow my finger." Zarefsky raised his index finger and moved it from side to side. Pennington slapped it away. "Fine. Have it your way."

He stood, then swayed, his head full of spikes. He rubbed the growing goose-egg on the back of his skull then drew his fingers lightly across the knot just in front of his left temple. "That Find woman is going to pay for this."

"You'll get no argument from me." Zarefsky stepped into the kitchen, poured a glass of water, and pulled a bottle of Advil from one of the drawers. "Here, take some of these. It should take some of the edge off."

"There's got to be another player, Doc. Why would a rich chick like Find involve herself in this? She's not the find-and-rescue type."

"How do you know what type of person she is?"

"I just know. And who is the guy with her?"

Zarefsky shook his head. "I don't have a clue. Maybe someone like you. You know, a hired gun."

"He's no operative, that's for sure. He didn't even put up a fight. I had him cold the first second I laid my meat hooks into him."

"Whatever he is, whoever he works for, he's got the boy."

"For now."

Zarefsky leaned over the counter. "I can't tell you how bad this is; how, really, really bad. You didn't see a car?"

Pennington shook his head and it hurt and the pain made him all the more angry. "I don't remember anything after my head hit the ground. I can't believe their luck."

"What about the mother?"

"She must be with them. Her body wasn't found in the house. We know our mystery man and the Find woman got away, so we must assume she did too."

"So we've failed to keep the boy, we've failed to kill the mother, and we have no idea what to do next. This isn't going to go over well. My people are going to blow a gasket and that means our lives are worth diddly."

"I'll get him and dole out a little payback along the way."

"Forget revenge, just get the boy. You've failed twice, I can't protect you a third time."

"I'm not afraid of your people." Pennington stood, his fists clenched.

"Then you're not paying attention. Get the boy. Get him soon."

"Don't worry, I will."

Zarefsky studied the man. "Any idea how?"

Pennington thought for a moment then said in ice-hard words, "If you can't find the one you want, find the ones they love."

"Do what you must. Pull out the stops. Just make certain nothing comes back to my doorstep. Having the police rummage through my home was ... unpleasant. I don't want a repeat."

"Certain sacrifices must be made."

Zarefsky snorted. "Like what?"

Pennington didn't reply.

Abel sat on the sofa eating a grilled-cheese sandwich and drawing oily potato chips from a bag. Ida had awakened from her nap and sat close to her son, running her fingers over wayward wisps of black hair. Abel took it in stride.

Judith nibbled a turkey sandwich and sipped from a plastic bottle of cranberry juice. Ida picked at a chicken salad and Luke was making headway on an Angus hamburger. As Judith ate she studied Abel. In some ways he was unlike any boy his age she had ever met; in others he seemed normal. Most kids his age would show signs of insecurity at having been abducted then barely being rescued. He had witnessed the violence against Luke, yet he seemed undisturbed.

"Abel," Judith began, "you mentioned the others. What others?"

"Like I said, the other children like me. The different ones." He took a large bite of the sandwich, the cheese leaving a small greasy smear on one cheek. He wiped it off with his sleeve.

"What makes them different, Abel?

"They're different like I'm different. Special."

"I don't know what that means." Judith felt frustrated. Was Abel being evasive? She looked at Ida.

"This is the first I've heard of it," Ida said.

"Abel, how do you know there are other children like you?"

"I overheard Dr. Zarefsky and the man he called Pennington talking. They were going to take me to the others."

"Take you to the others? Did they say where?"

184 / FINDER'S FEE

"A place called Ridgeline. I think it's in the mountains."

"It is," Luke said. "I've been there. San Bernardino Mountains. Small community not far from the ski resorts. Not terribly far from Ontario."

"And you heard Dr. Zarefsky say this?"

"When they first brought me to his house, they made me sit on his sofa while they talked. They whispered but I could hear them. I hear lots of things. They didn't know I was listening. Was that wrong?" He looked at his mother. "Was that wrong, Mom?"

"I don't think so, sweetheart."

Another odd trait, Judith thought. He seems unusually concerned about right and wrong for a boy his age. "Did they say why they were going to take you to the others?"

He shook his head. "I don't think Dr. Zarefsky liked talking about it, especially to Mr. Pennington. I don't think they're friends. Dr. Zarefsky said that he and Mr. Pennington would drive me there after Mr. Pennington got back from Fresno."

Judith shot a questioning look at Ida, who shook her head. She hadn't told him about the destruction of their home.

"Did they say anything else?" Judith prompted. Abel nodded and looked away from his mother. Judith could see that he didn't want to say any more. "Abel, sweetheart, it's important that you tell everything. It's the only way we can help. You know we only want to help you, don't you?"

Abel gazed at her for a long moment. "There is truth in you, but not all truth. You want to help yourself."

Judith felt herself flush and she sat back, uncertain what to say.

"Honey," Ida said, "that's not nice."

"No," Judith said quickly, "he's right. I do want to help myself, but I also want to help you. It is why I'm here."

"I believe you."

"That's good." Judith gave her best motherly smile. "Now what else did you hear?"

"They were going to send us somewhere." He stopped eating as if the admission drained his hunger from him.

"Do you know where?" Luke asked.

Abel directed his gaze to Luke. "A place called Singapore."

Luke choked. It took a full minute for him to clear his throat enough to speak. "Singapore? Are you sure?"

"I remember everything."

Ida agreed. "He never forgets anything he sees or reads."

"Eidetic memory." Luke returned to his seat and took a sip of soda.

"What's that?" Judith asked.

"Some people call it a photographic memory, but the correct term is eidetic memory. It's the ability to remember things with great accuracy. Apparently our young friend is gifted with it."

Judith thought of the Bible verse Abel had quoted. He had the kind of memory that let him recall anything he read. "What's the importance of Singapore?"

Luke chewed his lip before answering. "I don't have the memory skills that Abel seems to have, but my gray matter still works pretty good. If I recall, Singapore is a leader in biotech, pharmaceuticals, genome research and the like. They're extremely evangelistic about their work, recruiting the best scientists in the world with money, the best in research facilities, and prestige. A few years ago they built Biopolis, a two-million-square-foot biomedical complex. They want to lead the world in bioengineering and related fields."

"And scientists move there?" Judith asked.

"You bet they do. Remember Alan Colman? He and his team cloned a sheep they named Dolly. He went to Singapore. Scores of the best minds end up there. There are many incentives, but one is greater than them all. They can do their work without the restrictions they face in countries like the United States."

"And you know this how?" Judith asked.

"Come on, Judith. We've been through this. I spend most of my day trading stock and researching companies. I've got a lot tied up in biotech firms. It's my job to know who's doing what." He stood and began pacing. "It's starting to take form. I don't have the details but I'm starting to get it."

"Well, let us in on it."

"Do you remember that talk you and Ida had in the restaurant? The one I needed an interpreter for with all that ART, GIFT, ZIFT talk? Put the pieces together."

An idea formed in Judith's mind and it came with a glacial wind that chilled her blood.

"I don't follow," Ida admitted.

Luke sighed and looked at Abel. Ida remained puzzled.

"He doesn't want to talk in front of me, Mom."

"Your perception blows me away, kid. I gotta admit, I really like you." Luke paused then added, "This is kinda grown-up stuff."

"I told you what I know," Abel said and for the first time seemed more child than adult. "You're being unfair."

"It's up to you, Ida," Luke said.

The woman lowered her head in thought. She pulled her son close and kissed him on the head. "He's a special boy in so many ways." After a deep breath she said, "Say it."

Luke resumed pacing, this time in slow steps, his hands behind his back, and his head down. He spoke softly. "Okay, we know that Dr. Zarefsky treated you for infertility and used a procedure called—" He looked to Judith for the answer.

"Zygote Intrafallopian Transfer."

"Right, a procedure in which the fertilized ovum is implanted in the fallopian tubes and the pregnancy follows course after that. We know that Abel is special in some ways which makes me think that there was something special with the zygote."

The chill in Judith dropped several degrees. "Are you suggesting that the zygote was tampered with? I'm not sure that's legal."

Luke laughed. "As if that matters. Illegal stuff goes on all the time. Just because a law says something can't be done doesn't mean that it won't. Scientists are people and like any group of people there are those who will do what they want regardless of laws. It's those very laws that make things like Singapore's Biopolis so attractive. No legalities to worry about and deep pockets to pay for research. Who knows what other research facilities are doing. They have a different view of research than we do."

"And the other children ..." Ida began.

"The same as Abel. Genetically altered for some reason that is still unclear to me."

"But why kidnap Abel?" Judith asked, then stopped. She had just arrived at the same conclusion. "No. You can't be serious."

"I bet if we could check Dr. Zarefsky's date book, we'd see he plans a long stay in Asia and he's taking some children with him."

"They're a product to him," Judith whispered, unable to gather enough air to speak louder.

"While he remains in the country, he can keep tabs on his ... er ... progeny. I'm betting that some Asian country got wind of his research and offered him a pile of gold and the equivalent in research space and assistants. Of course ..."

"Of course what?" Judith prompted.

"If he stays in the country, word may get out about what he was doing eight years ago. The kids are growing older and maybe every one is as unique as Abel. If so, sooner or later, someone's going to catch on. That wouldn't matter in a place like Singapore. Bringing the kids may be part of the deal. They're collateral."

"Worse," Judith said. "They're guinea pigs."

Judith lay awake on the sofa unable to sleep despite eyelids that felt filled with lead shot. Her body hurt from a day of stress, travel, and of course, smacking a man upside the head with a tightly held cell phone. She hadn't told anyone, but her right arm, shoulder, and back hurt from the exertion. What good would it do to share the news? Everyone had pains, either emotional or physical.

After they ate, she volunteered to go to the gift shop on the first floor and buy whatever pain reliever she could find. After purchasing several small packets of ibuprofen, each priced as if they were the last pills on the planet, she returned to the room. Luke had wanted to go but after Judith made him look in the mirror at the lump on his forehead and the darkening circle under his eye, he yielded the point.

Luke slept in the living room chair, his sock feet propped up on the coffee table. Ida and Abel had taken the bedroom. They had discussed again using both rooms but Luke couldn't make himself comfortable with the idea. He wanted everyone in the same place.

Who was this Luke? She had met him only twelve hours before and they had traveled to Fresno on the company jet, barely escaped death in a house rigged to explode, flown to San Diego, learned that her own stepson might be attempting a coup d'état in her absence, ferreted out enough information from that provided by the Puppeteer and through the Internet, confronted a man who no doubt was a killer or at least some kind of criminal, overpowered him with surprise, returned to the hotel and learned from a child that other children were in grave danger. All of this she had done with a man unknown to her yesterday. Now she lay on the sofa wishing for a few hours' sleep while the paranoid man snoozed nearby.

The scenario was nutty and even though she had lived it she had trouble believing all that had happened. If she could sleep, then she might awaken in her own bed, in her own home, and learn that it had all been a hyper-real dream. She knew it wouldn't happen that way. The pain she felt was too real, the look on Ida's face when Abel bolted into the car, the fear she endured when she saw the man Abel called Mr. Pennington knock Luke to the ground. All of that made any hope of a dream evaporate.

She closed her eyes and tried to imagine herself someplace else: somewhere where peace and security were the norm, where the next person down the street would certainly be a friend, a place where she could feel safe.

Luke began to snore. "One more thing I've learned about you," she whispered.

She thought of his secret and his reluctance to speak of it, then she thought of her own. Guilt rose in her, seeking its outlet in tears, but she fought it. The last thing she wanted to do was lose control and the last thing she wanted Luke to see was her as a trembling woman.

The business, the television shows, the commercials, the money, the prestige—everything seemed to be the dream now, a dream that began and ended a generation ago. Fear could strip away pretense faster than sandpaper could remove paint.

It took effort, but Judith took control of her breathing, timing each inhalation and exhalation. Sleep slipped into the room and covered her.

She dreamt of children in the mountains.

Children with lavender eyes.

twenty-nine

At 5:00 a.m. Judith phoned the front desk to inform them they were checking out. Five minutes later she sat in the front passenger seat content to let Luke drive. Ida sat in the rear, Abel's head resting on her lap as he continued to sleep.

Luke was sullen but still cautious. They exited the parking lot, drove down the main street, turned into a residential area then repeated the process two more times, checking his rearview mirror every few seconds. Before pulling from the lot, he had circled the rental car twice and ran his hand in the wheel wells looking for tracking devices. He found none, but that fact did nothing to change his disposition. He didn't need to explain to Judith that a professional could hide a device in a way that only a detailed search or the use of electronic detection equipment would reveal it. They didn't have the equipment or the means to adequately search the car. Before starting the engine, Luke popped the hood and spent a full ten minutes looking at everything. It couldn't have been easy. The sun had yet to rise. All Luke had was the light of a nearby streetlamp.

Satisfied that no one tailed them, Luke pulled onto the I-15 and headed north. Judith seldom drove at this hour and the sight of lines of traffic, their headlights and taillights stringing the freeway like jewels, surprised her. San Diego came to life early—if it ever went to sleep.

Judith looked over her shoulder and saw Abel enfolded in the peaceful sleep of a child. She envied him. Her eyes burned from weariness and her back ached from reclining on the sofa. Her eyes moved from Abel to Ida. She looked pale and drawn, and Judith doubted she slept more than an hour.

"We need to make some decisions," Luke said. "I don't even know where we're going. I turned north out of reflex. It's the way home."

"I have no ideas." Admitting the fact did nothing to alleviate her tension. "Abel is back in his mother's arms but the danger still exists."

"For all we know, it may be worse. It certainly is worse for us. I don't think that Pennington character is going to forget last night."

The thought had crossed Judith's mind too and she wished it hadn't. "What about the Puppeteer?"

"I don't know. I just don't know. We've done what we were forced to do, but things don't add up. We could never have found Abel if we hadn't been given the photo. Who took the photo? How did the Puppeteer get it? If he knew where

Abel was in the beginning, then why not just tell us? Better yet, why bother with us at all?"

"I have no answers," Judith sighed. "Nothing, nada, zilch. I keep running these questions through my brain but nothing comes out. The only conclusion I can reach is that finding Abel is not the ultimate goal."

"The children," Ida said from the back. "Could that be the goal?"

Luke objected. "No. Don't even go there. There is no way we can rescue a bunch of kids. Getting Abel out almost cost me my life."

"Still . . ." Judith said.

"Still what?" Luke's question came fast and hot.

"I can't give up on them, Luke. And I don't think you can either."

Luke slammed his hand against the steering wheel but kept his voice low. "I used to think I was in control of my life, of my privacy, and now this."

Judith said nothing. She felt the same frustration. Sometime today, Marlin would meet with the board of directors and try to pull a fast one. She should be there, she thought. Have Terri find out what time the meeting is and then crash it. Of course there would be questions about her disappearance and why she fled the scene of an explosion. The police would want to talk to her and the media would be all over that. She corrected herself—they were already all over it. Visions of news vans parked in front of her building played on the screen of her mind.

"I dreamt about the children last night." Luke spoke the words softly, just above the drone of the tires on the pavement.

"Really?" Judith asked.

"Yeah. I don't remember much. Several kids, maybe a dozen, I don't know. They were huddled around me. They all had the same eyes as Abel."

"What were they doing?"

"Staring at me." Luke shuddered. "It gave me the chills."

"Their eyes?"

"No, the dream. You know how dreams are. Most of the time they fade like steam from a teakettle. One part of it stuck with me. They hovered over me while I lay on the ground. I was bleeding. I'm pretty sure I was dying."

"That's horrible."

He nodded. "But you know what? For some reason it seemed ... right."

"I didn't sleep so I didn't dream, but images of the children came to mind and wouldn't go away." Judith gazed in the predawn dark. "There was a little girl, with long, straggly brown hair."

"What was she doing?" Ida asked.

"Holding my hand." Judith raised her right hand. "I can still feel it."

"This is nuts, crazy, bonkers. We have got to find a way out of this; a way back to normalcy."

"I can never be normal again." Ida's voice cracked. "No home, no husband, no money."

"But you have Abel," Judith said. "And don't worry about money for now." She wanted to say more but couldn't form the thoughts. A few moments later she asked, "What happens if we just go to my house?"

"My first fear would be that someone has it under surveillance and it's probably bugged." Luke changed lanes and drove slowly, utilizing the same trick he used the previous day. It would be difficult to follow a slow moving car without being noticed—at least according to Luke. "My second fear is that the police will be keeping an eye on the place and stop by with more questions than we can answer."

"Is that so bad? We've done nothing wrong."

"We fled the scene of a crime; we, well more specifically, *I* entered property uninvited—*two* properties since Abel and I snuck around the wall onto the adjoining lot; you assaulted a man with a cell phone and we both left him in the street."

"That was self-defense."

"I know, but how do you prove it?"

"Okay, then, what about an attorney? I can have our corporate attorney dig up the best criminal lawyer. We can go to him. We both have money—at least I think you have money."

"I'm comfortable."

"Okay, we both have plenty of money. We have the lawyer work out a way that we can talk to the police without getting held for questioning."

"Maybe."

"And maybe he can find a way to protect Abel," Ida said.

"Yeah, maybe." Luke switched lanes again.

"What's on your mind, Luke?"

"The kids. I know I snapped a few minutes ago and said we couldn't rescue them but … It's just that I can't get them out of my mind. They're haunting me and I've never met them. Maybe it's Abel."

"What do you mean, Abel?" Judith turned to face Luke, his face lit only by the auto's instrument panel.

Luke smiled. "I kinda like the kid."

"I like you too."

"What?" Luke glanced over his shoulder. "You've been playing possum, you little sneak."

Abel giggled then sat up.

"That's it," Luke said, "I'm going to pull over and tickle you until you beg for mercy."

"Bring it." Abel laughed.

It was the most pleasant sound Judith had ever heard.

thirty

The sun had just begun its work when Marlin stepped into the private gym. A longtime member, he usually arrived at 6:30 a.m. and put in a solid hour at the weight machines and treadmill. Like all things in his life, he worked out to an extreme. A part of him knew he was compensating for his short stature but that didn't matter. The key to life was making the most of what you have, not whining about what you don't.

As he stretched legs, arms, and back, he thought of the pot of gold handed him. He couldn't be sure what was going on, but he knew enough to recognize that mommy-dearest had somehow gotten herself in a world of hurt. He'd be a fool not to capitalize on her blunders.

Today it would be his upper body that got the workout, but it would be his mind that would do the most exercise. He could barely sleep last night for the thoughts and plans ricocheting in his overstimulated mind. Once his muscles were warm and stretched he settled into the weight machine and began pumping his pectorals, feeling the smooth motion of his arms as they hoisted the weights.

With each exercise he reminded himself that what he was doing was for the good of the firm. The duty to defend the firm fell to Judith, but she had abandoned her post and apparently become the catalyst for corporate injury. As senior vice president, he had to act. The mantle of responsibility fell to him and he could not allow outside forces to destroy what his father had built even if that outside force was once the chief insider.

And there were the stockholders to consider. He had a responsibility to those who had invested in the firm. Of course there were the board members, all heavily invested. If Judith ruined the company, then some of them would suffer financial harm and at least two of them were facing retirement in the next year. He could not allow Judith to jeopardize them and their families.

Sure, there would be those who would accuse him of selfish motives. Privately, he wouldn't deny it. So what if protecting others happened to help him in his goal of leading Find, Inc.? He couldn't be blamed for that. Business people understood the bottom line was always the deciding factor in decision making.

Marlin moved from the weight machine to the curl bench and free weights and began to work his biceps. Eight reps in he began to feel the burn and it made him smile. Nothing he did in the gym today could remove the giddiness inside. Perhaps he should feel guilty.

But he wouldn't.

The black TwinStar AS355 business helicopter skimmed through the air at 150 miles per hour. Pennington sat alone in the passenger cabin taking one of the four beige leather seats and watched the ground, newly lit by the sun, scroll past. The rental company had come through for him, as well they should. Cal-Genotics poured a lot of money into their pockets over the last ten years. They had been good about not asking questions.

The pilot banked northeast as they passed over Riverside and headed toward the San Bernardino National Forest. He had made this trip before and knew what to expect. Soon the pilot would change directions again to skirt the controlled airspace of San Bernardino International Airport, then move back on track to the pine-covered mountains where his destination lay nestled in trees and accessible by only one road.

Pennington wondered what was happening at Dr. Zarefsky's house. Surely the crime scene people were scouring house and grounds alike. And while he sat in the comfort of the business chopper, Danny "Silk" Saccio was being grilled by the police.

Saccio earned the name Silk with his smooth talk and ability to lie with impunity. The rest of his name was a fabrication. As a young man he wanted to be thought of as the guy with mob connections. Truth was, despite his name, he was more Irish than Italian. The stupidity of the desire dawned on him one day while reading a newspaper report about a mob hit on one of its own. He decided a new goal was in order. In the end, Silk Saccio became a private detective and made a good living fingerprinting corporate execs, doing background checks, and following cheating spouses. He had one other attribute that put him on the top of Pennington's first-call list: loyalty. Saccio had an odd ethic but he could be counted on to never roll over on a client or a buddy.

The events of a few hours before replayed in Pennington's mind.

"You're kidding me, right?" Silk Saccio sounded more stunned than he looked. "A body?"

"Yeah. His name is ... was, Dr. Zarefsky. Got that? Alex Zarefsky."

"Alex Zarefsky. I got it." Silk took no notes. He knew better.

"Alex Zarefsky is a famous and rich infertility doctor. Early this evening, the police were here because someone reported shots fired."

"And they wouldn't leave without poking around and making a nuisance of themselves."

"That's right, Silk. Apparently, someone snuck in when the gate was open for the police and hid. We don't know when, but he got in the house. There was a struggle; things got knocked over including some silverware. Zarefsky took a knife in the back. As he was bleeding to death he used a fork to scratch a name in the wood floor of the kitchen."

"Name scratched into the floor. Got it."

"You were called because I recommended you for some security work at his home and clinic. He told you some woman has been harassing him and he didn't know why."

"Which means I don't know why."

"Right. He called you to come over and check the grounds. He told you he didn't want to call the police—"

"Because they made a hash of things the last time they were here and he was also afraid they wouldn't believe him."

"I like that last part. Good thinking. Here's what I want you to do. Walk into the house but only as far as the end of the foyer. The kitchen is to your left. There's an opening, so you can see into it. You look, you see the body, you walk back out and call the police and wait for them."

"And that's all I know, right?"

"Right. If they remember that I was here earlier and ask about me, tell them you don't know where I am but you have my cell phone number. I'll give it to you. Encourage them to call. I'll take it from there."

"You know, this is no small thing you're asking me to do, boss. The cops are liable to drag my fanny downtown—"

"One hundred thousand dollars." Pennington smiled. He understood where Silk was headed. "Cash if you want it that way."

"That'll do it."

"Remember, you touch nothing. When all is said and done, they will find no evidence to hook you into this. No fingerprints, no blood splatter on you, nothing. Just tell the story as I gave it to you."

Silk nodded then stared at Pennington for a long moment.

"No," Pennington said. "I didn't kill him. I'm leaving because I made a promise to protect some of his property. You don't need to know about that. I can be reached."

Silk continued his gaze then gave a reassuring nod. Pennington fought the urge to smile. Silk wasn't the only one who could lie on a moment's notice.

"Five minutes." The pilot's voice pulled Pennington back into the moment.

"Understood."

It was going to be a long day and timing was everything.

"You sure you didn't touch the body?" The detective stood tall and slender and looked like he had just crawled out of bed. The newborn day cast a pale light on his features as he stood close to Silk. He gave his name as Detective Jed Cary.

"Of course, Detective. I'm a professional private investigator. I didn't get my license out of a cereal box. I know not to mess with a crime scene. Especially a murder scene." Silk pulled a pack of cigarettes from his coat pocket. "Mind?"

"Yeah, I do."

"Come on, Detective. It's not every day I see a client face down in his own blood. It may be everyday work to you, but it's a shocker to me."

"You seem a little nervous, Mr. Saccio." The cop looked at the driver's license, PI license, and business card Silk had given him.

"And if I was all cool and calm and collected, then you would suspect something else was wrong. Of course I look nervous. I *am* nervous. I didn't get here in time to save a client."

"Judging by the size of this house, he must have paid you pretty good."

"Not a dime yet. We were negotiating for some work for his firm. He's a fertility doctor. You know, he helps women get pregnant who can't get pregnant. Fixes their plumbing or something."

"I know what a fertility doctor is, Mr. Saccio. What's the name of his firm?"

"Ah, the ol' let's-test-the-suspect's-statement approach." He fingered the unlit cigarette and struggled to recall what Pennington had told him. "Coast Fertility Care Center is the business he talked to me about. I wouldn't doubt he has other enterprises. I was hoping to score some work on those too. I guess that won't be happening."

"So you didn't scratch the name in the floor?"

"I told you, boss, I didn't go in the kitchen. I made it as far as the foyer, saw him dead on the floor and exited."

"You didn't try to see if he was alive?"

"No. The gigantic pool of blood and unblinking eyes made me think that his day was done for good. Dead is dead, Detective. You know that. Sometimes you can just tell, and this is one of those times."

"Did you see the name he wrote?"

"Not really. It looked like a word not a name. *Find* was what it looked like to me, but like I said, I didn't go in the kitchen."

"It's a name. He wrote two words: Judith Find. Any idea why he would do that?"

Silk stuck the cigarette in his pocket. "No. The name means nothing ... wait a sec. Judith Find? Isn't she that interior design chick I see on television every once in awhile?"

"Maybe. Do you have any reason to believe that's her?"

"Not that I can think of."

"I need you to go downtown for a few more questions. Oh, and I'm going to need your clothes."

Silk had expected this. "Okay, here's the deal. I'll go downtown. You can have everything I'm wearing from shoes to skivvies. I'll get my old lady to bring some fresh duds. But while I'm there, I want you to take whatever else you need. I give you permission to swab for DNA, take hair samples, examine and photograph my hands, the whole nine yards. But let's do it all in one fell swoop, shall we? I don't want to keep driving to the station because you need one more thing. I hate downtown traffic. So do it up right, Detective. I ain't got nothing to hide."

Fifteen minutes later, Silk slipped into the backseat of a patrol car and wondered how he'd spend the one hundred thousand dollars coming his way.

thirty-one

Two hours later, after they left the La Jolla hotel, Luke found a Jack in the Box and bought breakfast sandwiches for everyone, pulled through the drive-up window and backed into one of the more distant spaces on the fast-food parking lot. Judith didn't need to ask for the odd parking decision. Her own paranoia had grown sufficiently that she too wanted a clear view of the lot and the street. In fact, it had been her idea that they eat in the car for fear of being recognized. That morning she had decided to pull her hair back and to avoid makeup.

The food tasted wonderful. Nerves and apprehension had made her famished. Judging by the way the others ate, the affliction was shared. Luke had killed the engine but left the key turned enough to allow the radio to play. He found a news station which struck Judith as being a radio station of commercials occasionally interrupted by news. Traffic reports were given every ten minutes and national and local news orbited the reports. Earthquakes, crimes, and political intrigue took a backseat to the need to know what was happening on the I-10 and other freeways. In Southern California, transportation was everything.

Judith didn't want to listen to the news, much preferring the chirping and singing of birds in a nearby tree. She recognized the symptoms. Ever since childhood, when life became difficult, when pressures threatened to crush her, she would displace her thoughts, traveling the corridors of imagination, living in a place outside herself. At the moment, she'd love to be someplace else; *be someone* else.

The voice of a traffic reporter in a helicopter somewhere over the I-210 bounced around the interior of the rental car and Judith took little notice of him. The reporter finished and the news anchor took over.

"That was Bob Relnic in the traffic copter helping you get where you need to be. A strange story just in from police in San Diego."

Judith snapped her head around and faced the radio as if doing so would make the report stop.

"Uh-oh," Luke said.

The anchor continued. "Homicide detectives are looking for Judith Find, the well-known executive of Find, Inc. Police are not releasing details but have said that she is wanted for questioning in the murder of prominent physician Dr. Alex Zarefsky in La Jolla. We'll stay on the story and provide more details as they become available. Hmm. Does this mean another decorating diva is going to jail?"

Luke switched off the radio. "Used to be that news stations just gave the news without commenting on it."

"Did ... did he say Dr. Zarefsky has been murdered?" Ida's words tumbled out.

"Yes," Luke said.

Judith looked at him.

"Hey, don't look at me. I didn't kill him. I didn't go near the house, did I, kid?"

"Nope," said Abel. "Didn't go in the house."

Judith turned to face Abel. He looked pale. So did his mother.

"Who would kill Zarefsky?" Luke bunched up the remains of his sandwich in its wrapper and threw it in the bag. Judith had lost her appetite as well.

"And how are they connecting it to me? No one knows I went to San Diego. I didn't step foot on the property."

"You're being set up," Luke answered. "That has to be it."

"But why me?"

"Because the guy at Fresno named you. He saw me too but doesn't have a name to go with my face. He knows we're together. Especially after you coldcocked him. He can't find us, so he gets the police to chase after us. That puts us on the defensive and maybe he thinks it will frighten us off."

"He's pretty close to right." Judith folded her arms over her stomach and leaned forward.

"You're not going to be sick, are you?" Luke said. "If you're going to hurl—"

"I'm not going to be sick. I just ... I'm just stunned beyond all reason. I need a moment."

"Mr. Pennington killed Dr. Zarefsky." Abel's voice sounded hollow. Eight years old and he had endured an abduction, been held captive, chased, seen adults fighting, and now was exposed to murder. "He has no truth in him."

Luke turned. "What does that mean, Abel? You said the same thing at Zarefsky's house when we first met. You said I had truth in me and now you say that Pennington doesn't."

"You have truth in you. Mr. Pennington doesn't. The evil is on him—in him."

"I don't understand, Abel. How do you know that?"

He shrugged. "I see it."

"You see evil in people?"

"Yes, and good." He took a bite of his sandwich. "We all do."

"Who is 'we,' honey?" Ida asked.

"The children like me. The ones in the mountains. The ones in danger. The ones we're going to save."

"You've met these children?" Judith asked.

"No." Abel seemed unbothered by the incongruity of his statement.

"Then how do you know they see the same things you do?" Judith pressed.

"I don't know."

She repositioned herself in her seat. "I am so confused."

"That makes two of us," Luke said. He turned to Ida. "Has Abel always been like this?"

"Yes, although I don't understand about the seeing of truth and evil on people. He's always been different. I had to homeschool him because the other children would torment him because of his eyes and because he was so much brighter than them."

"We are going to save the others, aren't we?" Abel sounded worried.

"I'm not sure what the three of us can do. It seems every hour the danger increases, the mystery deepens, and the futility of it all becomes apparent."

"Four of us," Abel said with authority.

"I can't take you into a dangerous situation, kid." Luke looked defeated.

"We're already in danger. I was in danger when you came for me. It's the same thing."

Luke sighed. "I'm too tired to argue with you, buddy. Besides, I think you'd win. You're probably smarter than all of us."

"The truth is in you and Mrs. Find too. The truth will win. The truth always wins."

"How can you know that?" Judith asked.

"I dunno."

"We're going in circles." Luke started the car and pulled from the parking lot.

"Where are we going?" Judith asked.

"To save the kids. Abel is right. You're right. We can't let them be shipped off to Singapore to be lab rats." He paused. "Who knows, maybe by saving them we can save ourselves."

A new frozen fear pressed in upon Judith's soul. Never had she been so frightened; never had she wanted to run away more than at that moment. She bit her lip. She rubbed her hands together. She shifted constantly in her seat. Her eyes flicked from the view in front of her to that out the side window to that in her mind.

Oh, God. Dear God. Judith couldn't remember the last time she prayed and she was making a shambles of it now. Terri would be glad to know her boss had taken up the habit of prayer, even if she didn't know how to do it right.

"I see more truth in you, Mrs. Find."

Judith turned and looked at Abel through teary eyes. He smiled.

Something tickled the back of Judith's brain.

The helicopter rested on the ground for less than two minutes, just enough time for Pennington to exit and make his way to a waiting H2 Hummer. The moment he closed the door to the large vehicle, the chopper lifted off scattering dust and debris from the dirt landing pad.

Behind the steering wheel sat a painfully thin man with hollow cheeks and sallow skin. He smelled of cigarette smoke and cheap beer. The fact that the clock had yet to see seven made the smell of booze unsettling.

"Ready, Mr. Pennington?" His voice sounded like he frequently gargled thumbtacks.

Pennington stared at the man for a moment then reached across the seats and seized him by the front of his worn T-shirt. With a savage yank he pulled him close.

"What ... what are you doing?"

Pennington sniffed. The man had been drinking. He reached for the keys and removed them from the ignition, exited the vehicle, and walked around to the driver's seat. Three seconds later the driver lay on the ground. "You live around here?"

The frightened man stammered. "Y-yes."

"Good, then you'll know how to walk home." Pennington slipped into the driver's seat.

"It's a good five mile walk." The driver stood and dusted himself off.

"Lucky for you it's still early in the day." He slammed the door, started the engine, and then rolled down the window. "By the way, who hired you?"

"My brother, Ernie."

"Do you have a cell phone?" The man said he did. "Here's what you're going to do. You're going to call your brother and tell him that I don't tolerate drunks working for me. If he knows what's good for him, he will be gone when I get to the camp. If he's not, then I'll run him over. Clear?"

"Clear."

Pennington slammed the accelerator down and the tires of the large SUV spun, kicking up dirt and stone. Pennington's mood had gone from bad to worse.

Ridgeline exemplified the perfect postcard mountain community. Like many of the smaller towns in these mountains, Ridgeline had a single main road through it, with shops and retail stores along both sides of the road. Tucked behind these were the small mountain homes of the residents. The mountain mansions were reserved for spots further up the grade and around the larger bergs of Lake Arrowhead and Big Bear. Those without the wealth of kings lived in the smaller communities. Signs pointed the way to several rustic motels ideal for family getaways or a place to hang one's skis during the snow season. None of those interested Pennington. His destination lay five miles down a dirt road nestled in a sheltered valley with tall pine and fir trees. Field grass carpeted areas not shaded by forest and wildflowers lay in patterns that demanded appreciation.

Pennington wasn't in an appreciative mood. What should have been a smooth, even, uneventful plan had begun to unravel like a cheap rug. He had, on behalf of a dummy corporation created by Cal-Genotics, purchased the remains of a Christian youth camp built in the late fifties. Over the years, the various owners had upgraded buildings and facilities, but the place had fallen on hard times. The owners were glad to be rid of it. After Pennington and Cal-Genotics were finished with it, it would be left to the forest to reclaim what had been stolen from it.

Heavy shadows cast by mountain and trees from the early morning sun darkened the narrow road, giving way moments later to bright sunlight. He drove with purpose but so as not to attract attention from any hiker who might be nearby. As he drove his mind bounced back and forth between all that had just happened and what needed to happen next. His desire— his almost overpowering longing—was to track down that Judith Find tramp and her friend and finish the fight begun the night before. He rubbed the lump on the side of his head, then the one on the back. They had been lucky. Next time, no amount of luck would save them.

But such work was for a later time. For now, he had to focus on executing the plan he had worked so hard to formulate. Already things had gone askew. Killing Zarefsky had not been part of the plan, but the man was expendable. On paper, he appeared the head of Cal-Genotics but Pennington knew better. That position was held by a man he had never met who employed men that frightened even him, and nothing frightened him.

The tree-lined road gave way to an open expanse of field, lush with green, yellow, and purple wildflowers. A wide creek, fed by the snowcap, burbled through the salubrious setting. The field had plenty of room to accept a landing helicopter but such things gathered attention. If anyone wanted to know why a business helicopter was landing in the mountains, he wanted them going in the opposite direction of his true destination.

The Hummer lumbered down a long grade and onto the campground, leaving a trail of dust behind it. Pennington hit the brakes hard and brought the bulky vehicle to a halt. He slipped from the seat and stopped. He heard nothing. Letting his eyes trace his surroundings he saw nothing but buildings that looked abandoned and a yellow charter bus.

Pennington knew each building inside and out. There were six bunkhouses, each capable of sleeping twelve people, one administration building, one small house for the owner, a set of twelve small apartments for staff, and a large dining hall. At one time, the campground had been new and thriving. Black-and-white pictures hung from the dining hall showing tents spaced out in the open field, softball and volleyball games, children working crafts and learning to shoot a bow. The peeling paint and decaying wood showed the glory days had passed a half-decade before.

The sound of rusty hinges forced into action brought Pennington's attention to a man exiting the hall. He could see the similarity to the driver he left in the dirt near the landing field. Pennington marched to the steps that led to the porch around the dining hall.

"Where's Vince?" the man asked.

"I assume you mean the driver."

"Yeah. I sent him to pick you up. He's my brother."

Pennington stepped close to Ernie Braun. "I left your brother to walk home. He was stinking drunk."

A flash of fury crossed Ernie's face. At first, Pennington thought the temper had to do with his brother's treatment. "I told him. I told him no booze. This was a chance for him to make a little scratch and all he had to do was stay sober for two hours and pick you up."

"I told him to call you."

Ernie shook his head. "Cell phones are iffy up here at best." He took a deep breath. "I'm sorry, Mr. Pennington. Jose was supposed to pick you up but he landed in the hospital last night."

"Fall off a barstool?"

"No. Jose doesn't drink at all. He fell and broke his ankle. That left me alone with the kids. I had to get someone quick 'cuz I knew you were on your way. I'm sorry he let us down."

Pennington soaked up the words and the intent. He believed Ernie. He had to. With Jose out of the picture that left just the two of them to finish this assignment. Booting Ernie out now would only endanger everything else that needed to be done. "How are the kids?"

"Creepy. They don't talk. They don't want to run around. They just sit at the tables and wait. I gave them some paper and pencils I found in the office so that they could draw and play tic-tac-toe or something." He hesitated and Pennington watched him muster the courage to ask. "I know it ain't none of my business, but what happened to your head?"

"I ran into something. Take me to the kids."

Ernie opened the door to the hall and Pennington walked through. Twelve pairs of lavender eyes looked his way.

thirty-two

Ridgeline. Is that right? Is that the name you overheard Pennington and Zarefsky talking about?" Luke returned to the car he had parked in front of the pumps of a service station in Arrowhead. He had finished filling the tank, paid the cashier with cash, and purchased a local map.

"That's it."

Luke opened the map and Judith leaned close to examine it.

"Judith, you said earlier that you've been there?"

"It's been a couple of years. We shot a commercial spot about a new rustic line of products. There's a large log cabin we rented for the shoot. Beautiful."

"How much do you remember about the place? The town I mean, not the house."

"Very rustic, fairly small, one main road, small shops, lots of small homes."

Luke gave an understanding nod. "Well, we're not far from it. The problem is that even a small town has lots of places to hide."

"But they're hiding a group so the building has to be fairly large."

"Not really. People smugglers have been known to load lots of people in the back of a van."

The thought of children crammed in a small room or worse filled her with sadness.

Luke looked into the rearview mirror, shoved the map toward Judith, and started the car. Judith looked in the side mirror on her door. A Jeep Cherokee had pulled in behind them. They were blocking the way. Luke pulled forward and out of the gas station lot. The Cherokee didn't follow. Judith could see the tension leave Luke's body. He directed the car back down the mountain. Judith studied the map.

"Abel, are you sure they didn't mention where they planned to take you in Ridgeline?"

"Yes. All I heard was the name and that it was in the mountains. Oh, and Dr. Zarefsky said the place was perfect for kids. But I don't know what that means."

"What kind of place is perfect for kids?" Luke wondered aloud.

"Schools, playgrounds ..."

"Schools would be too noticeable. School is still in session. It would have to be an abandoned place. Playgrounds are too public. No way to keep the children out of sight."

"It's beautiful," Ida said. "So many trees."

Luke agreed. "The last time I was in the mountains was sixth-grade camp—"

"A campground?" Judith said.

"It would have to have buildings of some sort."

213 / alton GANSKY

"Aren't campgrounds public places?" Ida asked.

"Some, but some are privately owned. They're businesses. Schools, churches, civic organizations rent the facilities and the campground provides food, bathrooms, bunk rooms."

"It's perfect." Judith scanned the map for any indications of campgrounds. "There's only one campground in Ridgeline. That must be it."

"Maybe not, but it's the best we have. We can start there."

"And do what?" Judith folded the map. "I don't think we have a standing invitation."

"I need to think," Luke said.

"I need to go to the bathroom." Abel squirmed.

Luke frowned. "We were just at a gas station—never mind. I have an idea. I'm going to turn around."

"Why?" Judith said.

"Because I need to find a wireless Internet portal. Arrowhead is a bigger town. I'm betting they have a coffee shop with wireless. If not, I'll try some of the hotels."

"You're going to get a room to use their Internet connection?"

"No. Some places don't secure their connections. I might have to pay a service to access the Net but that won't be a problem."

"Will they have a bathroom?" Abel twisted in his seat.

"I'll make that a priority, pal." Luke made a U-turn and started back up the mountain.

"Why do we have to stay here? I don't like this place. The television is too small."

Terri looked at her aged mother perched on the edge of the bed staring at an early morning news show and mustered as much patience as she could. "It's only for a day or two, then we can go home."

"What about my shows? What about Perry Mason? This stupid television doesn't get the right channel."

Terri returned to the mirror and continued to brush her hair. She had no idea what she was going to do today, but at least her hair would be presentable. "The DVR is recording it. You won't miss a thing. Of course, you've seen every episode a dozen times."

"I don't care. Raymond Burr is a hunk."

Terri smiled for the first time that day. "*Was* a hunk, Mom. He's dead."

"Don't burst an old woman's bubble."

The television's volume rose dramatically.

"Mom, people in the other rooms don't need to listen to our television."

"You better see this."

Something in her mother's tone frightened her. A moment later she stood in front of the small set, her hairbrush still in her hand. "Oh no."

"Judith Find. Isn't that the lady you work for?"

"You know it is, Mother."

"Did you know she's a murderer?"

"'She's not a murderer. Judith wouldn't hurt a fly."

"That's not what the lady on the news is saying. She says that your boss killed a man."

"No, she didn't. She said Judith is wanted for questioning."

"Same thing."

Terri didn't respond. Every nerve came alive at once. Her mind raced but not a single, cogent thought emerged. It was all storm and wave and foam, no solid thinking.

The sound of her cell phone ringing made Terri jump.

"It's just the phone, girl. What's wrong with you?"

"Nothing, Mom." She raced to her purse and pulled the cell from it. She answered immediately. "Judith."

"No. It's Marlin Find, Ms. Penn. We need to talk."

"How did you get this number? This isn't the business cell phone, it's my private number."

"I have my ways."

"I'm not coming in today," Terri said. "I'm with my mother and can't leave right now."

"Ah, baloney," Mom said. She began to flip through the channels. "Stupid television."

"I assume you've heard," Marlin said. Terri was sure she heard a touch of glee in his voice. "My mother is wanted by the San Diego police. She's also wanted by the Fresno cops. It appears she's on quite a crime spree."

"I doubt that."

"Doubt all you want, you don't matter. What does matter is my ability to speak to her. Has she called you?"

"No."

"How do I know you're not lying?"

"You don't."

"I assume you've heard the news about the emergency board meeting. If, or should I say when, Judith calls, you make certain she knows about it. I've left messages everywhere I can, including her email. I don't want anyone telling me I'm working behind her back."

"That's exactly what you're doing."

"I don't need the likes of you to lecture me, woman. I'm calling out of courtesy. By the way, I've had the phones replaced in your office and in Judith's. They're ringing off the hook. Someone should come in and field those calls."

"I'm hanging up now." Terri closed the phone and tossed it on the table. Raising her hands to her face she covered her eyes and fought back the tears. She no longer knew what to do or what to think. Confusion soaked her mind and soul. Judith was a strong woman, a determined woman, impossible to intimidate, but she was not capable of murder ... was she?

Despite her best efforts, the pressure inside needed, demanded release. A silent sob slipped from her lips, then another.

A hand touched her shoulder.

A moment later, she wept in her mother's arms like she had as a child too many decades before.

The coffee shop was on the first floor of a two-story building that helped make up the U-shaped set of buildings filled with shops and stores all designed to attract the eye of tourists. Judith kept a lookout, watching carefully every shopper and patron that passed by. Luke had pulled in a parking stall that fronted the walkway at the front of the shop. He opened his computer and rested it on the steering wheel. He found what he was looking for: an open Internet portal.

"So the coffee shop has free wireless Internet access?"

"Nope," Luke said. "But the real estate office two doors down does."

"Someone should talk to them about security." Judith could see into the shop through the open door. Ida had taken

Abel to the back to use the bathroom. Now she bought coffee for herself, Judith, and Luke. She did so at Luke's request. Not because he thought they needed coffee but because he didn't want the employees remembering Ida as the woman who just used the bathroom but didn't buy anything.

Judith thought it a wise precaution especially since the coffee shop had few customers. One of those customers looked like a high school student who had decided to take the day off. He sat at one of the outside tables smoking, a white iPod resting on the metal bistro table and earbuds crammed into his ears. He bobbed his head to music only he could hear.

"I've got an idea." Judith reached for her purse and removed a small wallet. "I'll be right back."

"You should stay in the car," Luke said, his eyes still glued to the computer monitor. "Less chance you'll be noticed."

"Yeah. I know." She exited anyway and walked to the boy. He wore jeans that looked ready for their first wash in months and a black shirt with a stylized skull on it and the name of some band Judith didn't bother to read. His coal black hair, which Judith assumed was a dye job, hung in clumps. As she approached she could see that the teenager wore makeup that made his lips look dark and his skin pale.

She took the empty seat on the opposite side of the table. "Hey, kid. You want to make twenty bucks?"

He looked up at her but didn't respond. Judith's nerves had worn her patience paper-thin. She reached across the table, took hold of the wire leading from the iPod to the earphones, and gave a good yank. They popped out and fell to the table.

"Hey, watch it, you crazy—"

"I asked you if you wanted to make twenty bucks."

He studied her for a second then gave a leering grin. "What ya got in mind?"

"Wipe the smile off your face, Goth boy, or I'll do it for you. Do you have a cell phone?"

He sobered. "What if I do?"

"I'll give you twenty to let me make one call."

"No way. You'll call China or something."

"No, I won't. You have my word."

"Yeah, like that means something to me."

Judith clenched her jaw. "Should you be in school right now?"

"What are you, a truant officer? They don't want me in that place anyway. I'm too bad for their sensitive eyes."

"Are you going to let me use your phone or do I go to the cop car I saw down by the McDonald's and tell them you've been causing trouble? I'm betting they've met you before."

"Maybe once or twice, but I ain't done nothing but buy a double latte. And yes, I paid for it."

"Who do you think they're going to believe: you or me? Twenty bucks, one phone call, and I stay right here at the table."

"Twenty ain't much money these days, lady."

"Forty then, and that's it."

"I don't know. I mean forty is pretty good—"

"We're back to twenty."

"Okay, okay." He pulled a small phone from his pocket. It looked as dirty as his jeans. The thought of pressing it to her ear made Judith sick. "Let's see the cash."

Judith opened her billfold and extracted two twenties and exchanged them for the phone.

She dialed. Terri picked up on the third ring. "Terri?"

"Judith! I didn't recognize the caller ID. Oh, I've been so worried. Marlin just called. Everything is falling apart. I don't know what to do."

"He called you on this number?"

"Yes. I don't know how he got it."

"Maybe through my computer. Maybe he got my call list from the cell phone provider. Who knows? There's probably a dozen ways."

"They're saying ... I mean the news ... Marlin ..."

"Terri, listen. I don't have much time. I'm using a borrowed phone. First know that what you're hearing is wrong. Second, I want you to return to work. I may need you there."

"Marlin's planning a takeover. I'm sure of it. Can he do it? Can he really do it?"

"Maybe. It's happened to others. I'm certainly not immune."

"But if I go to the office, the police will certainly come and question me."

"That's all right, Terri. Tell them what you know. Tell them the truth. Also tell them that I will be in touch with them as soon as I can. I want you to do several things. First of all, you need to get the phones in our two offices replaced—"

"Marlin has already done that."

"Well, score one for him. I want you to go see Jim Gaines and tell him everything you know. Tell him I want him to be present if the—" She looked at the Goth kid. "If *they* come by to ask questions. If he needs to bring in ... help, tell him to do so."

"Why do I need the company lawyer?"

"It's a precaution, Terri. I also want you to do something else. You have to promise you will listen and not interrupt."

There was a pause. "Okay, I promise."

"When you talk to Jim, tell him that I'm installing you on the board. He is to draw up the necessary papers right away. Also, I want him to draw up docs that will transfer all my stock to you. Understood?"

"Judith, this is crazy."

"Yeah, it is, but it's all I can do."

"Won't you have to sign something?"

Judith sighed. "Probably. See what he says. Find a way around it. I can't come in and sign right now. I'll figure something out."

"Um, Judith. What if he doesn't believe me? I mean, transferring stock; he's going to think I'm trying to rip you off."

Judith hadn't thought of that.

"Come on, lady. You're wasting my battery." The kid reached for the phone. Judith pulled away.

"One more minute." Judith's mind sprinted between possibilities, then settled. "If he does, say to him, 'Judith asked me to bring up Everwood.' Got that?"

"What's Everwood?"

"You don't need to know and if he asks, assure him I told you nothing other than the name. I gotta go. I'm sorry to put all this on you. Whatever you hear, Terri, remember, I didn't do it."

She hung up and set the phone on the table, then walked away.

thirty-three

Pennington, normally a man of cultivated discipline, felt a strange disquiet deep inside. The children, each one with shocking lavender eyes, stared at him as if they could not only see through his clothing but count every bone, trace every vein, and outline each nerve. Worse, he felt they could read his soul like a comic book.

His years of experience, honed first as a field agent for the CIA and then, after the bureaucrats summarily fired him, as security expert for the largest firms and business interests in the world, had prepared him for anything. He learned to work for any company that could afford him. Their politics mattered nothing to him as long as they paid his exorbitant fees and didn't ask too many questions. He had a mental closet full of skeletons he never allowed to haunt him. Such a haunting required a conscience and that had been burned from his mind long ago.

Still ... their eyes ... their quiet nature ... their unblinking focus on him.

"What's wrong with them?" Pennington looked to Ernie. The children ranged in age from six to eight. Their hair color varied but was similar enough to indicate common stock.

"Beats me. We've been here a week waiting for each kid to arrive and this is as excited as they get. Sometimes they wander in the field, but most of the time they just sit in groups and stare. Sometimes they whisper to each other. To be honest, Mr. Pennington, it freaks me out."

"Abel was the same way. We gave him video games to play and he never touched them."

"Abel? Is that the last kid? The one you were supposed to bring?"

"Yeah. We encountered a little problem."

Ernie let his eyes drift to the blue knot on Pennington's head.

"Don't ask. Who else knows they're here?"

"No one. Just Jose, me, and you. I followed your instructions to the letter. Your operatives would bring their target, er, child to a park at the foot of the mountain. I'd check to make certain the kid was unharmed, pay the agent, and bring the child here."

"What about your drunken brother?"

"No, sir. Absolutely not. He was supposed to pick you up and drive you here, turn around, and leave. Then and only then would he get paid, and he sure ain't getting paid now."

"Jose was supposed to drive the bus."

"No problem, sir. I'm checked out on big rigs. Driving that bus won't be much of a problem."

Pennington gazed back at the lavender-eyed gazers. They hadn't moved other than to turn their heads to face him. The creep factor climbed a notch. He looked at his watch. "We leave in an hour."

"Yes, sir. What about the missing boy?"

"Not your concern. Be ready to go when I say."

"Understood."

Pennington began to turn when a motion caught his eye. A girl, hair the color of licorice, slipped from her spot on one of the benches. Her frame was frail, her eyes large, her lips full, and her skin pale. She walked with the tiny strides of a child two years younger. For some reason, Pennington's feet were welded to the floor.

Pennington didn't like children and had been uncertain around them all his life. He fought the urge to step back as if recoiled by her presence.

She stopped a foot away and looked up to his face that was three feet above her. "Mister?"

"Yes?" Pennington's word came out softer than he intended.

"You got evil on you. Lots of evil."

If Judith's heart had been made of steel instead of flesh, it would have melted under the heat of fear that came upon her when her cell phone rang. The familiar chiming alarmed her so much that she screamed.

"I thought that thing was out of commission!" Anger born of the unexpected sound fueled Luke's words.

"It was. Just like yours." Judith's heart stuttered.

It chimed again. She pulled it from her purse and looked at the caller ID. *Unknown Call.*

As the phone sounded the third time, Judith snapped it open. She heard a voice and everything within her began to dissolve.

"You have the boy." It was the same automated voice she had heard in her office. "He is not safe. You must do as I say. If you understand say, 'Yes.'"

"Yes." Judith said.

Luke snapped his head around so fast Judith thought she heard vertebrae snap. He pulled the car to the side of the road. "It's him, isn't it?"

Judith nodded and leaned toward Luke. He placed his ear by the phone as Judith pressed a button on the side to increase the volume. She could feel his hair touch hers.

"Ontario Mills Mall. Jake and Jill's Toy Store. Bring the boy. Just the two of you. Lead him to the toy train display. If you understand say, 'Yes.'"

"Yes." Judith had to force the word out. It slipped from her lips with a tremble.

"A woman will take him. He will be safe and well cared for. Do not follow. Do not speak to the woman. If you understand say, 'Yes.'"

"Yes."

"February 27. You know the date. You know what you did. If you understand say, 'Yes.' "

"Yes."

"Arrive no later than one-thirty. This is for the boy's own good. "If you understand say, 'Yes.' "

"Yes."

The line went dead.

"What?" Ida asked. "What's wrong?"

"The Puppeteer." Judith set the phone down and drew in a lungful of air. "He wants Abel."

"He can't have him." Ida's voice grew in volume and rose in pitch. "Do you hear me? I am not turning my son over to some stranger. I lost him once, I'm not losing him again."

"Ida—" Luke began.

"It's not your right." Ida was close to screaming. "Just because you found him doesn't mean you own him."

"Ida—"

"We're leaving. I'm not going to let you do this."

Luke hit the automatic door lock. Ida began to fumble with the handle then the lock.

"Ida, stop."

"No. I'll scream. I'll draw attention to you."

"SHUT UP!" Luke's voice echoed so loudly in the car that it hurt Judith's ear. "Just shut up for a minute." He worked his hands on the steering wheel, squeezing until his knuckles whitened. A moment later, he leaned forward and placed his head on the wheel. "I can't do this, Judith. I can't turn Abel over to the Puppeteer. I thought I could. Every hour I tell myself I can, I must. I can't."

Judith put a hand on Luke's shoulder. "I know. I gave up believing I could follow this thing through to the end awhile ago. I figured you did too since you're here looking for the others."

"It means our secrets will get out." Luke leaned back in his seat. "I don't know what your secret is but I assume it could cost you everything."

"Maybe. I suppose there are more important things." She looked back at Ida and Abel. Abel seemed untroubled. *To have a child's peace.*

"It's only been a day and a half but I feel like I've been reacting to one threat after another for a month." He paused and gazed out the window. "Okay, let me think. Nothing has changed. We still have to find the others and do what we can to help them."

"Maybe we should go to the police now," Ida said.

"Maybe, but I fear for the others." Luke started the car. "The same deal may apply for them."

"Besides, I'm kinda wanted for murder." Judith thought for a moment. "The Puppeteer didn't mention the others. He only mentioned Abel. Why?"

"There's no way to know. Maybe he doesn't know about the others."

"Maybe he does and doesn't want us to know." Luke let the car idle. "He said we should turn Abel over to a woman in a toy store in Ontario. Even if we left right now, we couldn't make it on time. That means—"

"He doesn't know we're up here in the mountains."

"But he knows we're not in San Diego," Luke added.

"He could guess that we would have left from the news reports." Judith's mind grasped for more clues, more details to help her understand, but she ran dry.

"Give me your phone." Judith handed it over and Luke deftly removed the battery. He did the same with his phone.

"I don't know how well connected or sophisticated this guy is, but so far he seems to be head and shoulders above anyone I've met. No sense in letting the GPS tracking in the phones broadcast our whereabouts."

Luke dropped the car in gear and pulled onto the road.

A few minutes later, he pulled up to a Dumpster, exited the car, and tossed the phones in.

thirty-four

The sound of tires changed from a dull hum to a crunching as Luke slowed and pulled from the narrow serpentine lane that led from the main road through dense forest and to the Christian campground. The map listed the site as Manna Creek Christian Camp.

"Why are you pulling over?" Judith asked. "We have at least two miles to go."

"I can't take Abel and Ida into danger. We don't know if Pennington and his pals are there, but it makes sense, and if he is, he's not going to be happy with unexpected company."

"So you're giving up?"

"No. I plan to walk the rest of the way using the forest for cover. With any luck, I'll be able to scope out the situation."

"Then what?" Judith folded the map.

"I have no idea. I'll figure that out when I get there."

"When *we* get there. I'm going with you." She unsnapped her seat belt. Her stomach twisted with apprehension that told her she didn't feel as brave as she sounded.

"No, you're not. I want Ida and Abel to stay here. I don't know why, but this feels real bad."

"The Truth is talking to you," Abel said from the back.

"That's nice, kid. I don't know what it means, but it sounds real nice."

Judith opened her door. "Say what you want. I'm going with you, and aside from knocking me unconscious, there's nothing you can do about it."

Luke took her arm in his hand. "There's no reason for you to go."

"Of course there is. Children respond better to women than men."

"Oh yeah, you haven't met my mother."

"Luke, you know that I'm right about this. Best we can tell, it was men who took them and it is men who are holding them."

"We don't know that." The protest was weak.

"We know Pennington is a man. He worked with Dr. Zarefsky. That's at least two men. All I'm saying is that having a woman along might be helpful." She turned to the backseat. "You like me, don't you, Abel?"

"I like you a lot."

"See?" Judith smiled. "I'm irresistible. Now, if we're going to do this, you need to let go of my arm."

Luke did and Judith slipped from the car. A moment later, Luke stood by her side. She watched him study the road and the tree line. "This way."

"I'm right behind you." Judith wondered if Luke could hear the thunder in her heart.

After just five minutes, Judith felt she had left the civilized world behind and was trekking through unmapped areas like Lewis and Clark. Trees, mostly ponderosa pine, towered around her like pillars. She pushed through the brush, doing her best to walk on loose pine needles in her pumps. Every step made her feet hurt. She had not dressed for this and imagined how ridiculous she looked hiking in business attire.

Having had no opportunity to change, Luke wore the same casual jeans and sneakers which were much better suited for the work, yet even he struggled at times. She marveled at his willingness to go this alone, with no knowledge of what lay ahead. Over the last two days she had come to admire the man, his keen mind, quick wit, and commitment. Of course, he was weird, paranoid, and a loner. In many ways, he was the opposite of her, his north to her south. She worked in a major business, a leader in her industry. She piloted a corporation that measured success in the billions of dollars; he apparently sat alone in his home typing on a keyboard, reading stock reports and placing money here and there. He had done well for himself, but the thought of spending hours alone working like he did would drive her crazy. Perhaps what she did would be equally insanity inducing for him.

They had not spoken once they entered the forest. Only the sounds of distant birds, the occasional tree squirrel added to the noise of their footsteps. They made no attempt to disguise their movements for the first twenty minutes. At first it concerned Judith but she said nothing, instead trusting Luke's instincts. She hoped he had instincts.

If they had walked along the road, then it would have been a fairly easy two miles of twisting path. Plowing through the forest made the distance impossible to determine. Would it be shorter because it was more direct? Maybe. It might also be longer.

Some of the difficulty in walking came from the sloping ground. Luke had pulled to the side after descending three miles along the winding road and therefore had not reached the bottom of the sheltered valley. So the distance they had to cover had to be made over inclined ground. *At least it is downhill*, Judith thought, then wondered what the trip back up might be like.

Minutes chugged by, measured in carefully made steps and the occasional slip. Perspiration dotted her forehead, the scalp beneath her hair, and behind her ears. For a moment she felt disappointment that Luke would see her sweaty and dirty, with pine needles in her hair. She quickly chastised herself for the thought. She had read novels where women were portrayed being more concerned about their feelings and appearance than the danger that loomed before them. She abhorred such shallow representations and determined not to prove the authors right.

Luke slowed and Judith caught up to him. His breath came in deep draws and she could hear a slight wheeze with each inhalation. "How you doing? Am I going too fast?"

"I'm okay. Want to trade shoes?"

He looked puzzled then gazed at her feet. "No, thanks, I only wear slingbacks."

The unexpected image of Luke in women's shoes made her smile. "Tell me we're not lost."

"Not at all. I just wanted to give you a moment to rest." He took several more deep breaths.

"Very kind of you. Of course, you don't need a rest."

"Are you kidding? I'm dead on my feet. I'm just trying to appear macho in your eyes."

"My hero."

"I also wanted to take one more stab at getting you to go back." His face softened, draped in a concern that Judith hadn't seen before. The iceman was melting.

"I can't, Luke. I have to see this through. I can't let you go alone, and if the kids are there, you're going to need help handling them."

"How did I know you were going to say that?"

"Maybe because we've learned more about each other in two days than most learn in two years."

Luke lowered his head in thought. "And still, we know nothing about one another."

The truth of that landed hard in Judith's mind. Luke couldn't be more right, yet without knowing details and history, the last two days had caused her to respect, even admire, the odd man named Luke Becker.

Luke looked at his watch. "We've been walking for about a half an hour."

"How far have we come?"

"Hard to tell. If we were walking on a flat street where we didn't have to dodge trees and lose our footing on pine needles, we could make maybe three miles an hour at a brisk pace. My guess is that we've done two-thirds of that."

"So at two miles per hour, we've come a mile. That means we have another mile to go. We're only halfway there."

"Not true. We had two miles of travel along the road. The road is pretty twisty. I think we're close. So we need to move slower and quieter."

"I'll let you set the pace. You've done a great job so far."

"Okay. Stealth is the key."

"Meaning if I fall down and break my leg I shouldn't cry out in pain?"

"Do your best not to fall. I'm not carrying you back up the hill."

"Again I say: my hero."

Luke resumed the trek down the slippery grade. Judith followed with careful steps.

The shadows cast by nearby trees and the far-off sun painted an abstract canvas of shade and stripe. Every footfall brought more sound than Judith wanted. In the near silence of the forest, each stride elicited what sounded like a cacophony of crunching. She pressed on, walking through spiderwebs, destroying hours of arachnid work and giving her the creeps. Every minute sharpened her senses. When they started she noticed only trees, needles, and leaves. Now, even the movement of ants marching along the crevices of tree bark caught her eye. Beetles scampered when their fortress of leaves was disturbed. Gnats flew in formless clouds. The smell of damp dirt and decomposing detritus wafted up in the still air, reminding her that she walked more on compost than on soil. For some reason, she thought of the actress portraying her in the ad agency's mock-up television ad. "I love the time I spend communing with the plants that make my garden an outdoor home." *If only they could see me now.*

Luke slowed and held up a hand. Judith stopped. A second passed, he waved her forward and pointed. A short distance ahead, the trees gave way to a meadow blanketed in wildflowers. California poppies and lilacs dotted long, green grass. A breeze made bud and blade dance in undulating waves. A creek split the meadow adding its burbling sound to the chorus of singing birds. Any other time, any other place, the site would be beautiful, but the serene panorama made Judith anxious.

Closer stood several buildings all needing the attention of a skilled handyman. The structures varied in size but shared a common design: clapboard siding with weather-worn brown paint, green trim, and shingle roofing. Judith guessed that they had been built in the late sixties or early seventies. They were rustic, but that was to be expected for a complex billed as "a camp." Several had broken windows. Judith wondered what it was about abandoned buildings that attracted vandals like a flame does a moth.

Luke pointed to the west side of the camp and Judith saw what had captured his attention: a yellow school bus. Nearby the large form of a Humvee rested.

Leaning close, Luke whispered in Judith's ear. She could feel the warmth of his breath. "Everything around the buildings looks dirty; the bus looks clean." Judith agreed. "The place looks like it's been abandoned, but the vehicles look like they've been here less than a day or two."

Judith understood the implication. The odds that this was the place they were looking for just increased dramatically.

Judith scanned the surroundings time and time again but saw nothing. She closed her eyes and tried to force them to listen beyond their ability. Surely children would make noise, wouldn't they? Still, she heard nothing.

The presence of the bus and Humvee could be coincidence. Maybe the SUV belonged to a contractor. Maybe the bus was just being stored here. Maybe ...

Something grabbed her attention. A vague, indistinct motion in one of the buildings. The grounds held six buildings. Three looked like bunkhouses, one appeared to be a home—maybe staff housing and offices; one looked like it could be a recreation building and one—longer than any of the others—she judged to be the dining hall. She came to that conclusion based on the number of dented trash cans at the back end, and a large metal pipe sticking up from the roof she assumed vented a large cookstove. It was all guesswork.

There it was again. Someone moved in front of the window. Judith pointed but said nothing. Luke had seen it too. He leaned close again and placed his mouth an inch from her ear as before. "I think the building farthest to the east is where campers slept. There might be some children in there. I'm going to work my way along behind the tree line and see if I can't sneak a peek."

"I'm right behind you." Her voice barely made a whisper.

Luke frowned but didn't object. He was in no position to argue.

Quietly as possible, Judith followed Luke up the slope and deeper into the woods. Once certain they couldn't be seen, they turned east and moved with slow, deliberate steps. *Haste makes waste,* Judith thought, *it also makes a lot of noise.* Slow was the only way to go if they wanted to avoid detection.

Ten minutes passed like an hour, their trek ending with them hunkered behind an oleander bush peering at the bunkhouse. They still heard nothing and saw even less.

"Looks empty," Judith whispered.

"Only one way to find out." They exchanged glances. Luke looked pale and uncertain. She could almost smell his fear and wondered if the terror she felt was as apparent as his. He took a couple of deep breaths, looked from side to side, then exchanged the shelter of the forest for the open gravel-covered ground that surrounded the buildings. A second later, Judith followed, wishing her shoes made less noise on the gravel.

Luke moved in a crouch and Judith mimicked the motion. When she reached the deck and stairs that bridged the distance from ground to raised floor, Judith's heart pounded like a piston and every nerve tingled. For a moment she thought her stomach would give up its contents. More than anything, she wanted to be far away from this place; to be in the comfort

of her home or even her office. Nothing in her life had prepared her for this. For a handful of seconds, Luke's pleading
that she stay in the car with Ida and Abel made impeccable
sense. But that was then; this was now. She had made her
choice and would now have to live with it.

Like a cat on uncertain ground, Luke moved up the stairs
first, Judith two seconds behind him. She calmed her breathing and listened for sounds inside. Nothing.

The door to the building had seen better days. Its edges
were worn and its face scarred. An aluminum vertical sliding
window allowed a view inside. Judith stood behind Luke as
he took a quick look through the filthy pane and immediately
snapped his head back. A moment later, he looked again, this
time lingering. Judith could see his shoulders relax.

He reached for the dented and crooked doorknob and
gave it a turn. It moved easily and without noise. Judith hoped
the hinges would be as cooperative. The metal protested only
slightly as Luke pulled the door open and slipped inside.
Judith took charge of the door and quietly closed it.

They stood in a mudroom, a small space where one could
shake snow and mud from their feet before entering the main
area of the building. It also provided a buffer against the
entrance of cold air in the winter. Once again they faced an
identical door and window. Luke gazed in for what seemed
like half an hour. Judith knew that only seconds had passed.

Again, Luke tried the doorknob and pulled open the
door.

Stale air, filled with the dust of decaying wood, assaulted
their senses. Luke moved inside taking steps like a barefoot
man on broken glass. He held the door for Judith and she
entered.

Dust covered everything. Spiders had made homes in the darker corners. They were the only inhabitants. Bunk beds lined both walls making use of every foot of wall space that had no window. It reminded Judith of boot-camp barracks she had seen in old military movies—a fondness held by her late husband and something she endured.

The dust on the floor had been disturbed by many feet—small feet, although Judith could make out adult-size shoe prints. Blankets were on the bed, left from the last campers to pass through the place, the owners not taking the time to remove the bed coverings when they abandoned the camp. The sheets and bedspreads were jumbled and askew. Judith approached one bed and could see a thin layer of dust on the corner of the sheets and the pillows.

On the floor next to the beds were hamburger wrappers and empty french fry bags from McDonald's. Paper cups with plastic straws littered the floor. Judith picked up one of the wrappers and studied it, then raised it to her nose. "These are recent. There's no dust on the wrappers and I can still detect the smell of hamburger."

"I guessed as much."

"That means the kids slept in these filthy beds." The thought disgusted her.

"I don't see any belongings. No clothing, no toys, nothing." He took a few steps. "There's a bathroom here." He went in then came back out. "Typical bunkhouse-style bathroom. There's a couple of showers but the floor is bone-dry as are the sinks. I didn't see any toothbrushes or combs. The kids brought nothing with them, which just further proves the abduction point."

"I was thinking the same thing." She dropped the food wrapper. "At least we know one place they're not."

"Time to move to the next building. The one where we saw the movement. I think you should stay here."

"And I think you need to give up that line. It's not working and it isn't going to work anytime soon."

"Can't blame a man for trying."

"I appreciate your concern, Luke. I really do. It's sweet in a hundred different ways. Now stop it."

This time Judith took the lead, walking through the bunkhouse and toward the doors on the opposite side of those through which they entered.

The next building, she knew, would not be empty.

thirty-five

This time it was Judith who paused at the windowed door and surveyed the scene on the other side. The only motion she detected was the start-and-stop dash of a squirrel. Laying hand to doorknob, Judith wondered if Terri was praying for her. The thought flashed like a strobe in her mind and even though it lasted only a moment, it brought a measure of satisfaction and hope. She wondered if she started praying now if God would know who she was. Terri would tell her, "Of course." Judith hoped her assistant was right.

The coolness of the knob seeped into her skin. Again, her senses had gone on hyper-alert. She could feel the blood streaming through veins and arteries. Her breathing became shallow. She forced deep inhalations, and then held her breath

237 / alton GANSKY

as she pulled the door open. Thankfully, no squeaky hinges. That settled it. Terri had to be praying.

Judith slipped outside, glanced around again, then made her way down the steps, across the ground and up similar steps to a porch on the next building. Luke moved so quietly, Judith had to turn to see if he was still with her.

This was the building she assumed to be the dining hall. The door on this structure was the same as the bunkhouse but it also had a screen, probably to keep flying insects out of the cooking area. A screen meant another source of possible noise, another set of hinges that could groan with movement and give away their position.

As Luke had done before her, Judith took a quick look through the windowed door then moved back. She had spent less than a second glancing inside. No people were apparent, just a kitchen. She slipped her hand into the screen door's handle and moved it one inch. No noise. She moved it another—

BAM.

Judith would have screamed if her lungs held enough air. Instead, she closed her eyes and bit her lip. The noise sounded like a gun going off and images of a dead child rushed into her unprotected mind. Then she heard a voice, somewhat distant.

Luke patted her shoulder and breathed in her ear, "Screen door slamming."

Judith's bones seemed to melt. Her knees shook and her heart no longer beat, it rolled like a ball within her. All at the same time, she wanted to swear, pray, weep, and scream. There was no logic to it, just a pure, raw emotion looking for escape.

Luke moved back down the stairs like a mime in slow motion. Judith gave him a questioning look. He held two fingers to his eyes and pointed at the corners. He planned to look around the edge of the building. He did then returned. "Pennington. Just him."

They had found the right place, but it brought her no comfort. For a while, she could tell herself that no one was here; that they had come to the wrong place; that they were still safe and secure.

That thought shattered.

Judith pulled the screen door open halfway and reached for the doorknob. The door opened easily and both stepped inside the kitchen. Luke feathered the door closed behind them. Moving across the wood floor they came to a pair of double metal doors like those in a restaurant. Judith stepped to the side of one door and Luke took the other.

One look told her what she wanted to know: the children were there, sitting on benches at long tables, quiet, almost stone still. One man, smaller than that Pennington character but with a look that made Judith uncomfortable, paced in the room. The children watched him as if he were a television show.

Judith telegraphed a questioning glance at Luke who just shrugged. Luke motioned her to the back door. "I'm going in. The guy's pacing like an expectant father."

"More like a tiger in a cage."

"We can argue metaphors later. Like I said, I'm going to slip in when his back is turned and see if I can't subdue him one way or another. If I can, I'll have a better chance of stalling Pennington while you get the kids out."

"And what do I do with them?"

"Slip into the forest and hide, unless—can you drive a bus?"

Judith shook her head. "You've got to be kidding. I drive an automatic transmission for a reason. Are you sure you can take this guy? When was the last time you were in a fight?"

"You know that. You were there last night."

"I was there. That wasn't a fight. It was a beating. I mean, when was the last time you exchanged blows with another person?"

He looked down. "Third grade."

"Tell me you won."

"No. She beat me."

Judith rubbed her forehead. "If we weren't in such danger, I'd find that hilarious."

"I'm open to ideas. What have you got in that business head of yours? Maybe you could subdue him with a discussion of midcentury modern architecture."

"I don't have any ideas."

"Look, Judith. I'm not trying to be a hero. I'm doing my best to keep from running into the woods screaming like a preschooler, but something has to be done and I don't see any other options."

Luke started for the double doors when Judith took his arm. He stopped. For an eternal second they stared at each other, then Judith stepped forward and gave him a hug, burying her face in his chest. "Be careful."

The door to the eating hall moved only enough for Luke to sneak through. Every brain cell in his head screamed about the stupid course of action he had chosen to follow. It was too late now. There would be no turning back.

Staying in a crouch, Luke moved to the end of the closest table. The table was empty, and the children were being grouped at the other end of the hall. At this distance, the table provided enough cover but Luke felt exposed. Once he left this perch, he would be in full view of the man guarding the kids.

If he was going to act he would have to do so soon. Pennington could return at any moment and Luke knew he couldn't handle both men. Pennington didn't seem the kind of man to let bygones be bygones.

He lifted his head above the top edge of the table and saw his target staring out the window, no doubt watching Pennington talk on the phone. Luke wished for a weapon, but the best he could see was a plastic knife. He doubted he could deliver more than a stinging scratch with it. He needed something more, something creative. With his mind snapping back and forth from idea to idea, Luke finally settled on the only thing he felt might be advantageous—a pepper shaker, one of the many remnants left behind by the owners. The shaker, a thick glass cylinder, lay on its side just within reach. After another quick check to be certain he wasn't being observed, Luke rose, seized the shaker, and resumed his crouch behind the table.

He fumbled with it and noticed his hands were shaking. It took three attempts, but Luke separated the top from the body of the shaker. Relief gave him a half-moment of joy before terror reassumed the throne.

Luke filled his left hand with black granules and held the glass shaker in his right. *This is crazy. This is stupid. I've lost my mind.*

He stood. He set his eyes on the man he planned to attack. He started forward.

In unison, the children turned to face him. Not one spoke; not one pointed.

Moving as fast as he could and stepping as quietly as possible, Luke sped forward.

When just a foot away, the man turned. "What—?"

Luke threw the pepper in the man's face. His aim proved on target. The pepper filled both eyes. The victim raised his hands and started to let out a scream, but Luke cut it off with a blow to the belly. He could hear the air rush from the man's lungs. Luke landed one more blow, this time to the back of the neck. The man dropped like a tree.

Luke's heart pumped his blood at racetrack speed. A sense of accomplishment rose in the darkness of fear, but he paid it no mind. It was no time to gloat.

"Come on, kids. That way." He kept his voice low and pointed to the back of the hall, back to the kitchen. "Hurry."

Judith opened the doors and motioned the children to her. "Come this way, children. Follow me. This way. Hurry … Luke!"

The warning came a half second too late. The door behind him swung open and slammed the wall. Luke spun and saw Pennington, his face frozen in fury. He looked down at his unconscious partner then back at Luke. His fists clinched into balls of iron.

Luke, who prided himself on his mind, his logic, his ability to reason through any problem, stopped thinking. Long buried instinct kicked in. Judith needed time. Luke would give it to her.

He charged.

He swung with a fist still clutching the glass shaker. It was a punch capable of dropping a heavyweight boxer, if it landed. It didn't. Pennington shifted to the side and Luke's swing missed its mark by two feet.

Pennington's punch didn't.

As Luke caught his balance, a fist caught him square on the nose. The pain blinded him, water flooded his eyes, and he staggered back a step. Something warm and thick flowed across his lips. He raised his hands to his face. Another blow landed on the back of his hands sending pain racing through his arms like lightning.

"No more of you, pal," Pennington said. "I have had my fill of your meddling."

Something hit Luke in the ribs. It felt like a demolition ball but he knew it was the fist of the man beating him. Something cracked and fire blazed just below the skin. Luke dropped to his knees. A second later, he rose and faced Pennington, raising his hands like a boxer—displaying the courage of the desperate.

Stall him. Give Judith a chance. Stall him for just a few minutes.

Like a man before a firing squad who refuses a blindfold, Luke faced his attacker, took a step forward, and threw the best punch his body would allow. It landed on nothing.

The next thing Luke felt was his feet leave the floor and his body flying over his head. Pennington had grabbed his extended arm and threw him over his shoulder. The floor took the last ounce of fight out of Luke.

He couldn't move. He could only stare at the ceiling.

Pennington stood over him. He grinned.

Judith began her sprint before Luke hit the floor. Leaving her shoes behind, she moved faster than she had since high school gym class. She let out a scream just as she leapt on Pennington, who still gazed down at his fallen prey.

She hit him with all her weight, sending both of them tumbling to the floor. The impact jarred Judith and the pain of it startled her but she had no time to think of it. She balled her hands into fists and began to pummel whatever part of Pennington's body she could find. The fact that she had somehow ended on top of him, straddling his abdomen, surprised her. Several of her blows landed on his face but the attack didn't last long. He reached up, seized a fistful of hair, and yanked hard to the side. Judith's head and body followed. Her scalp blazed with pain but she continued to throw punches.

A fist came out of nowhere and caught her on the side of the head. The room began to spin and sparkles of pain that delivered glittery drops filled her eyes. She raised a hand to throw another punch but her arms ceased cooperating.

Another yank on her hair and she crumpled to the floor beside Pennington.

He rose, brushed himself off, then reached beneath his coat and removed a dark object. The tears in her eyes slowed her recognition but two blinks later she saw a black gun in his hand. He aimed it at her, paused, then pointed the muzzle toward the still-unmoving Luke.

"No," she said. She had tried to shout it, but only a threadbare whisper emerged.

"I could make you beg for his life, but it would be a waste of time. I'd kill him anyway. Why pretend?"

Judith tried to rise, but the blow to the side of her head kept her down and kept the room spinning. "Pl ... please."

Pennington laughed. "I see. You think a polite request will work better."

244 / FINDER'S FEE

A movement caught Judith's attention. A small form stepped between the business end of the gun and Luke.

A child. A little girl.

Judith started to warn her away but words would not come. Another child stepped to her side, then another and another. The best Judith could tell, every one of the children stood between Pennington and Luke. Some moved by her.

"Get out of the way, kids. They started it. I'm going to finish it."

The children didn't move.

Pennington swore, reached forward, and pushed the closest child to the side. Immediately another child took her place.

"Don't make me angry, kids. Do what I say."

No one moved.

"Move! NOW!"

They stood their ground.

The young girl who made the first move looked at Pennington. "Mister, there's lots more evil on you. Lots more."

"Lots more," the children said in unison. "Lots more ... lots more ... lots more."

Judith's grip on consciousness slipped.

thirty-six

Pennington rubbed his chin. The Find woman had landed one decent shot and now his jaw ached. Oddly, he found it amusing. The bus rumbled up the grade, Ernie at the wheel. He had come to a few moments after Pennington had put the meddling twosome in their place. He gave him a few minutes to clear his head then ordered Ernie to load the bus with the children. To win the children's cooperation, Pennington had promised not to shoot Find and Becker. At least he had a name for the man now, a name he learned from rifling through the man's wallet. There wasn't much information, just a driver's license, a debit card, and some cash. Pennington had no interest in the latter. He tossed the billfold on the unconscious man's chest.

Duct tape provided the bonds necessary to keep Find and Becker from slipping away and calling the police. *Now that is a mystery, isn't it? Why hadn't they gone to the police already?* Perhaps they had but the cops didn't believe them. Although cops are generally stupid, this kind of problem should elicit immediate attention from even the dullest flatfoot. But there were no cops. Maybe the dumb ones were Find and Becker.

The bus rocked as it made turn after turn up the twisting road. He took hold of the metal rail that separated his seat from that of the driver. Pennington sat in the seat immediately behind Ernie. He gazed back at the children. They sat in pairs in the seats, hands folded in front of them, their eyes fixed on him. They were a strange bunch. No one cried out in fear when he delivered a beating to Becker then Find, and they had the courage to step in front of his Glock 9mm. There was something far more bizarre about them than their weird-colored eyes.

But that wasn't his problem. His job was to collect and deliver, and collect he did—all but one child. Twelve out of thirteen wasn't bad, but not perfect. His employers wouldn't be happy but nothing could be done about it at the moment.

He'd have to track down Abel Palek later. He did have a reputation to protect.

"Pull over, Ernie."

"Why? I just got a good head of steam going. This grade is a killer."

"I said, pull over."

Ernie sighed but did as Pennington ordered. The school bus slowed to a stop and Ernie set the brake to keep it from rolling downhill. "What's wrong?"

"I have one last job for you, then you can call it quits. Let's talk outside."

Pennington watched as Ernie gave him the once-over, his suspicion clear. Ernie popped open the door and stepped out. Pennington joined him and walked to the back of the bus. He looked up to see if any of the children were watching.

"I want you to go back and finish the job," Pennington said. "You won't have the kids to get in your way like I did."

"I don't understand." Ernie didn't bother to hide his reluctance. "Are you just going to sit here and wait for me?"

"No, your work is done. I'll see to it that you get extra pay for this. A lot of extra pay, if you know what I mean."

"Who will drive the bus?"

"Me. I'm checked out on any fixed-wing aircraft short of a 747, I think I can handle a school bus."

"I ... I don't know. I mean, I've done a lot of stuff I ain't proud of, but offing two people seems over the top."

Pennington took a threatening step forward. "Yeah? Well, don't forget, buddy, those two can identify you as one of the men who kidnapped twelve kids."

"I didn't kidnap anyone."

"No, but you're an accessory. Think about this: You have two strikes on you now. It's one reason I hired you. Three strikes will put you away forever and a day. I'm no lawyer, but I gotta believe that twelve counts of kidnapping, child endangerment, and who knows what else will add up to a lot of time in a federal penitentiary. I hear child abductors don't do well in prison. Not even the murderers like them. Are you catching my drift?"

"Yeah, yeah, I think I get the picture."

Pennington removed his gun and handed it to Ernie, who took it like a man very familiar with weapons. "It's only about a mile, maybe a mile and a half. After you do them, get rid of the gun. There's a septic tank on the property. The access port is visible. You should be able to open it and drop the pistol in. By the time the police find it, it will be too late. Be sure to wipe it down."

"Maybe I should burn the building down."

"Nice idea, but it will attract too much attention. Someone will see the smoke and the fire department will be called. We don't want the bodies found this soon. Just leave them to rot. It will be days before anyone finds them, maybe longer. By the time they're found, if they're ever found, we will be in far off places. Got it?"

"Yeah, I got it."

"Good. I left the keys in the Humvee. Use it to get as far out of town as possible. Now, start walking."

Ernie took the gun, wedged it in his belt and started down the road.

Pennington stepped into the bus and sat in the driver's seat. He closed the door, started the engine, then studied the controls for a moment. The hard part would be starting up a hill, after that, it should be a breeze.

"Where is the driver going?" one of the boys asked.

"I told you that I'd send someone back to free the man and the woman. They're bad people. They need to go to jail. Ernie will make sure they're okay and wait for the police to arrive."

. The boy wasn't buying it. "They had lots and lots of good on them. I don't think they are bad people."

"Shut it, kid. I have had it with all this good and bad stuff you kids pretend to see. I'm not going to play that game."

"It's not a game, mister. They had lots of good and you have even more bad on you."

"I said, shut up!"

Pennington threw the bus into gear, released the brake, and chugged up the grade.

Judith had never hurt so much. The ache in her head came in waves of migraine proportions that rolled through the rest of her body. Her scalp stung where Pennington had grabbed her hair and she could feel the swelling beneath the skin on the left side of her head. As bad as those things were, being bound with duct tape bothered her more. Arms tied behind her, ankles taped painfully tight, and a swatch of the gray tape across her mouth put her in a near panic. She forced herself to remain calm, taking deep breaths through her nose.

Despite her near-panicked state, she had a greater concern. Luke was choking. In his confrontation with Pennington he had taken a crushing shot to the nose. Blood oozed from it, swelling made it look a third larger. She held no doubts that Luke's nose was broken and he was choking on his own blood. Several times he had blown hard to clear his nostrils so he could inhale as much air as possible.

He stood a good chance of suffocating.

Like a caterpillar, Judith wriggled to where Luke lay. His skin had a slight blue tint that ratcheted her fear another notch. With greater urgency she inched along the floor until she lay face-to-face with him. Then she continued twisting and stretching until her belly was near his face. She rolled over to her other side and backed toward Luke, her taped hands close to his face.

She waited two horribly long seconds until Luke caught on and bent and squirmed until his face touched her hands. Quickly as she could, she worked her fingers along his skin until she felt the edge of the tape and began to pick at it, trying to get a corner she could grab.

The sound of Luke's wet breathing pressed her on. He couldn't be getting enough air. He coughed and convulsed. She waited until he placed his face near her hands. One second followed another like one day followed its predecessor. Tears ran from her eyes and fell to the dusty floor. How many minutes did she have? How long could Luke last before oxygen depravation plunged him into unconsciousness?

Don't think. Don't analyze. Just do. Focus on getting the tape.

A corner of the tape pulled from his skin. She couldn't see it but it was large enough to pinch between her fingers. Again, she explored his face blindly until she pinched the tape between index finger and thumb. She rolled, hoping with all her might that she could maintain her grip. She felt Luke pulling away.

The tape slipped from her grasp.

"No," she moaned through her gag. In desperation she searched for the loose end and found it. Again she rolled and Luke pulled back.

A new sound.

A loud puff followed by a wheezing inhalation. The sound repeated itself. She reached for the tape but couldn't find Luke's face. Panic descended until she recognized the sounds. Enough of the tape must have come loose for Luke to breathe through the corner of his mouth. The wheezing, puffing inhalation and exhalation became a beautiful sound.

Just as Judith's nerves threatened to get the best of her, reducing her to a weeping mass of woman, she felt Luke's face at her hands again. This time she got a good grip on the tape and Luke pulled away, leaving the tape in her hands. The sound of air being gulped by the lungful replaced the wheezing and puffing.

"I ... I thought that was it for me." Luke sounded like a man who just finished a forced marathon. "What a lousy way to go."

Judith allowed herself to relax for a moment. They were far from free but at least she didn't have to watch as Luke suffocated.

It took another five minutes, but Luke, using the same technique as Judith, removed the tape from her mouth. Both bore scratches from the nails of desperate fingers. Minutes passed as both rested.

"Judith?"

"Yes?"

"If we get through this; if we get free, I'm going to kiss you full on the mouth. I'm going to kiss you long and hard."

"If we get out of this, I'm going to let you."

Luke gave a pathetic laugh. "What makes you think you can stop me?"

"I've seen you fight."

Luke laughed again. This time it was genuine and deep, more a laugh of relief than humor. He coughed. She looked at him. His eyes were closed but his chest moved in an even rise and fall.

The door to the dining hall opened and the loud clap of the screen door slapping the frame filled the space.

"What have we here?"

Judith turned her head and saw the silhouetted figure of a man standing in the doorway.

"Oh, great," Luke said. "Just when I thought things were looking up."

The man stood with hands on hips, head tilted to the side. It took Judith a moment to realize the new arrival was too thin to be Pennington and too tall to be the other guy. It also occurred to her that she had not heard a vehicle drive up.

Judith noticed something else: the man reeked of booze.

"I don't suppose you guys have any beer?"

thirty-seven

Where's my brother?" the man asked.

"That depends." Luke tried to sit up but couldn't manage it. "Who's your brother?"

"Ernie. Ernie Braun. I'm Vince."

Vince moved away from the door and Judith could see him better. Thin, mussed hair, stubbly chin, and a sheen of sweat covered him. He looked nothing like his brother. "Do you work for Pennington?"

"The guy with the Hummer?" He laughed. "Yeah, I worked for him—for about thirty seconds. That's how long it took him to toss me out of the car. Can't blame him, though. I ain't nothing but a drunk. My brother gives me an opportunity to score some serious scratch and I blow it. I really need the money."

Luke spoke. "Vince, as you can see, we have something in common. We're not real high on Pennington's list of favorite people."

"Yeah, I can see that. I surely can. Looks like he busted you up pretty good. Did you get any licks in?"

Luke continued. "Nothing to brag about. Listen, Vince, birds of a feather flock together. Ever heard that?"

"Sure. I'm a drunk, not stupid."

"Sorry. I didn't mean anything. I'm afraid I got my bell rung a few too many times today. I'm not thinking straight."

"No problem. I've got a thick skin."

"Here's my point: Pennington tossed you and he tossed us too. We have that in common. He stiffed you out of your money, right?"

"You got that right."

"I can help you with that. What were you supposed to get paid?"

Judith stayed out of the conversation thinking Luke knew how to handle the man better than she.

"Two hundred solid for picking him up from the helicopter and driving him here, then following the bus."

"Okay, here's the deal. You untie us and I'll pay you the two hundred."

Vince studied Luke then Judith then his eyes fell on Luke's wallet resting on the floor. "That your wallet?"

Judith's hopes sank.

"Yeah, Vince, it is. You going to rob two battered and shackled people?"

"What better kind of people to rob." Vince picked up the wallet and peered in. "Whoa. You're not kiddin' ol Vince. You do have two hundred in here—wait, it's more like three hundred."

"Oh, come on, Vince. We need help here."

"I know it." He tossed the wallet on the closest table. Vince moved to Luke, knelt down, and swayed in uncertain balance for a moment. "The long walk must be getting to me. My head is spinning. That or too many years on the bottle. Roll over."

Luke hesitated turning his back to the man.

"You want me to get that tape off or not?"

"Yeah, yeah, of course. Sorry. It's been a rough day." Luke struggled to roll over. He lay on his belly. He looked nervous to Judith. Nothing like being helpless before a stranger to set one's nerves on edge.

Vince fumbled with the tape but finally managed to get Luke's wrists free. He smiled at his accomplishment. Luke rolled over onto his back. "Thanks, Vince—"

"Vince!"

Judith jumped at the voice. It was familiar. She had heard it a few times before Pennington drove off with the children. It belonged to the man Luke had knocked unconscious.

Vince shot to his feet, swayed, then steadied himself. "Ernie. You scared a year off my life. What's the matter with you?"

"What's the matter with *you*? What are you doing?" Ernie held a gun.

"They asked me to let them go."

"So you thought you would help them out."

"Yeah, of course. Wouldn't you?"

"I swear you get dumber by the week." Ernie entered and pointed the gun at Luke's head. Luke raised his hands. Judith's newfound hope shattered like crystal on concrete.

"What are you doin' with that gun, Ernie? You know guns make me nervous."

"Shut up, Vince. How did you get here, anyway?"

"You tell me to shut up then ask me a question. And they say my mind is going."

"Answer me."

Vince looked like a chastised puppy. "I walked. What do you think? The guy you had me pick up went off on me. Tossed me out of the car and threatened to run you over."

"I knew I shouldn't have hired you for this. I should have left you in your trailer swilling your booze. You lousy drunk. You good-for-nothin' piece of trash. You blow your chance then come here and mess things up even more. What am I supposed to do now?"

"I may be nothin' but a stinkin' drunk, but I ain't wavin' no pistol at helpless people."

"This helpless man threw pepper in my eyes then clobbered me with something hard. He nearly cracked my skull."

Vince looked at Luke. "That true, boy?"

"Yeah, Vince, it is. I was trying to save the children."

"What children?" Vince asked.

"Never mind," Ernie said. "That's none of your business."

Vince lowered his head. "What a pair we turned out to be, brother. You spend time in and out of jail, and I spend time in and out of bars and the drunk tank. We broke Momma's heart, we did. Sweetest woman on the planet and we turn out like this. First time in my life I feel glad she's dead. We can't hurt her anymore."

"You have to leave, Vince. I have to finish this."

"I ain't leaving, Ernie. I'm a no-good and I know it, but I know it ain't right to off two unarmed people who ain't done nothin' to me."

"Go on. Get out!" Ernie's hand began to shake. Luke closed his eyes. Judith forced hers to stay open.

"No way, brother. We're in this together. I'm not leaving. You blow them away, you blow your life away too, and then there's nothing else for me to live for. You might as well put that piece to my head and pull the trigger."

A tear escaped Ernie's eye. "You don't understand, Vince. You just don't get it."

"Probably not, but I get a few things. I get that year after year you been there for me. You been cleaning up my messes, covering my debts, lying to Mom when she was alive to protect her from the truth about me." Vince moved between Luke and Ernie, blocking any shot Ernie had. "Now it's my turn to look out for you."

"And do what, Vince? What do you think I should do? If these guys go to the cops and identify me, I'm finished. Do you understand? Finished! I got two strikes on me. One more and I'll never see a prison from the outside again. Is that what you want? You want me to be locked up for the rest of my life? Who will look after you then?"

"I don't know what the answer is, bro. You know I can only think about one thing at a time and that's usually about where my next drink is coming from. Right now I'm just thinking that I can't let you kill these people. You're not a killer, Ernie. You've done a lot of bad things, but you ain't no killer."

Judith wanted to speak, wanted to encourage Ernie to listen to Vince but she feared anything she said would inflame him. She bit her lip and watched.

"Come on, bro. Give me the gun. You take off and I'll stay here." Vince stepped closer. "Hand it over, Ernie."

"I can't."

Another step closer. "Yes, you can. This may be the only thing I get right in my life, I ain't flushin' it. Give me the gun." Vince's hand seemed steadier than Ernie's, maybe for the first time in years.

Ernie moved his head from side to side, slowly at first, then faster and faster. "No. I gotta do this. You don't know Pennington. You don't know the people he works for. I'm more afraid of them than I am the cops."

He pivoted and swung the gun toward Judith. She screamed.

"NO!" Vince grabbed the gun and pulled it away from Judith ... and toward himself.

The sound hurt Judith's ears. She recoiled the best she could, rolling away from Ernie.

"Vince? Vince!"

Judith rolled back to her side. Vince had the gun in his blood-covered hands. His eyes were wide and fixed on his brother. A trickle of thick crimson fluid trickled from his mouth. Ernie held him by the shoulders. Vince moved his mouth as if speaking but no words came.

His eyes rolled back, his jaw went slack, and he dropped to the floor.

"What have I done? Vince? Vince? Stay with me." Ernie knelt down by his brother. "Vince, I'm sorry. I'm so sorry. Don't die, man. Stay with me. I ... I need you, Vince."

Luke began to move. His hands were free, but duct tape still bound his feet. He reached, he stretched, he scrambled for the gun which lay two feet from the fallen Vince. In mad motions Luke squirmed toward the weapon—then seized it.

Ernie made no move to prevent Luke's actions. His eyes were fixed on the widening circle of red spreading from his brother's chest. He began to weep.

Luke struggled to put distance between himself and Ernie, inching away on his back, the gun pointed at the assailant. When he was several feet away, he sat up and started working on the tape around his ankles. It came free quickly.

Slowly, eyes pinned to Ernie, Luke rose. If Ernie saw him he gave no indication of caring.

Less than a minute later, Luke had freed Judith. "Here, hold this." He handed her the pistol.

"I don't want that."

"You got it." He forced it into her hand. It was warm.

Luke sprinted to Vince's side. Ernie wept from a torn soul. In a swift motion, he ripped Vince's blood-soaked shirt open. A gaping hole oozed blood from the left side of the man's chest.

"He's still breathing."

"He's ... he's not dead?" Ernie looked up.

"Give me your hand."

"Why."

"Just give it to me." Ernie extended his arm and Luke grabbed it at the wrist, and pushed it toward the wound. "Press here. Press hard."

Ernie did.

Luke sprang to his feet and looked around. A phone hung on the wall five feet from the entrance door. "Does that phone work?"

"I don't know."

Luke sprinted to the phone. "I got a dial tone." Judith watched him dial 9-1-1.

Returning to the fallen Vince, Luke examined the man again. Judith wasn't sure if Luke was being brave and noble or just foolish. Seeing him kneeling over a man he had known only for minutes and across from a hood who had come within a second or two of blowing their brains out filled Judith with warring emotions. They should flee. Let the assassin care for the drunk.

No sooner had the thought perched in the forefront of her mind than she felt awash in guilt. The man lying on the floor had saved their lives. It could have been, maybe should have been, them bleeding to death on the dusty wood floor. What did it matter that the man had an alcohol addiction? A hero lay dying. A hero unlikely in appearance and in life, but a hero nonetheless.

"His color is a little better," Luke said to Ernie. "Keep your hand there. An ambulance will be here soon. There's still hope."

Ernie looked up, his hand pressed to the hole in the front of his brother's chest. Thick red fluid seeped through his fingers. "I've killed my own brother."

"Not yet you haven't." Luke's words were firm. "He needs you to be steady, to be strong and focused."

"He was always useless, always following me around, always in some kind of trouble—just like me. A drunk. He's nothing but a stupid, worthless drunk." Ernie broke into tears, sobbing. Judith's heart gained ten pounds of grief. "I'll never forgive myself," he said. "Not in this life or any other."

"Hang in there." Luke rose to his feet. "The last page of the story hasn't been written."

Ernie looked up at Luke. "What are you going to tell the cops when they get here?"

"I don't plan to be here. I've got to catch up to your pal."
Luke paused. "Given the moment, I hate to ask this, but do
you have a cell phone?"

"Clipped to my belt."

"I have to take it. I can't have you warning Pennington."

Ernie gave a nod. "I understand. I'd do the same."

Stepping around to Ernie's back, Luke removed the cell
phone and slipped it into his pocket. "We gotta go. Help will
be here soon."

Ernie said nothing.

"I wish I could do more."

In a soft voice, Ernie said, "It's Becker, right? That's what
Pennington called you when he went through your wallet."

"Yeah. Becker."

Judith moved closer. Something inside Ernie had turned
down the volume.

"San Pedro. Pier F. *The Great Divide.*"

"*The Great Divide?* What is that?" Judith asked.

"It's a boat. A big yacht of some kind, I think. I've never
been to it, but I was supposed to drive the bus to the San
Pedro Bay, Pier F."

Luke moved in front of Ernie. "They're putting the kids
on a boat."

"I guess so. I don't know any more than that. Me and
another guy were to drive the kids there. He busted an ankle.
That left me so I hired Vince . . . and look where it's led."

"A boat?" Luke said.

The Humvee's engine roared as Luke pressed the accelerator closer and closer to the floor. Judith sat in the passenger
seat shaking from fear and the sudden realization that she

hadn't been killed. She wished for numbness; she wished for icy cold courage to replace the burning fear of uncertainty.

"Won't you attract attention driving so fast?" Judith pulled at her seat and shoulder belt one more time.

"There's no one to see us. Not yet. We might see the ambulance."

"Let's hope we don't *run into* the ambulance. That won't do anyone any good."

"You've never liked my driving."

Judith recognized the effort to make light of the situation. It wasn't working. "What's to like?"

Luke didn't respond immediately. She could see that something was on his mind. She knew what it was. The same fear had taken up residence in her thoughts. "Do you think they're okay?"

"I hope so but I fear the worst. I wish I had tried to hide the car. I just didn't see things happening this way."

"How did you see them happening?"

"I don't know. I just ... I don't know. Never, not even in my most paranoid dreams, have I imagined being in this kind of trouble."

Neither had Judith. No nightmare had been this terrifying. "There. I see the car." Even before Luke pulled to a stop Judith knew something was wrong. Her fear had been that Pennington would see the parked car and investigate.

The tires of the large vehicle came to a stop in a cloud of dust as Luke pulled the vehicle from the pavement. He was out before Judith could unfasten her seat belt. A second later she stood next to him and they peered into the car. Ida lay unmoving on the backseat. The right rear door hung open.

Judith moved around the car to the open door and bent over the woman. "She's alive." Ida's face showed red marks turning blue and black, the skin of her face drawn tight with swelling. Judith's stomach turned and her legs weakened. Her blood threatened to pool in her feet. She was uncertain what to feel. Pure anger demanded attention, but shock and sorrow wanted the front of the line.

Sirens echoed down the road.

"Get in the car," Luke ordered.

"What about Ida?"

"Get in the car." He moved to the Humvee and Judith followed.

"We can't leave her."

"We're not." He started the Hummer and pulled back to the road.

"This sure looks like leaving to me."

"There's nothing we can do for her now." He paused. "We've lost Abel. Pennington must have seen the car and taken him."

"Judging by the bruises on her face she put up quite a fight."

"The woman has guts, there's no denying that." Luke slowed at the sight of the ambulance, rolled down his window, and waved his arm, signaling the fire department vehicle to stop. The driver lowered his window. To Judith he looked barely out of high school.

"There's a car just a hundred yards down and on the right with an unconscious woman in it. I think she's been beaten."

"We got a call that someone was injured at the camp."

"I made the call. He's bleeding pretty bad. Both need your help."

"We'll take care of it. Procedure is to send a truck company on injury calls. We're ahead of them by a couple of minutes. We'll make sure both get taken care of."

"Thanks. You guys don't get paid enough."

The young man snickered and drove off.

"I feel horrible leaving Ida behind," Judith said.

"Me too, but what could we do? She might have head injuries that require hospitalization. We have to leave her to the care of experts."

"And we have to find Abel."

"We have to find Abel."

thirty-eight

Marlin fought not to smile. Before him sat ten of the twelve non-family board members; each looked stunned.

"I know it's hard to believe, and trust me when I say I take no pleasure in revealing this. After all, she is my mother. Still I owe you an explanation and I am obligated both by ethics and law to protect our shareholders. In the light of recent actions on the part of my mother, the president and CEO, I must ask that those titles be transferred to someone else, at least until these distasteful matters are taken care of."

"It takes a pretty big reason to justify such a change." The speaker was a gray-haired man in a suit that would cost most people a month's salary.

"I agree, Mr. Boyd, but since the corporate head of this company is wanted for questioning in a bombing in Fresno, a murder in San Diego, and since she has disappeared—

presumably to avoid the police—we are compelled to act. Who can argue with that? Anyone?"

No one spoke.

"I needn't remind this group that other companies have encountered great legal trouble and even gone under for the misdeeds of their CEOs. I don't want to assume the worst, but I do want to protect this company. Not to act is to appear either ignorant or to be a participant in a coverup. We must do everything possible to show that we are aboveboard and taking care of business. Executives can go to jail too. Shall I recite names of execs in major companies that now receive their mail in a prison inbox?"

Several members of the board grumbled.

The door to the conference room swung open. Jim Gaines entered. Terri Penn was right behind him.

Marlin smiled at Jim but when his eyes fell on Terri the grin evaporated. "It's good to see you, Jim. I was getting worried. We need our company lawyer more now than ever."

"I'm sorry to be late," Jim said to those seated. Marlin noticed that he didn't make eye contact with him. "An urgent matter kept me chained to my desk a little longer than I expected."

"Understood," Marlin said. He then addressed Terri. "Ms. Penn, I'm sorry, this is a closed-door meeting for members of the board."

Gaines walked to the front of the conference table and stood next to Marlin. He held a folder filled with neatly paper-clipped bundles of documents.

Marlin felt threatened. "Um, Jim, there's an empty seat at the other end of the table."

"The CEO usually sits up here."

Marlin gave a patronizing smile. "I'm afraid my mother is still missing in action."

"I wasn't referring to her, Marlin. I'm speaking of Ms. Penn."

"What kind of joke is this?"

"No joke." He opened the thick folder and began to pass around the documents. "Under the direction of Ms. Find, I have drawn up papers appointing Ms. Terri Penn as acting CEO. Included in these papers are documents showing the transfer of all of Ms. Find's stock to Ms. Penn. That stock equals the amount of 53 percent of all stock available. Of course, that makes her majority stockholder."

"Wait a minute," Marlin said. "I happen to know my mother only owns 51 percent of the stock."

"Still, that's enough. I've transferred my 2 percent to Ms. Penn also." Gaines drew himself to his full height and cleared his throat in solemn fashion. "Ladies and gentlemen. It is my honor to introduce the new CEO of Find, Inc."

No one moved.

Terri stepped to the front of the long table and looked Marlin in the eye. Fury boiled in him; fury that grew in intensity when she said, "I believe you're in the wrong seat, Mr. Find. There are some empty chairs at the other end of the table."

Thirty minutes had passed since Terri walked into the conference room. The time was spent discussing the problem of the missing Judith. Ideas were tossed on the table in rapid fashion. Only Marlin remained mute. When all had been said and done, the board agreed that a high-end private detective agency should be brought in to aid in the search if for no other reason than to show that the execs and board took a proactive approach. They also agreed that a complete sweep for electronic devices should be made of the building.

Terri called on the head of communications to prepare several news releases covering different possibilities and have them ready to go ASAP.

As soon as Judith had been gone forty-eight hours, she could be officially declared a missing person. Terri would work with the police on that angle.

Removing Judith as CEO and president had become moot when she divested herself of position and investment. No one challenged the documents drawn by Gaines but Terri knew that Marlin would have several high-powered attorneys go over every word seeking a loophole. Judith could not sign the documents so they had relied on Gaines's power of attorney—a right she had transferred to him a year ago when Marlin began making noise about taking on the president's roll. It granted him the right to act on her behalf should she be disabled by disease, accident, or in case of her absence. Gaines had told Terri that at the time, he thought it was overkill; now he thought differently.

Terri had yet to move from the head of the table. The others left ten minutes before, but Terri couldn't muster the strength to stand. She had never seen herself in the aggressor's role, not even in business. The last few hours—those spent with Gaines in his office and those long minutes in the boardroom—had wrung the last of her strength from her.

"You done good, kid." Gaines spoke softly. "Who knew you had that kind of talent."

"An act. Nothing but an act."

"You deserve an award. If I didn't know better, I'd think you had been doing this for years."

"I feel sick." She laid her head on the table and tried to quiet her stomach.

"Understandable. Can I get you anything?"

"A condo in Hawaii. I promise to return in a couple of years."

Gaines laughed. "That would be nice." He cleared his throat. "Thanks for not asking."

Terri raised her head. "About what?"

"Everwood."

"Oh. Judith ... I mean, Ms. Find—"

"Until Marlin gets Judith's decision overturned, you're CEO. You can call Judith whatever you want."

"She said to remind you of Everwood, but not to ask about it. I guess it's none of my business."

"It's not, but I think you have a right to know. Everwood is a drug rehabilitation clinic in Colorado. It's part of a private hospital outside of Denver. I spent ... some time there."

That made Terri sit up. "I had no idea."

"I can thank Judith for that. Cocaine. I started in law school. It cost me my family and what little fortune I had. It began to impact my work here. It reached a point where she was going to have to fire me. That would have pretty much put an end to everything for me."

"But she didn't?"

"She came down to see me. Marched into my office and unloaded on me with both barrels. That woman could burn down a forest with her words. She knows how to put a mad on."

Laughter rolled from Terri. "That's one way to put it. I always thought of it as the power to peel paint with words. I'm glad I've never been on the receiving end of that."

"Anyway, when she finished ripping me apart she gave me an ultimatum: I would go to a rehab center and do everything I was told, or I could pack my desk in a cardboard box. When I told her I couldn't afford a decent clinic, she promised to pay for it. The next day, I took an extended vacation." He scratched quotation marks in the air when he said vacation. "Those were the longest, darkest, most difficult days of my life. But here I am. I still have a great job, doing legal work which I love, and take one day at a time. I even got my family back."

"She's a remarkable woman."

"I tell you all this so you know about me, and so that you'll know that I will walk on hot coals for that woman."

"Thank you for your honesty. I'm going to need all the support I can get. I'm not cut out for this kind of stuff."

"Don't sell yourself short. You're smarter and stronger than you think. Besides, you have your faith."

Terri looked at Gaines. She couldn't recall ever speaking of spiritual things with him.

He smiled. "Yes, I know all about that. Judith's mentioned it. She admires your commitment."

"Really? I thought it might be a problem for her."

"Your faith makes you what you are, Terri. I don't know much about Christianity—you know that old joke about there not being any lawyers in heaven—but I know it suits you well. When we get through all of this, I hope you'll tell me more about it."

"Thank you," Terri said. "I will."

Karen Rose looked at the lined legal pad and skimmed the hieroglyphics of her handwriting that few could read. In a week, she might have trouble deciphering her pen scratching. She brought her eyes back to the computer screen then back to her notes. Her eyes burned from lack of sleep, her stomach soured from vending machine food and bad coffee, and her spine felt like it was twisting into a corkscrew.

Still, she stayed at her desk as the afternoon sun charted a course for the western horizon.

"You should go home," Dwayne said. "You look like—"

"Don't finish that," Karen said. "I know what I look like."

"What time did you go home last night?"

"Ten, maybe ten-thirty."

"Not too bad. At least you got some sleep." He leaned against the divider that marked off her cubicle.

"I didn't say I rested. I just said I went home. I have a computer and Internet access there too."

"Are you telling me you've been up all night and all of today?"

"Sleep is for the weak." Karen powered down her computer.

"And for the sane." Dwayne frowned. "You're no good to the station in this condition."

"Grab your coat, boss. We're going on a trip."

Dwayne cocked his head to the side. "Usually I'm the one to make assignments."

"Trust me on this." She picked up the phone and dialed.

"And just where am I going?"

Karen ignored the question. "See if you can find Cindy. Tell her to bring her gear."

"I hate playing twenty questions. Who are you calling?"

She stilled him with an upraised hand and spoke into the phone. "This is Karen Rose of KTOT television calling for Detective Ben Wilson. Please tell him this is an emergency."

Dwayne's expression changed from annoyance to puzzlement. He said nothing. Karen watched him jog toward his office.

thirty-nine

Although Terri had told Jim Gaines she didn't need an escort, he insisted. She stepped into the room that had been her office for the last several years and sat in her chair. She felt empty, cored out by mystery and fear.

"I wondered which chair you'd choose."

It took Terri a moment to catch Gaines's drift. "That's still Judith's office. I'm just holding her place." She swiveled her chair and looked through the open door between the two offices. The cleaning crew had done a fine job scrubbing up after the field forensics team, who had blighted the walls, jambs, and other surfaces with fingerprint powder. "This office suits me well, I plan on staying here—"

The phone on her desk chimed. She picked up.

"Ms. Penn, there are some people here to see you." The voice belonged to Darla Allison, first-floor receptionist and keeper of the executive elevator.

"Who?"

"Call me if you need me," Gaines said and started to leave.

"A Ms. Karen Rose and Mr. Dwayne Hastings of KTOT. There's a camerawoman with them. Also—"

"No interviews today, Darla. I just can't fit them in."

"Detective Ben Wilson is with them. He says it's urgent."

Terri blinked hard.

"Ms. Penn?"

"Hang on." Terri lowered the phone. "Mr. Gaines—Jim— you had better stay." She raised the handpiece back up to her ear. "Send them up—everyone but the cameraman."

"Camerawoman."

"Whatever. No cameras. Understood?"

"Yes, ma'am.

Even though she had ensconced herself in the meeting area of Judith's office, Terri could clearly hear the elevator doors open. She forced herself to breathe in measured breaths, taking long slow inhalations and releasing them a moment later. She didn't know why the odd mix of people wanted to see her, but she felt sure her brain would need all the oxygen it could get.

Waiting in the seating area of Judith's office was Gaines's idea. The room had been swept and pronounced clean of listening devices. At the moment, it was the only room in the building that could properly make such a boast. Gaines waited by the elevator. His voice carried through Terri's office and into Judith's.

"I'm Jim Gaines, senior legal counsel to Find, Inc. I understand that you've all already met the company's senior vice president, Mr. Marlin Find."

Pleasantries were exchanged and then they appeared, led by Marlin as if he were conducting a military march. Since Terri assumed the detective had news about Judith, she thought it right to include Marlin. She also hoped keeping him informed would take a few barbs off the ragged edge that had been created between them. She doubted it would, but at least he couldn't complain about being kept out of the loop on matters concerning his mother's welfare.

All the faces were familiar, but one. Just behind and to the right of Karen came a tall man with gray hair, a mustache, and a tiny patch of hair below his lower lip. He introduced himself as Dwayne Hastings, news director at KTOT television. Terri shook their hands, trying to offer a dry and firm palm.

"Please, sit down," Terri said.

They did. Terri took the leather seat Judith used when conducting meetings here. She felt like she trespassed on private ground.

Gaines spoke first. "Just so there's no confusion, Ms. Penn is acting CEO until Ms. Find returns."

"Really?" Karen said. She glanced at Marlin then back to Terri. "I hadn't expected that."

"It's complicated and temporary. Things will return to normal soon." Terri pushed a smile.

"And if they don't?" Dwayne asked.

"Then the board and senior execs will make a decision about permanent leadership of Find, Inc." She let the smile fade. "Did you come here to ask about who's piloting the ship? I'm guessing you didn't."

"No, ma'am," Karen answered. She hesitated and looked around. "I've brought my laptop; is there a way to connect it to the flat screen television? I brought an S-video cable. It should just plug in."

Terri nodded, stood, and made room for Karen to hook up. Within minutes, the connection was made and people had repositioned themselves to get a clear view of the screen.

"Now can you tell me what all this is about?" Terri said. Gaines and Detective Wilson moved Terri's chair to the best spot for viewing.

"Okay, first my confession." Karen spoke as she booted her computer. "A good reporter has a personality fault—she can't let go of things until she feels she has all the answers, and if presented with a mystery ... well, things just get worse. I knew you weren't being forthcoming with me, Ms. Penn."

"I didn't know I was obliged to be."

"You're not, but reporters like me live in a world where we think we are entitled to whatever information we want. We're not, but we act like we are. It's the only way to do our job. Once you put me off, I began to think that something was going on behind these walls. I interviewed Mr. Find and learned a few things, but the mystery continued to grow."

Terri looked at Marlin, who shrugged. "Go on."

"Dwayne and I spoke to one of our counterparts in Fresno. He tipped us off that Ms. Find had been seen at a house that exploded and burned. Well, that's not everyday activity for a wealthy business leader. Then came word about her possible involvement in a murder in San Diego. Murder! Conspiracies, bombings, murder: it's a gold mine for someone like me. But things weren't adding up."

"Like what?" Detective Wilson asked.

"I'll bet this week's salary that you've been wondering the same things." Karen worked the keyboard and mouse and the image of her computer's desktop appeared on the flat screen television.

"Bodies?" Wilson suggested.

"Yeah, bodies. That's a good place to start. In Fresno, a woman's house blows up and burns to the ground. Arson investigators discover enough evidence to know that someone planted an incendiary bomb of some sort. I imagine they're looking the scene over real hard. It's easy to get distracted by something as remarkable as a bomb. We ask, 'Who put it there?' Important question, but just as important is, where are the bodies? No one died in the attack. That's good. But where is the owner? Why hasn't he or she come forward?"

Karen took a breath. "Finding the owner's name was easy. I got it through public tax records then verified it with Fresno police: Ida Palek. I used LexisNexis and other tools to search newspaper articles mentioning her. I only found one, an obituary for her husband. He died less than two weeks ago."

"Her husband dies then someone blows up her home." The thought unsettled Terri.

"Ed Palek, coronary, died in his sleep." She returned her attention to the computer. The obit said he was survived by his wife Ida and their son, Abel, age eight. Where there is a child there is a school record. I contacted the elementary schools in the area and got lucky. He attended Grant Elementary School—for less than one year."

"What?" Dwayne leaned forward. "If he's eight he should be in second or third grade. Right?"

"Something like that," Karen replied. "At first, I thought maybe his parents put him in a private school. Lots of parents do that. I asked who taught his class and then made contact with the teacher. She remembered him. She told me that he was exceptionally bright but a little quirky. He didn't fit in and the other kids were merciless. You know how kids can be."

"So Ida Palek pulled him from the school?" Wilson asked.

"Exactly. But she didn't put him in a private school; she decided to homeschool the boy. That's also big these days."

"What do you mean he was quirky?" Dwayne asked the question.

"First, he showed unusual memory skills. Second, he seemed far more ... spiritual than a child his age should be; third—"

"What does that mean?" Marlin interrupted.

"It means that he seemed sensitive to spiritual things. I can't explain it. I'm not a very spiritual person. The teacher did tell me that Abel would often point at people and say things like, 'He has a lot of truth on him,' and 'He's got lots of evil on him.' She never figured out what that meant and thought he was pretending to have superpowers like kids that age do."

"Some superpower," Marlin said.

Terri wanted to get back on track. "You were going to list a third quirky thing about the boy."

"You know how schools have photography companies come in to take pictures of the kids? The parents buy packets of photos and teachers inevitably get copies from the students as gifts. She had one of Abel, scanned it, and emailed it to me." Karen punched a key on her computer. "This is Abel."

A photo of a dark-haired boy appeared on the screen.

"Look at those eyes." The sight stunned Terri.

"Yeah," Karen said. "No wonder the kids at school gave him a bad time. Anyone who looks different gets picked on. At least that's the way it happened in my school days."

"No wonder his mom decided to homeschool," Dwayne said. "Placing him in another environment would make no difference. Kids would tease him there too."

Marlin shifted in his seat, making no effort to hide his impatience. "What does this have to do with my stepmother? I don't see the point."

"You will, Mr. Find. You will." Karen turned to her news director. "Dwayne, what is it you keep driving home to the young reporters?"

"Dig deeper, then dig some more."

"That's what I did. The police in San Diego want to question Ms. Find about a murder in La Jolla. Now, why would she leave Ontario, fly to Fresno, then to San Diego to kill a man or aid in his killing? Detective, did you do a wants and warrants on Judith Find?"

"I did."

"And you found no criminal record, did you?"

"None. Clean as a whistle."

"I know that anyone can slip a cog and kill someone, but Judith Find seems the least likely person to do so. She has the kind of money to pay someone else to do her dirty business. If she is involved in the man's murder it must be self-defense or her mind snapped."

"I wouldn't dismiss the last option too quickly," Marlin quipped.

"Shut up, Marlin," Terri said.

Karen seized on it. "Has she been acting strange lately, Mr. Find?"

He shook his head no. "I question her judgment all the time, but I can't say she's crazy."

Karen turned to Terri. "What about you, Ms. Penn? Did you see anything in her words or behavior to indicate that something might be psychologically wrong?"

"Not a thing. She seemed as normal as ever."

"Okay, then. That's just one more reason to believe she did not kill the man. I made some calls and I bet Detective Wilson did too. How did Dr. Zarefsky die?"

Wilson took his clue. "I can't go into great detail but I can tell you he took a knife in the back. The homicide detectives found Ms. Find's name scratched into the floor."

"Sounds like a scene from a 1950s mystery movie," Dwayne said.

"That's what the detectives thought," Wilson said. "I spoke with the lead detective on the case and he doesn't think Zarefsky scratched the name in the wood floor."

"Why?" Terri asked.

"Two things. First, Zarefsky bled out pretty bad. He lay in his own blood. If he wrote the name there should have been blood smears around the arm and where his body moved while scratching the name in the floor. They found none of that. The second reason is more basic. They interviewed some of Zarefsky's employees. Typical research. They learned he was a lefty. Ms. Find's name was by his right hand."

"That means she didn't do it," Terri said. For a moment she had a reason to smile but Wilson squashed it.

"Not necessarily. It's not proof. Not yet. It does, however, raise a lot of questions."

Karen took over again. "I did research on the guy. He owns a corporation called Coast Fertility Care Center. It has a number of clinics in Southern California. He's a fertility doctor. He's also part of something called Cal-Genotics, a company that does research in fertility problems."

"What connection would he have with my mother?" Marlin asked.

Karen looked at him. "She's your stepmother, right?"

"Yes."

"Do you know if she ever had children of her own?"

Terri answered. "No. I know she didn't. We've talked about it a couple of times but not in detail. She's a private woman. She, however, did admit to being infertile." Terri remembered the conversation. She also remembered the look on Judith's face.

"Are you saying this Zarefsky guy may have treated my mother?"

Karen shrugged. "I couldn't find evidence of that, but they were connected—connected in a way you won't believe."

forty

"How are you feeling?" Luke slowed the Humvee as he entered the next hairpin turn.

Judith opened her eyes. They felt as gritty as she felt exhausted. "My head hurts, my face is swollen, my body aches, I'm scared to death, and I'm hungry."

"Hungry."

"I think so. It might just be another version of fear. I can't tell." She gazed through the windshield. "You're driving pretty slow."

"This thing isn't a sports car; it doesn't handle all that well around these mountain corners. Besides ..." He trailed off.

"Besides what?"

"We have a little time. Pennington's in a school bus. A speeding school bus would draw a lot of attention and calls to the police. He has to keep it slow. He's going to have more trouble with mountain roads than we are. The question is what to do next."

"We can't let him get away with the kids. Once they're out of the U.S. we'll never get them back. Who knows what they plan to do with them—or to them."

"It can't be good. This whole operation must have cost a fortune. Pennington has broken more laws than I can count. What puzzles me is why a boat? Why not load them on a charter plane?"

"Security concerns perhaps," Judith said. "Flying internationally may require a security check of some kind. Not to mention walking a bunch of kids with purple eyes through an airport terminal might draw unwanted attention."

"They could use a private airport," Luke said. "Maybe you're right. Who knows what their logic is?"

"So, what do we do if we catch up to them?"

"I don't plan to catch them. There's no way we can sneak up on Pennington in this thing. He'd see us a mile off and we don't have time to try and rent another car. San Pedro is a couple of hours away, depending on traffic. Once we hit the freeways, we can make better time than Pennington. Maybe we can get to the dock before him."

"Then what?" Judith rubbed her face. The swelling continued. She fought the urge to pull down the visor and look in the mirror. It couldn't be good. Instead, she looked at Luke again. He looked no better. He had endured two beatings and it showed.

He sighed and chewed his lower lip. "I've been thinking about that. I doubt he plans to sail a boat by himself. That means he'll have help. Frankly, I don't think I can take another beating."

"You've been very brave."

Luke's laughter surprised Judith. "I think you're the first person ever to say that."

"It's true. You rescued Abel and fought to save a bunch of kids you've never met. Most people would have written them off."

"Don't forget. I didn't volunteer, I was drafted—blackmailed."

"What you've done goes beyond that. The Puppeteer sent us to find one boy, not thirteen."

"I guess it doesn't matter at the moment. We had Abel and we lost him. I can't get the image of Ida's battered face out of my head. Pennington didn't need to do that."

"Pennington is a nutcase," Judith said. "He is far from sane."

"He's sane enough to get the job done." Judith closed her eyes again and longed for the deep, soft mattress of her bed. Home seemed a place she lived years ago, yet it had been only two days. "Maybe it's time to call for help."

"Maybe. I know I'm tired of jumping through the Puppeteer's hoops. Pennington is the real threat to Abel and the others. He's the one we have to deal with."

"So we call in the police?"

"Not yet."

The answer surprised Judith. "And why not?"

"Because Pennington has the kids and can hold them hostage. Imagine a police cruiser or highway patrol car pulling the bus over. Pennington has thirteen hostages. I agree that it's time to bring the police in, but we have to time it right. We have to do this in a way that protects the kids, not endangers them."

"So we're going to San Pedro?"

"Yes. Let's get on site and see what we're facing. We can call the police in. Let's make sure we get to the dock before

Pennington. Open the glove box and see if the rental company has a map in there."

"How do you know this is a rental car?"

"Would you use your own car? I doubt Pennington is from around here. According to Vince, Pennington came in by helicopter. I'm guessing he flew in from San Diego after killing Zarefsky."

The mention of Vince saddened Judith and she wondered if the man still drew breath. She forced the thought from her mind and opened the glove compartment.

It held a map.

Terri let the words settle in before asking the question on everyone's mind. "Karen, what do you mean Judith is connected to Dr. Zarefsky? Was he her doctor?"

"No." Karen rubbed her hands. "I'm trying to keep this simple. I've got a feeling it's more complex than any of us realize. This is one of those six degrees of separation things. You know, I've got a sister who went to school with a guy who used to live across the street from Tom Cruise. Given enough layers of connection, anyone can connect themselves to someone else. That kind of thing. This is much tighter than that." Karen keyed her computer again and a web page appeared on the screen.

"This is the Cal-Genotics website and I learned that Zarefsky is . . . was their president and CEO. I wondered what would happen now that he was dead. I ran down a few fertility doctors and asked them about Zarefsky. A couple wouldn't talk to me, one gave me an earful about 'never having opened a book on ethics,' and another told me he couldn't speak about the man because he had brought complaints about Zarefsky's work to the board that certified doctors in his specialty. I did find one doc who didn't mind filling me in on what little he knew. When I asked what would happen to Cal-Genotics now that Zarefsky had been cut out of the picture, he said, 'Nothing.' "

"Nothing?" Gaines spoke for the first time since the meeting began. "They must have a pretty tight contingency plan for the loss of key personnel."

Karen agreed. "That's what I thought, but that wasn't my source's point. He said Zarefsky served as a figurehead. The real decisions were made by a confederacy of several biotech firms. Zarefsky put an American face on a Singapore company."

"Why would an American doctor do that?" Marlin asked.

"Money and freedom," Karen said. "A quick Internet search shows that Singapore is known for biomed research and loose ethical guidelines. Freedom and money."

Terri's frustration grew. "How does this tie Judith to Zarefsky?"

Karen worked the computer and a page with Zarefsky's picture came up. "This is the man's bio page. He took two degrees from Stanford and a business degree from Harvard. During his Stanford days, he worked for and received financial support from a fertility clinic in Palo Alto. I got that last bit of info from my source."

"How does this *source* know that kind of information?" Detective Wilson looked suspicious. "That seems the kind of personal info that people keep under wraps. I doubt Stanford would tell you where one of their students worked and who helped him along his way."

282 / FINDER'S FEE

"That's where luck came my way, or fortune or fate or whatever you want to call it."

"Providence," Terri said.

"If you like," Karen said. "My source went to school with Zarefsky and worked at the same fertility clinic—and so did someone named Judith Maurer." She looked at Marlin. "What is your mother's maiden name?"

Marlin's skin faded a shade whiter. "Maurer. My step-mother went to Stanford? She told me she couldn't afford to attend the better colleges."

"Maybe she couldn't," Karen said. "Zarefsky went to Stanford. That doesn't mean Judith did. There are other colleges in the area. The connection isn't the university but the fertility clinic."

Terri struggled to take it all in. Every bit of information raised more questions than it answered. "Did your source say what Judith did for the clinic?"

"Called her a recruiter. Zarefsky and my source were lab techs. In exchange for their work, they earned some good money, picked up lab skills, and the clinic gave them money for tuition."

"Why do I feel like there's more to this?" Wilson said. "By the way, I'm going to want that source's name."

"We'll argue about that later, Detective," Karen continued. "According to my source, Judith did some office work but spent a good bit of her time as a recruiter."

"Recruiter?" Terri didn't like the sound of the word.

"The clinic paid for eggs."

No one moved. No one spoke.

"Excuse me," Gaines said. "It's the lawyer in me so I need to ask for a clarification. You're not talking about the kind of eggs that make for a good breakfast. You're talking about . . ."

"A woman's eggs. Ova." Karen paused as the words sank in. "Judith Maurer, later Judith Find, was hired to encourage young women to sell their ova."

Marlin rubbed his forehead. "Let me get this right: my stepmother used to approach a woman and say, 'Hey, lady, you want to sell a couple of your eggs?'"

"Nothing so crass. She was one of several recruiters who would select the best and the brightest and offer them money. Most were college coeds and some needed the cash. The clinic also recruited ... um, donations from high IQ men."

"The clinic was experimenting with selective genetics?" Dwayne said.

"Best they could in those days. My understanding is that the science has made great strides since the eighties."

Dwayne had another question. "Didn't someone else try to create high IQ children by selective fertilization? I read something about it. Graham ... Robert Graham? That's it. Didn't he try to improve the human race by preselecting donors for infertile couples?"

"Good memory," Karen said. "In the 1980s he launched the Repository for Germinal Choice. It became known as the Nobel prize sperm bank. He recruited high IQ males to make donations. Several had won Nobel prizes. Graham believed that he could improve the overall level of intelligence of the children born to chosen infertile couples. It's debatable how successful he was."

Emotion boiled in Terri. "You're saying that Judith, while a college student, worked for someone like Robert Graham?"

"According to my source she did," Karen spoke softly. "She worked at the same place as Zarefsky. I can't say she knew him. The timeline is a little muddled. My source thinks Zarefsky left before Judith got there. He wasn't certain."

"Still," Wilson said, "there may be motive."

"Don't be ridiculous, Detective." Terri's words came harsher than she intended. "Judith isn't a killer. And you said that there's reason to believe that someone is setting her up."

"I did, but I'm not allowed the luxury of concrete opinions until all the facts are in. You can bet the San Diego PD feels the same way." Wilson turned to Karen. "Is the clinic still around?"

"No. My source said it went belly-up. I checked news archives and confirmed it. There was a brouhaha in the mid-eighties. The head of the clinic got into deep trouble."

Dwayne asked, "What's his name?"

"Her name," Karen corrected. "Dr. Diane Corvino." She tapped a key and displayed a picture of a severe looking woman with brown hair pulled into a bun. Terri judged her to be in her late forties or early fifties.

Karen continued. "Dr. Corvino took degrees in medicine and genetics. A real rising star, the kind that gets a Nobel prize. Apparently, she was the impatient type, always stretching the limits. Authorities closed her down and brought charges against her."

"For what?" Terri asked.

"She made fertile women infertile. Some complained. Some donors sued. Corvino disappeared at the end of 1985. She hasn't been seen since."

Each revelation dropped on Terri like bricks—no order, no design, just a weight that grew heavier each moment. Missing mother and child, Judith disappearing, a bombed house, a dead doctor, a missing researcher, Judith's office bugged ... Her head began to ache. Yesterday, she was a personal assistant. Today she was interim CEO of her boss's firm.

Nothing made sense.

forty-one

The *Great Divide* rested exactly where Ernie had said it would and Judith had a clear view from her place behind a large metal shipping container. Luke stood beside her. The containers were stacked two high and set in rows forming narrow alleys between them.

Judith knew nothing about boats and sailing but she knew this vessel was huge. It had the feel of a yacht—sleek, white, and gleaming in the sun, but looked like a small version of a cruise liner. The windows in the superstructure—if that's what you called it—were all tinted dark. She could see nothing inside. Beneath *The Great Divide* was painted the word "Singapore." The site of it chilled Judith.

Despite the yacht-like appearance it displayed several differences. Judith had been on several yachts, attending parties held by business associates. Those vessels were long and fairly narrow. This boat, ship, whatever, was much wider than anything she had seen in a pleasure craft. She had heard the term "superyacht," and now she had seen one.

The vessel was impossible to miss. Not just because of its size, but because of where it had been moored. The ship immediately in back of it was a monstrous, ill-colored, battered container ship. Judith assumed the size of the *The Great Divide* prevented it from docking in the nearby marina.

"Wow," Luke said. He had parked in a lot a half mile from the pier, afraid that Pennington would see the vehicle when he arrived and know they were there. Unfortunately, the F Pier street ran right past the lot. Luke had done his best to hide the Humvee behind one of the many eighteen-wheelers that brought containers to the San Pedro Bay for shipping.

They had approached the area carefully, looking for guards and the presence of a school bus. As expected, they had been able to make better time than Pennington. Now the question rested on what to do next. "I don't see anyone guarding the yacht. I was afraid that Pennington might have called ahead."

"And done what? He wouldn't warn them about us. He thinks we're dead. And we know he didn't try to call Ernie because we have Ernie's cell phone."

"And his gun."

"Do you know how to use it?" Judith could see the pistol tucked in the back of Luke's jeans.

"I think I can figure it out." Luke pulled back into the shadow of the orange and blue containers. "I'm at a loss. If Pennington gets the kids on the boat and it sets sail, we may never get them back. We have to either prevent him from loading the kids aboard or somehow prevent the boat from leaving."

Judith's heart slowed as if it had grown too weary to continue beating. "I think it's time." The words came out as a whisper.

"Maybe I could sneak onboard and disable the ship. You know, slip down to the engine room and do something: pull wires, break a fuel line."

"No, Luke, it's time."

"The problem is a boat that size is bound to have several crewmembers. How do I get past them?"

Judith could almost see Luke's mind racing. His head was down, his eyes fixed on something only he could see. He wasn't hearing her. "Luke, you're not listening."

"Maybe the key is finding a way to keep the kids from ever getting on the boat in the first place. Maybe we could—"

"Luke!"

"What?" Startled, he spat the word.

"Listen to me." She stepped closer and placed a hand under his chin as if she were speaking to a child. "It's time we call the police."

"Judith, we've been through this. You're wanted ..."

"It doesn't matter. All that matters is the kids. I didn't kill Zarefsky. I'm sure a good attorney can prove that. I don't matter now. Only them. Do you understand? We can't fight our way onto the ship and we can't stop Pennington from arriving. We have to stop the ship from leaving. That's it. We need help."

"But Pennington can hold the children hostage."

Judith dropped her hand. "I know, Luke. I know. But there is nothing else to be done. It's the only way. It's crossed your mind. I know it. I must make the sacrifice."

"Judith—"

"No. No more talking. Give me Ernie's cell phone. You go back to the Humvee. There's no need for the police to take you."

"I'm not leaving you," Luke said. "Don't bother arguing."

"Sweet as this is, nobody's going to call the cops and the only place you're going is with me."

Judith spun on her heels. An Asian man in white pants, a white button-down shirt, and deck shoes stood at the opening of the alley. He also wore a dark blue coat that was much too heavy for the warm temperatures. His right hand was in the coat pocket. The pocket bulged more than it should. He was holding something.

She snapped her head around. Another Asian man dressed in identical clothes blocked the other end of the artificial corridor. He too had a hand in his pocket.

"You will come with us." The first man demanded.

"And if we don't?" Luke asked. Judith recognized bluster when she saw it.

"Then I will shoot the woman."

"Someone will hear," Judith said.

The man smiled. "Maybe. Maybe not." He addressed Luke. "I'll take that gun now."

Judith felt like wax in the sun. Her strength had left; her will to fight had grown thin and been replaced by weariness. She was too tired to fear.

Judith and Luke followed the man to *The Great Divide*.

"I told you I'd figure out a way to get on the boat." Luke's words were artificially light and devoid of humor.

Terri sat alone in Judith's office and tried to make sense of all that had happened in the last two days. Karen had presented a bulletproof case that Judith was somehow connected to the dead Dr. Zarefsky. That news had hit Terri like a cruise missile. The other news Karen brought had been just as devastating. Sitting in the same casual meeting area where Karen Rose had laid out her case, Terri replayed the information over and over in her mind.

Karen moved the mouse on her computer. "I had to look deeper." A list of names appeared on the screen.

Dwayne was the first to ask. "Who are they?"

"Missing children." Karen muttered the words as if they were painful to say. "I went back to the missing Ida and her son, Abel. I kept wondering why someone would blow up a house, causing it to burn to the ground. To kill someone seems a likely answer, but it is, for lack of a better term, over-kill. Why draw so much attention? Why not just suffocate, or shoot, or poison, or something else? That had me going."

"To get rid of more than a person," Wilson said. "The explosion kills the target, the fire destroys the evidence. It's just a guess at this point."

Karen agreed with him. "I came to the same conclusion. So that got me thinking. Were there any other such cases? I used a media archive retrieval service the station subscribes to and came up with some interesting things. By using several sets of parameters, such as search terms for house fire, bomb-ings, missing children, and so on, I developed a list of poten-tial events that were similar to what happened in Fresno. I found four that were close enough for me to begin making phone calls."

She worked her computer again and the photo of a child appeared, a girl who looked a little younger than Abel. Karen continued. "This is Sarah Thomason of Phoenix, age six. She lived in this house." A photo of a burned-out shell flashed on the screen. "The bodies of both parents were found in the home, but not Sarah's. No one has seen her. The newspa-per that ran the piece included her picture." Another image popped up. It showed a three-story apartment building. Fire-fighters were battling a blaze on the second floor. "Tucson. Again, a man and woman found dead. Neighbors told report-ers the couple had a seven-year-old boy; again, missing." The image of a child who looked much like Abel but thinner in the face looked back at Terri. Like Abel, like Sarah, he had pale lavender eyes. "His name is Jesse Barnett."

Another pair of pictures. "Henderson, Nevada. Explosion. Fire. Two bodies. Missing child—eight-year-old Liza Marshall."

Again photos. "Six-year-old Nelson Vines. His parents also died in an explosion fire."

"This is crazy," Dwayne said.

"I wish I had made it all up." Karen turned back to the group. "I think there may be more. I haven't had time to run everything down. I thought it best to get everyone on the same page."

"Why tell us?" Marlin asked. "This has to be the scoop of your career. Why bother with us?"

Karen looked at Marlin. "Some things, Mr. Find, are more important than career."

Wilson stood. "I've got to make some calls." He pulled his cell phone from his pocket and stepped from the office.

"What I can't figure out," Dwayne began, "is whether Judith Find is part of the problem or one of the victims."

"I can't say," Karen admitted.

Terri had gone numb. Running away sounded so sensible to her. Instead, she asked, "Earlier you said that this woman doctor or researcher or whatever she was, made women infertile. How?"

Karen paused before answering. "When a woman goes in for fertility treatment, the doctor harvests some of her eggs. Usually, then as now, hormones are given to mature the eggs. The doctor then harvests the cells. The same is true for women selling or donating their eggs. Today a woman can make tens of thousands of dollars by selling her eggs. Since a woman produces at least one egg per month, selling or giving away a few shouldn't hurt her chances for children later. Companies advertise in college newspapers because college-age women are younger, healthier, and in greater financial need. Diane Corvino apparently tried new procedures and new medications. Remember, this was over two decades ago. In her zeal, many women were damaged in the process. There were even allegations that she let nonmedical personnel do some of the procedures but that hasn't been proven."

"Am I the only one appalled by this?" Terri asked.

"No. In 2006 a congressional effort to make the selling of eggs illegal was begun. It is illegal in some countries like Great Britain. In our country, there are in the neighborhood of 100,000 egg-harvesting procedures. Not all of those women are selling their eggs. Some are done for infertile couples as part of an IVF procedure."

"You think these children are somehow different, don't you?" Terri stood.

"Aside from the odd eye color and the fact that at least one of them, Abel, is unusually bright, I can't say."

"What does your reporter's instinct say?"

"It says something really weird is going on."

forty-two

Hold 'em." The command came from the first captor they had seen. "He'll be here in a moment."

Judith looked around the room. They had been led up a sturdy metal ramp that bridged the gap between boat deck and concrete pier around the cabin structure and into a large space that nearly spanned the width of the boat. Judith's practiced eye couldn't help noticing that the space was beautifully designed and appointed. In less stressful times she might have taken notice of the furnishings, the carpet, and the wall treatment. At the moment she had trouble looking away from the man with the gun. Once on the monster yacht, he had ceased hiding the weapon.

She didn't know much about yachts but the few times she had attended parties on such vessels she learned that this room was called the salon—the equivalent of a large living room in a mansion. Tinted windows ran the perimeter of the space; the smoke-colored glass complemented teak panels.

Luke moved to the set of windows overlooking the dock area.

"I didn't say you could move." The gunman raised the weapon a few inches.

"Then shoot me. After what I've been through the last two days, you'd be doing me a favor." Luke returned his attention to the window.

Judith joined him. The gunman said nothing.

The tint darkened the view of the outside but the view remained clear. She could see the stacks of shipping containers waiting to be moved to or from the container ships that loaded on this part of the pier. She could see the wide expanse of asphalt they had been forced to walk before being led up the ramp to the yacht. She could also see a bright yellow school bus pull onto the lot and park near the ramp.

Pennington had arrived with the children.

The overpowering sense of helplessness she had been fending off for two days returned with irresistible force. One thought ricocheted in her mind: we failed.

The door to the bus opened and the children filed out in quiet order, like students following a teacher from the classroom to the auditorium. They looked helpless. All separated from their parents; all held in the grip of a man with no conscience. She and Luke were no better off.

Abel stepped from the bus last and took his place at the end of the line. He paused, looked puzzled, then gazed at the window through which Judith gazed as if he knew she was there looking back at him.

One of the men who had taken Judith hostage trotted down the ramp and spoke to Pennington. Pennington gave him a slap on the shoulder. The man stepped to the head of the line of children and led them up the ramp. Pennington followed at the line's end, a step behind Abel.

A set of stairs at the stern side of the salon ran to the lower deck. The crewman at the front of the line made a sharp turn and started down the steps. The children followed. Not one cried. Not one seemed upset or worried. Each child did, however, take the time to look at Judith and Luke.

Judith wanted to run to them, to take each one in her arms, but a man with a gun stood in her way and any confrontation would only endanger the children.

The floor vibrated and a guttural rumble rolled through the yacht.

The engines had come alive. The nightmare grew worse, something Judith didn't think possible. She looked out the window again and saw men removing the mooring lines.

"Not good," Luke said.

Judith had no response.

Pennington appeared at the top of the stairs. Judith felt a fury that came from a dark place in her she didn't know existed. For a long moment, she had the urge to launch herself at the man; to push him down the steps; to strangle him; to find something hard and beat him until he couldn't move.

Pennington paused and then smiled. He walked toward them in casual, easy steps. "Mr. Becker, we meet again."

Luke doubled over as Pennington buried his fist in his belly.

"Don't—"

A backhand quieted Judith and she dropped to the deck.

"I don't know how it is that you are still alive," Pennington spat, "but you have meddled in my affairs for the last time."

Luke straightened the best he could and Judith struggled to her feet.

Pennington smiled again. "I was beginning to think you two were clever; worthy adversaries and all that. Turns out you're just a pair of lucky idiots. You should have hidden the Humvee better."

"Not many hiding places around here." Luke coughed and Judith expected to see blood. Thankfully, she didn't. "Nothing here but open pavement for parking or shipping containers. And just for the record, I did hide it behind an eighteen-wheeler."

"You see, that's the difference between us. I would have known that the truck's driver could return and drive off in his rig. You're not devious enough, Becker. Not by a long shot. Personally, I would have flattened a tire or two on the truck. It takes a long time to get those things changed. But you didn't and I saw the Humvee when I drove by the lot. All I had to do was send a couple of crewmen to find you and bide my time driving in circles until they did. Now, here we are."

"I take it we're going for a little trip." Luke struggled to get his words out. His hands still clutched his stomach. "Say ... to Singapore."

"How do you know about Singapore?" Pennington's smile dissolved.

"My Humvee hiding skills may be weak but I have other talents."

Judith braced herself to see another punch launched at Luke. It didn't come.

"What are you going to do with the children?" Judith tried to sound forceful but to little effect.

"You got the Singapore thing right. I'm going to take the kids on an ocean voyage. This yacht is designed to sail across the Pacific, but most of all, it's designed to stay at sea for long periods of time. When we get close to the island of Singapore we'll take on a few more passengers."

"Who?" Judith pressed.

"People who work for the company that owns this vessel and several others. The people who own the children."

"Own the children? You can't own another person."

"Sure you can. Slavery still exists in some countries, but I'm talking about something else. I'm sure you've noticed the children are different. They're genetically engineered or so I'm told. As such, they are as much product as people."

"Engineered for what?"

"I don't know. I'm not a scientist. I just work for those who are."

"What are their plans?" Luke finally lowered his hands.

Pennington shrugged. "Beats me. They hire me and pay my exorbitant fee and I do what I'm told. Then I disappear for a long time. With what I'm making on this gig, I may disappear forever."

"You don't care what happens to the children?" Judith couldn't believe what she had just heard.

"In a word, no. I don't care one bit. I only care what happens to me."

"What do you plan to do with us?" Luke asked.

"Ah, the movie question."

Judith didn't understand. "Movie question?"

"In the movies, the abducted always ask something like, 'What are you going to do?' Dumb question. No one in that situation really wants to know. They're just buying time. But since you ask: I plan to get rid of you once and for all. When we're out of sight of other vessels, you're going for a swim. Having you around dead or alive is a problem. Dead bodies are annoying in so many ways."

"You plan to throw us overboard," Luke said.

"You are bright. Of course, I'll have to weight your bodies. I can't have some current carrying your corpses to shore. If you're nice to me, I might suffocate you before putting you over the edge." He turned to the gunman. "Take them below and lock them away."

forty-three

The room reminded Judith of those found on cruise liners, small and packed tight with a single bed, a short dresser, a mirror, and a bathroom. One difference stood out. The lock on the door operated from the outside.

"It's like they were planning for us to be here." Judith looked at the doorknob.

"Not us, the kids." Luke worked his way around looking in every drawer, behind anything that would move, even removing the lightbulb from the lamp on the dresser. "This operation has been planned to the smallest detail. My guess is that some of the kids were supposed to be locked in here. They must have doubled them up in one of the other staterooms."

"Can this boat really make it all the way across the Pacific? I thought you needed a big ship for that kind of voyage."

"Much smaller vessels cross the oceans all the time. Columbus's ships were quite a bit smaller than this thing." Luke stood on the bed and removed the diffuser over the ceiling light and studied the bulbs and wires. Judith didn't need to ask what he was doing. She no longer thought his paranoia was misplaced.

It took another fifteen minutes for Luke to satisfy himself that no listening devices or spy cameras were in the room. "I'm not surprised," he admitted. "They wouldn't need to listen in on the children and they didn't know that we would be ... joining them."

"How much time do you think we have before ... you know?"

"We sleep with the fishes?"

"Not funny."

"Sorry, humor is my last resort of sanity." He sat on the edge of the bed. "Not long. The engines don't sound like they're laboring and the boat's motion indicates that they're pulling through the harbor at a leisurely pace. I imagine there's some kind of speed limit for ships entering and leaving port. They're too smart to draw attention to themselves by plowing through the water faster than they should." He worked his lips as he thought. "Pennington won't do anything until we're well out of port. The boat is pretty stable right now, so we must still be in the calmer waters of the bay. We should be able to tell the difference when we hit open water."

A long but narrow window was in the outboard bulkhead, the side of the room where the bed sat. Luke stood on the bed and looked out. "I can still see the shore. We can't be more than a mile out yet."

"But every minute puts us further away." Judith stepped on the bed and took a look for herself. It brought her no comfort.

Luke sat on the bed again. Judith joined him. "This is as bad as it gets." He lowered his head into his hands. "I can't think. I'm out of ideas."

Judith put a hand on Luke's knee and squeezed gently. "We can't give up now, Luke. We've found a way out every time. I thought everything was over when Ida's home went up but you pushed along. We got past Pennington in La Jolla and in the Ridgeline camp. Every time we faced the impossible something right happened. We did what we had to do. Now we have to do it again. The first thing we have to do is get out of here. Everything hinges on that."

"Easier said than done … What did you say?"

"I said we have to get out of here—"

Luke's head snapped up. "No, you said everything hinges on us getting out." He stood. "Morons," he whispered and stepped to the door. Keeping his voice low he said, "You can reverse a lock on a door, but it's much harder to reverse the hinges. I need something strong and narrow; something like a nail."

"Where are we going to get a nail?"

"We're not, but we might find something similar. Start looking."

Judith stood and glanced around the room. The decor was plush but she saw nothing that could be used as a tool. She had to think outside her normal perceptions. *Stop seeing what is and see what can be.* "The bathroom."

Judith led the way and the two crammed themselves in the small space. Judith forced her eyes to trace the objects before her: toilet, small shower, lavatory ... "The sink."

"What about it?"

She reached for the rod that worked the sink's stopper. "There's a rod that works a device on plumbing below the sink." She pulled it up. "It's an old and proven system. We have a line of faucets and we worked hard to move away from this system; it's too old-fashioned for us."

"Fortunately, these people haven't caught up to you." Luke dropped to his knees, grunting as he did. The pain on his face reminded Judith that the poor man had taken two beatings. This posture had to set every nerve on fire.

"Let me do it."

"I'm already here." He opened the cabinet. "I see the plumbing. Typical P-trap. Almost everything is plastic."

"PVC," Judith said. "Can you see the plunger rod?"

"Yeah, but it's not a rod, it's a strap. It won't work. Too wide."

"Wait a sec. Let me think. It's been over a year since I looked at the designs. I wanted to change everything but my advisors reminded me that below the sink everything works pretty much the same." She closed her eyes. "Okay, what you're seeing is the adjustment strap. It has a series of holes, right?"

"Right."

"Okay, the pop-up rod attaches to the strap at the top. You might have to feel for it, but there should be a set screw that holds the rod to the strap."

Luke grunted. "Man, this hurts."

"Want me to do it?"

"No. That would get me kicked out of the male chauvinist country club." He groaned. "My side feels like it's on fire ... found it."

"You'll have to loosen it."

"The head of the screw is knurled. I was ... ow ... afraid that it would need a screwdriver of some sort."

Three painful grunts later, Luke pulled his hand from beneath the counter, a screw in hand. "We got lucky. It wasn't that tight."

Judith saw blood oozing from Luke's fingers and it shredded her heart. She reached for the plunger rod behind the faucet spout. It came free easily. In her hand she held a chrome rod about six inches long.

Helping Luke up, Judith waited for him to catch his breath and for his pain to settle. Perspiration dotted his forehead. The job might have been easy for a man not beaten into unconsciousness earlier that day.

"I don't know how all this is going to end, Luke, but I want you to know, you're the bravest and noblest man I have ever met." She kissed him on the cheek. To her surprise, he blushed.

He pushed away from the lavatory and Judith noticed that he carried his arm across his chest. He didn't say so, but she could see that the injured ribs had been damaged even more.

At the door, Luke placed the blunt end of the rod beneath the pin on the top hinge. There were three hinges, smaller than those found in a home but still large enough to require a pin for setting. He paused then stepped away from the door.

"What's wrong?"

"I need a minute." He looked at the door. His breathing came in gulps. A full minute passed before he spoke again. "There may be a guard on the other side of the door. We're going to have to work quietly and be ready to fight should he come barreling in. I'd feel better if we had some kind of weapon."

"Like what?"

"Cattle prod, machine gun, bazooka. I'll take anything right now."

forty-four

I don't want to be morose but this is going to be our last chance." Luke looked into Judith's eyes and for a moment it seemed her insides were trying to rearrange.

"I know." It took a moment for her to realize it, but Judith worried more for Luke than herself.

"There's a good chance that by breaking out we are going to get ourselves killed."

Judith pursed her lips. "If we don't get out, Pennington is going to kill us anyway. I think I'd rather die on the boat than under it."

Luke nodded slowly. "We don't have much time, but maybe I should take a moment to tell you my secret. After what we've been through, you have a right to know."

Judith raised a finger and put it to his lips, silencing him with a gentle touch. "Not now. It doesn't matter, anyway."

"It might. I could be a cannibalistic ax murderer."

"You're not," Judith said.

"How do you know?"

"Because Abel says there's truth in you and that's good enough for me."

"Okay, but this is probably the only chance you'll have to hear it." He stood.

Judith placed a hand on each side of his head. He winced when she touched the knot left by Pennington but didn't pull away. She drew him close and kissed him. Their lips touched for only a second but it seemed to Judith to contain a lifetime of pleasure and an encyclopedia of communication.

He returned the kiss, then turned his face to the door. "I'm ready. If we manage to get out and get past the guard if there is one, we should split up."

"Is that wise?"

"I don't know how large the crew is. My guess is that it's small. Fewer mouths mean less talking about secrets. I'm hoping that's the case. We have two things to achieve. First, we have to signal for help and I think I know how to do that."

"Won't the radio be where the people are? You're in no condition to fight your way past them."

"You're right. I'd have to subdue them; I don't think I'm the man for that job. But I have another idea. When we were looking at the ship, I noticed what looked like a dinghy. That got me thinking. What happens if they have to abandon ship? They won't want to be in a dinghy with an outboard motor. Not in the open ocean. I think ships this size have modern life rafts."

"I didn't see a life raft."

"You wouldn't. It's probably in some large container. It would have to be easy to get to and open, as well as launch.

It's probably at the back end of the yacht. A ship this size needs a way to get passengers and crew back and forth to shore in shallow waters—that's what the dinghy is for. Maybe they call it a tender. I don't know. The life raft is meant to keep people alive in rough seas for several days. It must carry some electronic communications and maybe even an emergency beacon."

"Makes sense. So you're planning to activate the beacon?"

Luke shrugged. "It's the best I can come up with. We can't go toe-to-toe with these guys. If I can get the beacon activated then the Coast Guard will pick up the automated signal. If there's no beacon, maybe I can use the emergency radio. There has to be some electronics on that thing. I wish I knew more about this stuff."

"What should I do?"

"I'd like to disable the engines, but I don't know if you can do that."

"I can try. What would I need to do?"

Luke thought. "I'm sure they're diesel engines. The way to kill any engine is to deprive it of fuel, air, or disrupt its electronics."

"Will there be someone in the engine room?" Judith tried to imagine herself creeping through a massive, oily engine room like those she'd seen in movies.

"I doubt it. This is a superyacht but I doubt they have men stoking boilers or oiling machinery like old ships. My guess is that you'll find a room with a couple of big diesel engines. Everything is controlled from the bridge above."

She bit her lip. "I'll do what I can."

"I know. It's all we can do." Luke started to the door but Judith grabbed his elbow.

"Do you believe what Abel said ... back in the hotel, I mean."

Luke looked puzzled.

"Wait on the Lord and He will save you. Remember. He said it was in the Bible."

"Are you suggesting that we do nothing?"

"No, he said waiting wasn't doing nothing; it was doing something. I think I have that right. Abel seemed so certain about it. At first, I thought he was just quoting something he read. After all, he said there was a Bible in the room. I assumed he had been reading it, but now I'm wondering if he has more up his sleeve. He is so ..."

"Spiritual?"

"That's it," Judith said. "Terri's tried to talk to me about faith and about Jesus many times, but I keep putting her off. Now, I wished I had listened."

"Somehow, I think God knows."

"Do you really think that?"

"I feel it as much as I think it." He took her in his arms.

"Can we pray?" she asked.

"I don't know how."

Judith stopped fighting the tears. "Me either, but I feel the need to try."

She felt his head touch hers. "Okay."

To Judith's surprise, the hinge pins came out easily. Maybe because the doors were thinner than those in a home, maybe because the superyacht was well taken care of; whatever the reason, Luke had been able to use the metal rod pulled from the sink to push the pins free of the hinges.

After setting the pins aside, Luke pressed the rod into the space between the jamb and the edge of the door and used it as a lever to pry the door free on one side. The door fit snugly and Luke had to work the rod several times to get the hinge side free. With his right hand on the doorknob he quietly pulled the door free and set it aside.

Judith could see beads of sweat on the back of Luke's neck. She didn't know if it was from the work or from fear or pain. In the end, it didn't matter. She stepped close to him as he peeked into the corridor that ran by the door. The passageway ran two-thirds of the length of the cabin deck. When they had descended from the salon above, they first entered a smaller salon similar to the one above but more intimate. The rest of the deck had staterooms on either side of the corridor.

"No guard," Luke said. "Of course, where can we run? I don't think they consider us a problem any longer."

"Let's prove them wrong."

Luke stepped from the room and Judith followed. She looked up and down the passageway and wondered which room or rooms the children were in. It was a question she'd have to answer later—if there were a later.

Judith followed Luke who came to an abrupt stop at the foot of the stairs that led to the salon above. He tilted his head as if straining his ears to hear a distant sound. Then he looked up the circular stairway. He motioned for her to go around him and the steps, to the other side of the stairs, which led to the lower deck.

The time had come to part company. She took his hand and gave it a squeeze, inhaled a bushel of air, and moved.

Luke tiptoed up the steps, fearing several of the crew might be waiting for him in the salon. If such was the case, then his plan was dead before it had a chance to live. Slowly he slipped up the steps. He heard no voices; heard no movement. Fighting fear that made his hands shake and acid boil in his stomach, he emerged, his eyes looking for any movement. He saw none.

Where is everyone?

He looked through the open doors of the salon and at the stern deck. Lounge chairs sat empty waiting for passengers who would never come. This wasn't a pleasure cruise. He doubted there would be much sunbathing going on.

A voice trickled into his ears. He tensed. It came from above. While studying the yacht from the pier he had seen a superstructure he took for the bridge. He listened carefully. There wasn't much conversation but enough for Luke to guess that at least two people were manning the controls. Most likely one was Pennington and the other one of the two who had captured him and Judith.

Returning his gaze to the deck again, he easily identified the dinghy, a rigid hull inflatable. He doubted that had what he needed. He had to find where the life raft would be stowed. The superyacht looked like it could hold twenty plus people. Did they make rafts that large? Would there be more than one emergency raft?

Something caught his attention. To either side of the deck were white, rounded fiberglass containers that reminded Luke of fuel tanks. But they couldn't be fuel tanks—not on the main deck. He moved closer and his mind raced with hope. Each had writing on it and a nylon strap encircled the capsule-shaped containers. EMERGENCY FLOTATION. The words looked painted in gold to Luke. All he had to do was open the large canister and find the emergency beacon. That required stepping into view.

There was no other way.

He slipped through the doors and looked up at the bridge. He saw no one but knew at least two men were there. He couldn't turn back. The odds of his success were miniscule but they were the only odds he had.

The strap, a two-inch wide nylon belt with a metal clasp like those used on seat belts decades ago, came off easily. He set it down at his feet. The container had two handles locking the top half to the bottom. Releasing them he pried open the top and peered inside. He couldn't make sense of what he saw. Maybe if he had thrown back the lid he could better see the folded mess of what looked like canvas, rubber, and other materials. He did find something else: a rectangular nylon bag with strap handles. Printed on the side were the words "Abandon Ship Bag."

He removed it, lowered the lid, picked up the strap, and eased his way back into the salon. He had an idea and glanced around the room. On the inboard side was a bulkhead with a narrow door. A man/woman symbol told him it was the room he was hoping to find. A few moments later, Luke had locked himself in the head.

Setting the bag on the small sink he pulled open the zipper that kept the contents inside. The bag opened into two parts with pockets. Some things he recognized easily: flashlight, signal mirror, can opener, whistle, extra batteries, something that looked like a collapsible drinking cup, patches he assumed could be used to repair the inflatable part of the raft, and a few items that were foreign to him. He also found a yellow electronic device with an antenna. Printed on the front was a brand name and EPIRB in large letters.

EPIRB?

He turned it over and read. "Emergency Position Indicating Radio Beacon."

"Bingo," he whispered. He found the switch and turned it on. A light on the case began to strobe. Luke set the device down. Something else had captured his attention: three orange-topped cylinders marked "Smoke Signals—1 Minute." He slipped them in his pocket. He allowed himself a moment's hope, a hope that melted when Luke heard the rumble of the engine increase and felt the yacht gain speed.

They were headed for open water.

forty-five

Judith moved down the stairs, forcing herself to take careful steps. In an ironic emotional turn, she felt the urge to throw caution out and simply run to the engine room for all she was worth. Instead, she ignored her emotion and fear-fueled desire and moved as smoothly and quietly as possible.

She had no idea where she was going. She followed instinct and some bit of logic that said the engine room would be in the back of the boat. After all, wouldn't a designer want to put the engines near the propellers? It made sense to her. To her surprise, she found it faster than expected. Someone had even provided a nice sign that read ENGINE ROOM; probably to keep passengers from entering.

Luke filled her mind. In one sense, he was close, just two decks above; in another sense, he was miles away. Everything he said made sense. Splitting up was the right thing to do but she didn't like it. If she was going to die today, she'd rather not do it alone and down here.

"Please, God. Let the room be empty." She turned the doorknob and it twisted easily. She stepped in. Alone. Two large engines filled the small space, one on either side of a metal grate walkway that ran between the noisy behemoths. Closing the door behind her, Judith moved along the metal walk uncertain what to do next. She could feel the steady vibration of the engines through her feet. An aluminum safety rail separated her from the mechanics. She could easily reach over it and assumed they were there to keep a workman from falling from the deck into the rolling seas.

"Now what?" she said, but the noise made it impossible to hear herself. What had Luke said? A person could stop an engine by depriving it of fuel, electricity, or air. She assumed by electricity he meant something like spark plugs. No, diesels didn't have spark plugs. She heard that somewhere. Nonetheless, they had to have some kind of circuit to run. For the first time in her life, she wished she was a mechanic rather than an interior designer.

She continued to study the stupefying mess of hoses, metal lines, and wires having no idea what any of them did. "This is hopeless."

Something moved.

The engines rumbled louder and Judith felt herself leaning against the acceleration. They were speeding up and she knew that couldn't be good. They must have left the bay.

What had moved? A wire. A thick wire—cable might be a better word. It moved and the speed changed. A throttle cable? She studied the cable and the L-shaped metal bracket it was attached to. The cable emerged from a protective sheath and attached to one end of the L-bracket, the other end was attached to a thick spring. *They push a lever upstairs, a cable gets pulled down here, and more fuel is sent to the engine. Cut the cable and the spring pulls the L-thingy shut. Maybe. It's a place to start.*

Easy in concept but how could she cut the cable? And if she couldn't do that, how could she disconnect it? Cutting was preferable; it would take longer to fix. "There's got to be a toolbox. No one spends millions on a boat like this and not put a few tools on it."

She found a large red metal tool chest at the back of the room. It was bolted to the deck and bulkhead. It had a dozen drawers. She pulled on one but it didn't open. Locked. No. She fingered the drawer pull again and jiggled it. Nothing. She pushed it in and then pulled and the drawer slid open easily. *I guess it's not good to have drawers of tools opening by themselves in rough seas.*

She found a pair of wire cutters and for a moment thought she could cut the cable but the pliers-like tool seemed too small. She doubted she had the hand strength to pull it off. She needed something bigger. The search continued until she reached the bottom drawer and found a small pair of bolt cutters. They were twelve inches long and had padded handles. They were smaller than she expected but much larger than the wire cutters. They would do.

Judith closed the drawer and returned to the diesels.

"Time to ruin someone's day."

Luke would have been happy to hide in the salon head until help arrived, but he had Judith and the kids to think about. Hiding the satchel next to the toilet, Luke slipped from the bathroom, the emergency smoke markers in his pocket.

The salon remained empty and he relaxed for a moment. Now to find Judith.

"Where is it?" A horribly familiar voice.

Luke turned to see Pennington, gun in hand.

"Lose something?"

"You're about to lose your life." Pennington took a step closer.

"You keep saying stuff like that. No wonder you don't have friends."

Pennington chuckled. "I've killed quite a few people, and every once in awhile I get someone like you who thinks he's funny. Now where is it?"

Luke shrugged. "You'll have to be more specific."

"The Coast Guard just put out a bulletin for all craft to look for a vessel in distress. It seems they've received a signal from an emergency beacon and the GPS signature puts it in our area. I had to tell them that it was a faulty unit."

"And you feel bad for lying."

"Not at all, but if I don't silence the thing, we'll be paid a visit from some folks I don't want to see." Pennington looked at the door to the head. "You stow it in there?"

Luke said nothing.

"Go get it."

"No, thanks. Do your own retrieving."

The yacht slowed and the subtle rumble of the engines quieted. Pennington looked puzzled.

"It's hard to get a good superyacht these days." Luke started across the salon.

"Don't move."

"Shoot me, pal. I'm beyond caring." Luke strode to the open doors that led to the open deck. He put his hands in his pocket.

A bullet whizzed by his ear followed by the loud report of the gun.

Luke sprinted forward.

Another shot.

Judith had made only three steps away from the engine room when the sound of a gunshot pressed its way down to the lower deck. She ran to the stairs, sick with apprehension. As she pushed through the next deck she passed a man in the same white uniform worn by the two who had held them at gunpoint. He ran toward the stairs.

She didn't hesitate. To do so would put her within reach. No longer concerned about the noise she moved as quickly as she could, feet pounding the stairs.

"Come here!"

Judith ignored him but she did come to a stop the moment she cleared the steps and entered the salon.

Fire?

How the second shot had missed, Luke couldn't be sure and he felt no compunction to give it much thought. He had other things on his mind. The first smoke signal device ignited on the first try and Luke threw it into the salon. Designed to produce thick, billowy orange smoke the device filled the space, engulfing Pennington. Luke drew another from his pocket, set it off, and tossed it into the dinghy. An orange plume crawled through the air. A quick look told Luke that several ships and sports craft were in sight and if he could see them, they could see smoke.

"Hey!"

Luke spun and saw a uniformed man on the deck of the bridge. He was running to a chrome ladder that spanned the main deck from the upper deck and bridge. Luke removed the third smoke signal stick, struck it, and tossed it at the man, not to hit him, but to give him another problem to deal with.

Coughing to his left made Luke snap around. Pennington ran through the opening and into the clean air. He still held the gun but had yet to spy Luke.

Luke charged.

The man behind Judith emerged, seized her arm, then froze as he saw the orange smoke. "What?"

Judith pulled free, turned, and shoved as hard as she could. The sailor backpeddled two steps and fell back down the circular stairs. She ran through the smoke toward the sunlight and arrived in time to see Luke run by, shoulders lowered. She heard the impact before her mind could process what she saw.

There was a thud, an "oof," and another thud.

The smoke stung Judith's eyes and she wiped at them, trying to clear her vision. Eyes still blurry, she could see Luke drive Pennington into the side rail. The man doubled over but for less than a second. He straightened and in the same motion brought a hard backhand across the side of Luke's head. Luke's legs looked like rubber but he remained on his feet.

Pennington's gun came up and leveled at Luke's head. "No!"

A thunderous thumping pounded from overhead. Pennington looked up. Judith started to follow his gaze but instead kept it on Luke, who delivered one punch, a punch with every ounce of his weight in it, a punch that struck Pennington on the chin.

Something snapped in Luke's hand, a knuckle, a finger, something impossible to identify because of the fire that raged up his wrist and arm. Even his shoulder hurt. The pain vanished for a moment as he saw Pennington's eyes glaze and his knees buckle. He folded to the deck.

"Ow, ow, I broke something ... Look out!"

Luke was clutching his wrist when he shouted a warning and pushed her to the side.

The loud pop made Judith duck and cover but she still saw Luke stagger, clutch his stomach, and fall facedown. Blood oozed from him and stained the teak deck.

"Luke! Luke." She ran to him. Knelt by him.

"Back up, lady."

Judith didn't. She struggled to roll him on his back. He coughed. He moaned. She pulled at his shirt.

"I said, back away, lady, or you'll get the same thing."

Judith refused to move. Luke's eyes closed. Waves of sorrow rolled from her.

The thunder continued, louder and louder. The gunman swore.

"*Great Divide*, this is the U.S. Coast Guard. Lower your gun."

Judith looked up and saw the white-and-orange Coast Guard helicopter overhead. A motion off the stern also caught her attention. A Coast Guard cutter was bearing down on them. "If you're going to shoot me, you had better do it now. I think your time just ran out."

The gunman's eyes grew cold and he started to raise his weapon.

"And what about the kids," she added. "You going to kill them? Are you going to be the one who goes down in history as killing two adults and thirteen children?"

"I'm a citizen of Singapore. Your laws don't apply to me."

"Wanna bet?"

Three other men appeared on the deck. One surveyed the situation and stepped to the gunman. "Don't make things worse." He took the gun.

Judith looked at Luke, bent, buried her face in his chest, and wept.

The darkness around Luke seemed warm. He could hear thunder in the sky and people talking but none of it made sense. He also felt something touch his chest and heard sobbing. Why, he wondered, was Judith so sad? His pain had disappeared.

The darkness got darker.

He was dreaming again. He seldom repeated dreams but the one from last night had returned. He lay on the ground, wounded, and the children stood around him. The dream was blurry this time and filled with noise.

He saw Abel.

Abel smiled.

Luke rose into the air.

The few miles' trip back on the Coast Guard boat was the longest Judith had ever taken.

What followed were endless questions from the Coast Guard, police, FBI, and others. She answered the best she could, but worry over Luke's life, the stress of two days of fear and mystery, a beating, and more had fogged her mind. She did the best she could, telling what she knew and revealing what she didn't. By late evening, with Jim Gaines there to help, she had answered every question, including those asked by San Diego homicide detectives who had driven up to press her for answers.

No charges were brought but every agency said there would be more questions. She didn't doubt it. The hands of the clock moved past midnight before she made it to the hospital, her swollen face making her look more like patient than visitor. Judith learned that Luke was in surgery.

She waited, Gaines and Terri by her side. Terri had driven in with Gaines and tolerated hours of waiting while Judith endured a seemingly endless interrogation. At the hospital, Judith passed the time listening to Terri tell of all that happened at Find, Inc.

At 2:00 a.m., Judith, against her wishes, fell asleep in her chair.

At 4:00 a.m., she received word that Luke would live but that he had some long days ahead. Judith determined she would make those days as easy as possible.

Then her mind turned to the children.

epilogue

One year later

Luke sat at a picnic table playing chess with Abel. He held his head low, shifted in his seat, then scratched his head. Abel must be winning again. Judith stepped from the refurbished dining hall with a pitcher of lemonade in one hand and a bowl of ice in the other.

The month of May brought an early summer to Ridgeline. Although not nearly as warm as the air in Ontario, it was still warm enough to justify the lemonade. She walked slowly down the stairs and across the finely manicured grounds. Even though he had his back turned to her, she could see how much he had improved over the last twelve months. The weight he lost from his injury and subsequent surgeries had finally returned. She had thought him thin the first time they met, but he had grown skeletal after his injuries.

The battle had been a long one for him. The bullet had struck him in the abdomen and exited his back. By the grace of God it had missed spine and aorta, but it had done enough damage. Twice, she had been told, his heart stopped. Twice he had been revived. Even a year later, one of Judith's saddest memories was watching him rise from the deck on a metal stretcher and be swallowed by the Coast Guard helicopter.

It had taken three months to make the formerly Manna Creek Christian Camp livable again, and another nine months to expand it with better housing for the children and caretakers as well as a top-of-the-line security system. Pennington and some of his crew had been taken out of the picture, but the people who hired him still slept snug in their beds, no doubt dreaming of new ways to get what they wanted.

As Judith set the lemonade down on the picnic table, Luke said, "Don't ask."

"I don't need to. Abel always wins."

She looked around the camp and felt a sense of achievement greater than anything she had felt before. Some of the children played ball in the field; others played by the creek;

still others read in the shade of trees. It was Saturday and they were free to do what children do. Judith could also see several caregivers watching the children; several other men and women moved along the tree line across the field and moved through other areas of the camp. They were the private security hired to keep the next Pennington at bay.

After the incident on the yacht, authorities took the children into protective custody, then farmed them out to foster parents—a situation Judith considered intolerable. She put Gaines to work, who with the aid of a hand-chosen legal team, began to plead the children's case—all but one now orphans.

Legal matters were still pending, but they had achieved their goals. The idea came from a slowly recovering Luke. "They're special kids, Judith. They need a special place to grow up and we're in a position to make that happen."

The sight of it all was as beautiful as it was costly. Luke and Judith poured much of their personal wealth into the camp's renovation and the hiring of the best teachers.

The sound of an approaching vehicle caused Judith to turn. A limo, long and white, rolled slowly along the small parking lot. A Jeep Cherokee with the words SECURITY painted on the doors escorted the limo. Judith had been expecting it. Security had called a few minutes before.

The limo stopped and the driver exited, stepped to the back door, and opened it. Slowly, an elderly woman wearing an ankle-length white dress exited. She paused to gain her balance then straightened. Standing by the open door, the woman gazed around the camp and smiled. Then, with the help of a cane in one hand and the support of her driver, she walked toward the picnic table.

Judith glanced around the camp and could see that the other security personnel had noticed the arrival. Judith then looked at Abel and raised an eyebrow.

"Mostly truth. New truth. Lot's of old evil."

Judith had come to understand the strange speech. Abel and the other children could see what others could not, the nature of the soul—more accurately, the intent of the soul. Abel had just told Judith that the woman had done evil things in her life but had changed. He and the other children distinguished between the "truth" and "The Truth." The former referred to their intent, the latter to the giver of truth, Jesus— the Way, the Truth, and the Life.

Abel had become Judith's and Luke's teacher in many ways. Judith had never realized how often Jesus used the word "truth" in His ministry. He claimed to be the Truth, prayed His disciples would be sanctified in the truth, promised the spirit of truth, and scores of other references. Abel had also taught them that truth was not relative or subjective. Truth came from the Truth. Abel didn't use those terms, but he got the idea across.

After almost a year with the children, Judith still had many questions and sought answers diligently, but despite their great wisdom and insight into human nature, the kids were still kids, unable to explain everything they experienced. To top that, they seemed to be changing in subtle ways. Judith doubted she had seen the end of their remarkable nature.

"Checkmate," Abel said.

"What?" Luke studied the board. "I just wanted you to feel good about yourself."

"Yeah. Right. Sure. Whatever you say." Abel giggled.

"Don't you ever lose?" Luke asked.

"Sure. Eva beat me yesterday."

Luke frowned. "Eva is two years younger than you. Somehow, that doesn't make me feel any better. Go play."

"I'm going to go help Mom. She's baking cookies."

Abel disappeared into the dining hall. Ida would love the help. She lived at the camp, working as one of the cooks, a job she seemed to be enjoying.

"May I sit?" The elderly woman stood by the picnic table.

"Yes, please," Judith replied. "Would you like a chair?"

"The bench will be fine. I won't be long." The driver helped the woman lower herself. She dismissed him with a wave and he returned to the limo, taking his seat behind the wheel.

The woman looked vaguely familiar but Judith couldn't place her. Luke, however, looked stunned.

"Thank you for seeing me," the woman said, her voice worn by years of life. "I'm sorry I couldn't give you more warning."

"You told security at the gate that you had information about Abel." Judith sat and poured three glasses of lemonade. One she placed in front of the woman who took a courtesy sip and set it down.

"Dr. Corvino?" Luke whispered the question. "Diane Corvino?"

Judith stiffened. Luke was right. So many years had passed and the woman had aged so much that she didn't recognize her. When Judith had last seen the woman, the scientist's hair had been chestnut brown, her skin smooth, her blue eyes bright. The woman on the bench looked nothing like that now.

"Yes, Luke. I'm Dr. Corvino."

"Wait." Judith turned to Luke. "You know her?"

He nodded. "Many years ago. When I was a graduate student."

Corvino's smile was window dressing. "Am I to assume that you have not exchanged your secrets?"

Judith's mind began to spin. Missing pieces of the story were swirling in her head like leaves in a tornado. "No. We no longer believe our past matters."

Nodding, Corvino said, "It doesn't, but knowledge of it might be helpful. You deserve the truth." She chuckled then coughed hard. "Have you heard that word much lately? The word 'truth,' I mean."

"All the children talk about seeing truth and evil." Luke seemed edgy.

"I hadn't expected that. Actually, I hadn't expected much of what has happened. The problem with being told you're smart, that you're a pioneer, is you begin to believe it. That ruined me in many ways."

"I don't understand," Judith admitted.

"I don't have much time, so let me explain, then I will leave you to this Eden you've created." She closed her eyes as if imagining events of decades before. "I imagine you're starting to suspect that I am the one who set you off on your journey. I am the one who sent you the phones; the one who drafted you."

"You?" Judith made no effort to hide her disbelief. "It was a man's voice ..." She caught herself. "The voice was electronic. I started thinking the Puppeteer was male and never challenged my assumption."

"Puppeteer?" Corvino chuckled again. "I like that. Very creative. Yes, the voice was a fabrication, a simple electronic voice that can be bought on the Internet. The electronics were not that sophisticated and I hired a good computer genius to pull it all together."

"And my cell phone service being interrupted?" Judith pressed.

"Same computer genius. He's a kid, really. He hacked the system. That's what he called it, hacking. I paid a lot of money so he could hire someone within the cell phone firm to help him pull it off. That's the thing about this world. There's always someone who can be bought because of their greed or because of some great need. Money still makes things happen. I imagine it always will. I also hired a man to make sure the packages were delivered, including the one under the bench in the park."

"You arranged for all of this while you were out of the country?" Luke asked.

"Of course. Distance no longer matters. That changed with the telephone. The Internet has made it even easier."

"Why?" Judith asked, her anger coming to the surface. "Why me? Why Luke? We were almost killed."

"Because, Judith, you could be manipulated. You were always inclined to carry guilt with you. It was your weakness decades ago and it is your weakness now. The same goes for you, Luke."

"What you did is nothing short of heinous." Judith started to stand, but Luke placed a hand on her arm.

"Hear her out."

Judith froze.

"Please let me get through this, then I have a favor to ask."

"A favor?" Judith snapped. "You have the nerve to ask favors after what you did to us?"

"Yes, I do." Corvino seemed unbothered by Judith's outburst. "The first thing we must do is clear the table of secrets. I plan to tell you mine, and then it's time you tell each other yours. Or shall I tell it?"

"I don't see that we have to do anything you suggest, except call the police." Judith's temper had not settled.

"If you want to send an old woman to jail, go ahead. I'll never see trial and I have enough money to bail me out of any jail. Even if I could live long enough to stand trial, I can hire enough attorneys to stall things for years."

Luke looked puzzled. "What do you mean, 'live long enough'?"

"I'm dying, Luke. Cancer. It's spread to enough organs to make me terminal. My existence is measured in weeks." She looked at Judith. "It's not a sob story. We're all dying. I just happen to know what's going to get me."

"I'm sorry to hear that," Luke said.

Judith said nothing.

"I've worked through the emotion and am at peace with it, but I don't want to go to the grave without you two knowing the part of the story that affects you. It's one reason I'm here. I tell you now, or you will never know."

Luke turned to Judith. "I began my career in graduate school. My father hired me on as a stockbroker in his firm. It turned out I had a knack for it. My instincts were good and some considered me a bit of a prodigy, a whiz kid at the market. I became interested in a growing industry—the biotech sector. Most of the brokers in the firm were still pushing the industrials and the growing silicon market. I did well in those, but my interest lay in the biotech companies. I didn't always understand what they were researching but I could pick those that had potential. I became aware of Dr. Corvino's work in infertility and research through a professor who wanted my opinion on investing. I approached her with an idea that I felt would make us all rich. I pulled together investors."

He paused as if waiting for the memories to catch up with his words. "I didn't care about her techniques. Actually, I didn't know enough to ask. What I saw was the desperation factor. Infertility treatment had everything going for it. It helped others, women desperate to have children. Any time the desperation level is high, the potential for high fees is present."

"So you funded her research?" Judith said.

"In a way. I brought in the money people. My father followed my lead and invested his clients and himself. Then she left. She just took off. My people lost truckloads of money. Some lost everything because I invested too aggressively. My father's reputation was tarnished and mine ruined. The Securities and Exchange people investigated me and although I was cleared I never worked for another firm." He looked at the table. "Some of the people I invested for didn't take the loss lightly. Two attempts were made on my life. I moved and locked myself away in my home, always looking over my shoulder."

Corvino shook her head. "I didn't just disappear. I fled for my life."

That was more than Judith could take. "You fled because you left scores of women infertile."

The old woman didn't respond at first. "Where did those women come from?"

Judith's jaw tightened.

"Judith?" Luke took her hand.

"Some of them came from me. She hired me to recruit women to donate eggs. Back then a woman could make a few thousand dollars donating her eggs."

"How does that make them infertile?" Luke asked. "I'm under the impression that egg donations have been done safely for many years."

"I'll answer that," Corvino said. "I got greedy. You both know about greed. I could no longer harvest eggs and treat patients as fast as I would like. And the research was eating away most of my day. I wanted everything, so I hired people to help and taught them the procedures."

"People who were not qualified to do the work," Judith said. "They mismanaged medications, screenings, and technique. In the end, close to one hundred women were rendered infertile—including me. I'm partly responsible for leading women to barrenness—women who felt they were doing something noble and making needed money. Most were college kids like me."

Corvino looked to the blue sky as if trying to read her next line. "I had an associate then, a fresh-faced young man just out of med school and internship. He started as a tech while an undergrad. I paid him well and helped with tuition. I was pretty good at buying silence. Lawsuits were mounting against me, and I took the coward's way out. I fled the country and found a new home in Singapore. Alex Zarefsky took over my clinics, research, and everything else."

The revelation stunned Judith. "Zarefsky worked with you? I never met him."

"Why would you?" Corvino said. "Think, Judith. Other than those who performed your procedure, how many of my doctors, nurses, and techs did you meet? Not many. Of course you never met Zarefsky. Your functions were vastly different. Anyway, he kept the inventory."

"Inventory?" Luke said. "You mean—"

"The harvested eggs and frozen embryos." Judith felt certain her conjecture was right, and she hated the use of "inventory" to describe the zygotes and embryos.

"Yes. In that inventory were several zygotes I had been experimenting with. You know of Dr. Robert Graham's work?"

"We've discussed it," Luke replied.

"He combined sperm from high IQ men and combined them with ova harvested from the mother in order to produce brighter children. I wanted to go a step further. I selected donations from men and women of special skill and intelligence, or beauty or athletic prowess. Remember, we were still on the cutting edge of things back then. We know a lot more now. I noticed certain zygotes reacted differently after conception. I'm still not sure why. I froze them waiting for a suitable donor. That's when my legal troubles began. Years later, I learned that Zarefsky had begun implanting the zygotes I left behind. Medical science had made the likelihood of success greater so he was willing to risk what I had described as my special babies." She waved a hand at the playing children. "You see the result."

"This is so hard to believe." Judith had to ask. "Why are they different?"

"I don't know," Corvino said. "At first, I thought it was all my doing. Serendipity is a powerful force in science. Now, I don't know if I'm the cause or just an observer. Maybe we should be talking to someone with more knowledge." She pointed to the sky.

"If you're the Puppeteer, you sent a photo to us—"

"Yes, a photo of Abel and you're wondering how I could have a picture of Abel in Zarefsky's home. Zarefsky sent it to me."

Luke narrowed his eyes. "And why would he do that?"

"Blackmail," she said. "Once he became aware the children were different, he wanted to do some testing and felt he stood a better chance of doing that without legal interference if he set up shop overseas. He needed a place to work and convinced a Singapore biotech firm to help him for a full share of the knowledge and any marketable product that could be developed from the study. That's where Cal-Genotics comes in. On the surface it looks like a U.S. company headed by Zarefsky but under the skin was a group of biomed businesses. I owned one of those interests—something not known to Zarefsky. It was one of the ways I kept tabs on him. Since he thought I'd never return to the U.S. and was getting too old to care, he cut me out of all operations in the States. I funded all his clinics and took a share of the profits. Once he had money flowing in from the Singapore people, he felt invulnerable—or at least he acted that way. He sent me the photo to extort money from me. He had promised to deliver twelve children and he had thirteen. One was expendable. I could have the child for a large sum of money. I knew he'd never honor that promise."

"So you sent us?" Judith said. "Not the police. Not the FBI. Us. Two businesspeople. Why?"

"Because you're smart, you're caring, and you have resources. I had no idea where Zarefsky lived. I know that he kept several homes all bought under various names. That and I feared everything would be traced back to me. Singapore is fairly safe for me and I didn't want to take a chance on losing that."

Luke tapped the table. "And Zarefsky wouldn't go to the police because they might start asking questions that could ultimately implicate him."

"Correct. He doesn't have to lose his freedom to be ruined, just his reputation. Trust me, I know. People will go to great lengths to protect their image. Isn't that true, Judith?"

"I don't appreciate the implication."

"You don't debate the truth of it either." Corvino winced. Something inside her was causing pain. For a moment, Judith felt sorry for her. "I've been getting treatment for my cancer and was hospitalized for a time and unable to participate in the Cal-Genotics decision making. Part of my requirement for participation was that my name or picture never be used. I was afraid it would tip off Zarefsky. Some decisions were made in my absence."

"To bring the children to Singapore?" Luke said.

"That and to hire the man you know as Pennington. The pretense was that Pennington was helping Zarefsky gather the children from different states. The truth was, Pennington was the guarantee the children would be brought to Singapore. Zarefsky thought he was in charge. He never was. As it turns out, neither was I."

"Why not hire a private detective?" Judith asked. "You entrusted Abel's life to two amateurs."

"Because they would want information I couldn't give. I had to press you two into service. I had something to hide and I needed people with something to hide working for me. I could motivate you with your secrets, and I could hold them over your head later if I needed to."

Luke looked like he had aged several years. "The children never arrived. I'm guessing there are some unhappy corporate types in Singapore."

"Unhappy is one word. You must be careful. They may try the whole thing over again. I won't live long enough to stop them."

"And you never found out why the children are special," Judith said. "You actually have no idea or are you just trying to keep us in the dark?"

"I honestly don't know. I do know one thing." She looked Judith in the eyes. "Three of the children are yours."

Judith felt like a candle in an oven. "What?"

"Like those you brought to the clinic, you donated eggs. And it's true our carelessness left you infertile. We did, however, harvest eggs during those procedures. I know that's a lot to take in, but I'm not feeling well so forgive me for getting to my favor." She motioned to the car and the driver reappeared carrying a briefcase. He set it on the table and returned to the limo.

"Money doesn't solve everything," Corvino said. "It doesn't take away a single ounce of guilt, but it can be used for good. I've made a great deal of money through my research and investments. It won't do me any good in the grave. I want you to oversee the use of it for the benefit of the children. I've set aside more than enough to meet my needs for several years although I doubt I'll live several months. No strings. This is the last time you'll see me."

She motioned to the limo again and the back door swung open. "I'm afraid you've been laboring under a misconception. There aren't thirteen children—there are fourteen."

A boy about the age of twelve emerged and walked slowly their way. Even at a distance, Judith could see the familiar eyes. "No need for great detail here. Suffice it to say that his mother was a surrogate and Zarefsky didn't get all the inventory. She lived with me for a year prior to Isaac's birth. After he was born, she went home a wealthy woman."

"Isaac?" Judith said.

"It's a Hebrew name that means 'laughter.' In the Bible, Isaac is born to Sarah, a barren woman. I was well beyond childbearing years when I implanted the zygote in the surrogate woman. That was ten years ago, a year before Zarefsky started experimenting with my research."

The boy stood quietly by Corvino.

"Hello," Judith said.

"You have much truth on you."

"Thank you," Judith said. "I think you probably do too."

Corvino took Isaac's hand and patted it like a grandmother does with a grandchild. "At about six he started talking about seeing truth and evil on people. As time passed that ability grew. I hate to tell you what he saw on me. A year later, he developed a fascination with spiritual things and with the Bible. Have you found that true with the children?"

"Yes, very much so." Judith studied the boy. He seemed unworried and comfortable around strangers.

"I wish I could be around to see what other talents develop." She winced again and looked more frail than when she first arrived. "Over time, he convinced me that I needed the Truth. That's Truth with a capital T. By that he meant I needed Jesus. I haven't had much need for spiritual things in my life, but that's probably because I never looked at myself. If I had, I might have seen what I had become. Isaac saw it every day. He never preached at me and never condemned me, but also never held back. The thing about truth is that it is so clear when you look for it and so hard to see when you don't. I saw it just a few months ago. I wish I had seen it decades ago. If I had, we wouldn't be having this conversation. The Truth changed me. Do you understand what I'm saying?"

"Yes," Luke said. "We understand it very well."

"Take care of Isaac. He needs a place where he can be among his own. I don't want to leave him alone." A tear ran from Corvino's eye.

"We will," Judith said softly.

"The briefcase has all the papers you need. Just countersign them and have your attorney file them with the appropriate banks. The money will be yours to use for the children." She stood and wavered a moment. "Take me back to the car, Isaac."

"Yes, Mother."

Judith and Luke walked with them. The driver opened the back door, but before Corvino seated herself, she turned to Judith. "You never asked."

"Asked what?"

"Which of the children are yours. I've been able to find out."

Judith looked around the grounds and noticed the children walking toward them. A few moments later, they had all gathered around Isaac. Judith pulled a couple of them close to her. "Dr. Corvino. As far as I'm concerned, they're all my children now."

Three ways to keep up on your favorite
Zondervan books and authors

Sign up for our *Fiction E-Newsletter*. Every month you'll receive sample excerpts from our books, sneak peeks at upcoming books, and chances to win free books autographed by the author.

You can also sign up for our *Breakfast Club*. Every morning in your email, you'll receive a five-minute snippet from a fiction or nonfiction book. A new book will be featured each week, and by the end of the week you will have sampled two to three chapters of the book.

Zondervan *Author Tracker* is the best way to be notified whenever your favorite Zondervan authors write new books, go on tour, or want to tell you about what's happening in their lives.

Visit *www.zondervan.com* and sign up today!

ZONDERVAN.com/
AUTHORTRACKER
follow your favorite authors